CHRISTINE WASS

THE POWER AND THE GLORY

BOOK ONE - JOURNEYS

Romaunce Books

1A The Wool Market Dyer Street Cirencester Gloucestershire GL7 2PR
An imprint of Memoirs Publishing www.mereobooks.com

First published in Great Britain in 2019
by Romaunce Books, an imprint of Memoirs Publishing

The address for Memoirs Publishing Group Limited can be
found at www.memoirspublishing.com

The Memoirs Publishing Group Ltd Reg. No. 7834348

Typeset in 9/12pt Century Schoolbook
by Wiltshire Associates Publisher Services Ltd.
Printed and bound in Great Britain by Biddles Books

CHAPTER ONE

"You there! Move that wagon out of the way!"

Hearing the threatening shout, Flavius Quinctilius Silvanus drew back the curtain of his litter. He frowned as he saw one of his bodyguards brandishing a flaming torch close to the wagon driver's face.

"You stupid bastard, you almost collided with the litter!" The bodyguard continued to shout and threaten the driver with the torch. As the angry, cursing driver struggled to force his ox-drawn wagon out of the way, a second bodyguard came out from behind the litter, sword drawn, ready for trouble.

After much shouting and cursing, the driver managed to move his bellowing oxen and wagon aside, and Flavius heaved a sigh of relief. He yanked the curtain back in place and settled back onto his cushions, confident that the bodyguards would be more than capable of dealing with any further trouble.

His father had hired the services of the two ex-gladiators after they had won their freedom in the arena. With their bull necks and huge muscular arms and legs, Flavius knew he would be safe; they were not the kind of men to argue with.

The litter lurched as the bearers swerved to miss yet another wagon. Flavius began to feel sick with the constant sway of the litter and the aroma of different foodstuffs mixed with the smell of horse and ox-dung emanating from the many vehicles hurrying into Rome. He sighed. It was the same aggravating nightly ritual: the streets of Rome filled with dozens upon dozens of vehicles in their mad scramble to bring in their wares during the hours of darkness, in a desperate bid to beat the city's dawn curfew.

He gingerly touched his cheekbone and winced. It had been a rough night in more ways than one. Not only had he lost a great deal of money at the tavern where he'd been drinking and playing dice, he'd also been involved in a fight, leading to his unceremonious ejection into the street by two burly men employed by the tavern to deal with troublemakers. He'd stopped his own bodyguards from joining in, not wanting to involve the Vigiles, who would most certainly appear and break up the disorder in the street, possibly leading to him and his men being arrested and causing more trouble.

The new moon was waxing as Flavius entered his

father's estate, set in the hills above the sprawling city, and the four litter bearers carrying him approached the luxurious family villa. Outside the villa door, Flavius climbed out of the litter, then dismissed the litter-bearers and the bodyguards with the order to return quietly to their quarters in the extensive villa grounds. He tapped on the door. The door porter immediately pulled back the grille, then quickly unbolted and opened the door. Once inside, Flavius nodded to the grinning porter. He jumped nervously as he heard the grille and bolts being secured again, then, composing himself, walked unsteadily into the atrium.

Flavius was glad he'd reached home in one piece. He trod softly, not wishing to disturb his family, especially his father, Senator Gaius Quinctilius Silvanus.

He stopped suddenly, his heart pounding, as he saw a figure carrying an oil lamp come out of a side room. The flame from the lamp cast an eerie shadow onto the painted walls. He swore under his breath as he recognised his father walking towards him. He tried to put on a brave face, but knew he was in trouble.

"Father! You startled me."

"Where have you been, Flavius? It is almost dawn." His father's voice was hard.

"Out with my friends," came his son's curt reply.

"You do not speak to me like that!"

Flavius' relief turned to unease. He did not wish to rouse his father's temper.

"How do you keep getting past the porter?"

"It's not his fault, father, I told him weeks ago that if he didn't let me in late at night, I would accuse him of stealing or of some other misdemeanour."

Gaius tried hard to control his anger. "Go to your bed, Flavius! I will speak with you in the morning. I'll deal with the door porter too."

Flavius wanted to protest, but thought better of it. Without a word he walked in the direction of his bedroom. Tired, his head throbbing, he threw himself down onto his bed, knowing he would be facing the same familiar argument in the morning.

The next morning as the servants brought the family their breakfast, the tension in the room was palpable. Sensing that all was not well, the servants beat a hasty retreat.

Gaius glared at Flavius. "When you came in this morning you stank of the Subura gutters. Look at you! Your eye and cheek are swollen and bruised, your lip is cut. What happened? Did you fight over a whore in one of the squalid taverns you frequent?"

Flavius was indignant. He shook his head. "No father, I didn't fight over any woman. I caught a man trying to cheat me at dice. What was I supposed to do?"

His father brought his fist down heavily on a nearby ornamental table, shattering its delicate obsidian inlay. Ignoring the damage, he went on "Don't you realise how upsetting all this is for your mother, Flavius?"

Flavius looked across the room and saw his mother,

the elegant Lydia Flavia Silvana, lying on her couch, her lovely face pale and drawn. He loved her very much and was mortified to think that he had inflicted pain on her.

"I'm sorry, mother. I will try and behave myself in future."

She gave him a wan smile.

"You had better!" came Gaius' stern voice. "I warn you, if you do not, there will be consequences."

Peace descended upon the household for the next few days, Flavius came home at a decent time and ate his meals with the family.

That peace did not last. On the sixth evening Flavius came into the dining area. He was hungry and ready to do justice to the evening meal. He stopped when he saw his father pacing agitatedly around the room.

Gaius stopped pacing when he saw his son. "Sit down, Flavius." His voice was commanding.

Flavius frowned. What was he being accused of now? He stood there, a defiant look on his face.

"I said, sit down!"

Hearing the anger in his father's voice, Flavius sat down on a dining couch.

"We had a visitor today. Senator Marcus Virilis."

Flavius knew what was coming next and sat anxiously awaiting the explosion.

"He came here to tell me that he had walked in on you and his daughter, Marcia, in her bed!" He loomed over Flavius, who sat with head bowed, deeply embarrassed by this statement in front of his mother and younger brother, Marius.

"Virilis warned me that if his daughter becomes pregnant, he will force you to marry her."

Flavius smiled inwardly at that, for he knew he was not alone in bedding Marcia. Her reputation was well known in certain circles of society. He knew Virilis was also aware of that fact, although he would never admit it.

Gaius continued his diatribe. "Virilis has had his door porter executed for letting you into the house, and his daughter's female slave has also been killed for allowing you into her mistress' bedroom. It has cost me a great deal of money to compensate Virilis for the loss of his slaves and to pay him for his silence to avoid scandal being attached to our family name." Gaius' temper exploded. "Don't you understand that this family's reputation – my life – is on a knife-edge? It is only by the will of the Emperor that I – we – are alive now. Too many problems like this one today involving another member of the Senate and the Emperor could change his mind."

Over the past few years, to keep all of their lives and estates safe, Gaius had been forced to make some brave but dangerous choices.

"You are a disgrace to this family. Why can't you be like Marius? He has never brought shame on this family."

At these words Flavius frowned. His younger brother had always been his father's favourite. Even as small children the brothers had never got on. Marius was too serious. He was always to be found in the family library with his nose stuck in one scroll or another taken from his ever-growing collection, usually one about law or politics, or his favourite subject, the life and times of the great Republican Dictators, Gaius Marius and Julius Caesar being his heroes. Flavius was only interested in the present, not in the people and events of a hundred years and more before; it was all far too boring and dry for his tastes.

He was brought out of his reverie by his father's icy voice.

"You, as my heir, should be setting an example, not drinking, womanising and gambling with the low company you keep. I am ashamed to think that one day you will be following me into the Senate. I have already warned you, one more mistake and you will feel the full weight of the consequences I promised you."

Gaius sat down heavily on his couch. "I'm ordering you to stop wasting your life and start thinking about your future. I've made arrangements for you to join the Army to learn some discipline. Make no mistake, if you wish to keep your inheritance, you will do this."

Flavius was horrified. "It's my life. I will not go."

Lydia Flavia had tears in her eyes as she leaned across to her son and covered his hand with her own. "Your father wants only what is best for you, Flavius. Please obey him. It will be better for you." She turned away and spoke quietly so Gaius couldn't hear "It will be better for us all."

Seeing his mother's distress, Flavius knew he had to

obey, if only for her sake. He looked at his father and said reluctantly "Father, I will obey you."

Gaius had arranged for him to join the Legion 1 Italica. They were camped not too far from Rome, making it easy for Flavius to return to the city and continue his dissolute activities whenever he was free from his duties. This went on for several months until on a brief visit home, Gaius, who had heard rumours of his son's return to his old ways, gave him a final warning.

"I am shocked and angry that you seem to have learned nothing," he said. He put his face close to his son's. "For Jupiter's sake, you are twenty-three years old! Remember who you are, who I am! When will you face up to your responsibilities?" He pointed a finger at his errant son. "I warned you of the consequences. You must understand that I am very close to disowning you. I want you transferred away from Rome to a proper legion based in a place that will make a man of you. This is my final word."

Gaius knew that Judaea was looked upon as the most troublesome province in the Empire. He turned to his wife. "Lydia, please write a letter to your cousin, the Procurator of Judaea, Pontius Pilate. Ask him to find a post for our son at the Garrison in Jerusalem. Do not reveal the real reason for the transfer, write only that Flavius seeks to further his ambitions before entering the Senate."

He was pleased when the official scroll from Pilate arrived containing the Governor's agreement to the transfer. He called Flavius to him to tell him the news, adding: "A stint in the East away from Rome's temptations will do you no harm. In fact it may help you to finally grow up."

Marius was standing outside the door listening. When the Senator left the room, he approached Flavius, sniggering. "Perhaps it *will* make a man of you, brother, if you can handle the discipline and stay away from the women."

Flavius was furious at the sneering comment and wanted to slap his brother, but instead he kept his temper and walked away.

Flavius spent a restless night. He hated his father at this moment for ruining his life. Why should he give up his pleasures? Why should he be forced to go to this hostile land, perhaps to die?

The following morning, when he'd calmed down, he thought of his father's words about having to tread carefully in the Senate, of having many enemies waiting to strike and that his life and the family fortunes were on a knife edge. All of this was true. To protect his family and estates, his father had publicly supported Lucius Aelius Sejanus, once Commander of the Praetorian Guard. With the Emperor Tiberius in Capri, Sejanus had plotted and murdered his way to the top and had gained total control of the City. He was feared by everyone in Rome. His spies had been everywhere and they were ready to condemn anyone, even high-ranking Senators, for speaking out against his atrocities. Flavius knew that his father's support was only an act. He had heard Gaius tell his mother how much he hated the 'usurper'.

When Sejanus was killed, his father had gone to the Emperor and explained his position, begging forgiveness and re-stating his loyalty. Fortunately Tiberius had accepted his father's explanation and forgiven him. Flavius was relieved that his father had been allowed to live and continue being a senator. He had witnessed Tiberius' revenge on the followers of Sejanus, carried out in many cruel ways in Rome and beyond. Some of the tyrant's supporters had committed suicide rather than face the Emperor's wrath. He shuddered at the thought of his father's body, or what was left of it, being found washed up on the banks of the Tiber. He felt ashamed. His own recent behaviour had contributed to his father's tension.

Thinking of these things, he realised it was for the best that he should be sent abroad to make his father's life a little easier, and put an end to the distress he had caused his mother. He hoped that by sacrificing his dissolute life in Rome, he would one day make Lydia Flavia proud of him. He knew she loved him, despite his selfish ways.

As for his brother, despite the animosity between them, Flavius felt a little sorry for Marius. He knew deep down that his brother was jealous of him, of his good looks, and of his position as elder son and inheritor of the family fortune and estate.

In the days before Flavius left for Judaea, Marius grew ever more spiteful, constantly making remarks about his brother's lifestyle. One day it grew too much and Flavius retaliated, saying "Marius, the gods only know, you will die without ever having lived." Marius went straight to their father and complained about Flavius. Gaius immediately took Marius' side against Flavius, causing more bad feeling in the family.

The day came when it was time for Flavius to leave the family home. He placed his saddlebags across the back of his magnificent black horse, Saturn, then went over to his mother, who stood watching with Gaius and a smirking Marius. He tenderly kissed his mother goodbye. The goodbyes of his father and brother were cold and stilted. Flavius was relieved to go.

He arrived in Ostia and reported to the Port Commander. After presenting his credentials, he sought out his ship, a military trireme which was riding at anchor in the harbour. He introduced himself to the marine centurion and naval captain in charge, then boarded the vessel. He made sure Saturn was safely stowed in a horse pen, then watched as the ship began to fill with legionaries travelling to the East.

The ship's captain roared out orders and the sail was unfurled. The oarsmen readied their oars. The sound of a drumbeat filled the air, its rhythm communicating to the oarsmen the rowing speed. The ship slowly negotiated its way out of the busy harbour. Flavius stood on the deck watching until the port was out of sight and the ship was on the open sea.

Over the next few days, when Rufio, a marine centurion, had spare time, Flavius would while away the boring hours playing dice with him, and they struck up a friendship. Rufio had been to Caesarea many times, but never to Judaea.

"I'm sorry, Tribune, I don't know enough about Judaea," he said. He cleared his throat. "But I tell you this, I've heard many bad reports about that area. I wish you good fortune and the protection of the gods, if that's where you're heading."

Flavius stared at Rufio and swallowed. What had he let himself in for? As each day passed, Flavius grew more and more apprehensive.

After many days and nights, the ship docked at Caesarea. Flavius wondered what awaited him in this hostile land.

CHAPTER TWO

Flavius stared at the grim fortress rising up before him. He removed his helmet and wiped the sweat from his forehead with the back of his hand. Shading his eyes, he looked up at the sun which beat down unmercifully, creating a shimmering landscape.

"By all the gods!" he swore quietly. "I've never known such heat. Even Rome in high summer is not as uncomfortable as this." If his father had purposely chosen this post to punish him, at first glance it looked like he'd succeeded.

He replaced his helmet, then guided Saturn up the steep slope leading to the fortress entrance. He identified himself to the Roman Guards who stood at attention outside the massive gates. One of the guards went into the fortress, returning quickly with a Duty Officer. Flavius introduced himself.

"I am the Tribune Flavius Quinctilius Silvanus, seconded from Rome for duty here at this fortress," he said.

"Sir!" The junior officer clenched his fist, brought his arm across his chest, then extended it in front of him in full military salute. "I am the Decurion, Julius Cornelius Vittelius. The Commander is expecting you. If you will follow me, sir."

Julius led Flavius to the horse pens, where two slaves waited.

"Sir." Julius pointed to the elder slave. "This is Zeno, he's been appointed by the Commander to make sure your horse is well cared for, sir." Julius saw Flavius' troubled look. "Zeno has been with the legion for many years sir, he is an expert at taking care of the fort's equine stock."

Flavius would have preferred to look after Saturn himself, but he knew he had to hand over his precious mount whilst staying at the fortress. He looked at Zeno, who stood waiting patiently for his orders. "My horse needs a good rub down," he said. "Cover him with a clean blanket, he's sweating and mustn't chill, then give him water, food and rest. Let him settle today, then tomorrow morning have his hooves checked by the farrier, it's been a long, hard ride from the coast to Antipatris, then on to here. Make sure the bronze horse pendants are cleaned and polished too."

Zeno bowed. "He is a fine horse, sir. I will take extra care of him."

"See that you do. Saturn was a gift from my family."

Flavius removed the leather bags draped over the saddle. In them were stored his personal possessions. He adjusted the bag which was slung across his shoulder, then stroked the magnificent black horse's neck and spoke softly to him. "You've done well, Saturn, you've earned your rest," he murmured. Saturn nuzzled his hand.

Zeno turned to the young groom standing at his side. "You heard the Tribune's orders. See to it."

Flavius watched as the young man, under Zeno's watchful eye, led the horse into an empty stall, removed the bridle, the four-horned saddle and girth strap and the elaborately stitched saddle blanket and put them to one side ready to carry out the Tribune's orders. Flavius hoped Saturn would be well looked after.

Julius coughed discreetly. "Sir... the Commander is waiting."

Flavius realised that it would not be wise to keep his Superior Officer waiting too long. It would be a bad beginning to his new career. "Yes, of course Decurion. You had better take me to the Commander now."

The Decurion saluted, then led Flavius to the Garrison Commander, whose office was based in the administrative centre of the Via Praetoria. Julius knocked once and entered, announcing the arrival of the new Tribune. The Commander of the Fortress Antonia, Quintus Maximus Piso, rose from his desk and stepped forward to greet Flavius. Julius saluted his superior officers, then marched out, closing the door to the Commander's austere room behind him.

Flavius stood rigidly to attention, even though every bone in his exhausted body screamed for rest.

"Welcome to Jerusalem and the Fortress Antonia, Tribune. Welcome to the Tenth Fretensis." Quintus pointed to his saddlebags. "I take it you've left your horse at the pens?"

"Yes, sir."

"Zeno is head groom here. He's very conscientious and a fine groom. I chose him for you myself."

"Thank you, Commander." Time would tell if Zeno was indeed a good groom.

"Put your saddlebags over there." Quintus pointed to a table in the corner of the room. Flavius did as he was told; he then produced a dispatch from his shoulder bag and presented it to the Commander. Quintus read it quickly, then cast a steely gaze over the younger man. He frowned when he saw the broad purple band hemming Flavius' short tunic. He was a Tribune Laticlavius, a Tribune of the Broad Stripe – an aristocrat who would use the army as a stepping stone to a political career. In his experience they usually meant trouble.

"So, Flavius Quinctilius Silvanus, you are the son of Senator Gaius Quinctilius Silvanus. You are to serve a short term with the Army before entering the Senate." He hesitated. "I take it you do intend following in your distinguished father's footsteps?"

Flavius drew himself up. "Yes, Commander."

"You'll find it very different here from Rome, Tribune. Tell me – why Judaea?"

"To further my ambitions." He saw the questioning look on the commander's craggy face. He didn't want to reveal that it had not been his choice at all, that he would much rather have stayed in Rome. "I have heard Judaea is a difficult place to serve in. I wanted a new challenge, the chance to experience some action, before I enter politics."

Quintus tried hard not to laugh out loud. How foolish and arrogant Rome's aristocrats were. He was tempted to say, "Jupiter boy, I hope you haven't made the biggest mistake of your life," but kept his thoughts to himself.

He changed the subject. "How much military experience have you had?" He didn't think it would be much.

"I've spent a year with the One Italica in Italy, sir."

"Not much then." He saw the hurt look on the younger man's face. "You have other despatches there?" He pointed to the bulging leather bag.

"They are for the Governor, Commander. Private letters from my mother, the Governor's her cousin."

"I see. I hope you won't seek special privileges because of your family's connection with the Governor." Quintus spoke sternly to test his latest recruit.

A flash of anger, quickly suppressed, crossed Flavius' handsome features. "No sir. I expect to be treated like any other officer. I'm prepared to work hard and do my duty"

Quintus nodded, satisfied with the answer.

"Well Tribune Silvanus, I suggest you go to your quarters and unpack, then find your way to the garrison bath-house and clean yourself up. The Governor's in Jerusalem, so I'll send word to him of your arrival. No doubt he'll send for you soon."

Flavius saluted the Commander and turned to go.

"Dine with me in my quarters tonight," the Commander added. "I want to hear about Rome – and I want to tell you more about your new posting."

"Thank you, sir. It will be a pleasure."

Quintus smiled grimly "I hope it stays that way." He shouted for one of the legionaries who guarded his door. "Show our new Tribune to his quarters."

Flavius saluted, picked up his saddlebags, and left the room.

The legionary led Flavius to his designated quarters. Being a senior Tribune, he had a small two-roomed house to himself in the cavalry block a short distance from the Via Praetoria. Zeno was waiting for him with a freshly-blanketed Saturn. Zeno stabled Saturn in the front room of the house, where clean straw had been laid and fresh fodder and water waited. He placed the saddle and tack onto hooks set in the wall and the elaborate saddle cloth onto a small shelf. Next to it were the now gleaming horse pendants.

Flavius saw a ditch had been dug and covered with stone slabs so the horse's urine could go through to the ditch below. He grimaced. How primitive this was, compared to the luxurious stables on the family estate, but he was in a frontier legion now and would have to get used to it.

He spoke harshly to Zeno. "You will make sure this area

is kept clean. I don't want my horse to suffer any infection."

"It is part of my job to make sure that doesn't happen, Tribune. I will have the area thoroughly cleaned every day."

Flavius nodded, then walked through an interconnecting door into a back room. Waiting for him in there was a personal body slave also assigned to him by Quintus. Flavius studied the tall, well-built slave. He judged him to be about forty years old. "What's your name?"

The slave looked down, not meeting his new master's eyes. He spoke softly "Gebhard, Tribune."

"Where are you from?"

"Germania, Tribune."

"How long have you been in this fortress?"

"Nine years, Tribune."

Flavius marvelled at the answer. "Nine years?"

"Yes, Tribune, but I have served the Commander for many more years. A long time ago, when the Commander was stationed in Germania, I was his personal slave. I pleased him, so when he was transferred from my country, he ordered me to travel with him to wherever else he was sent." Gebhard paused. "He has been a good master. I hope I meet with your approval too, Tribune."

"If the Commander recommends you, I am sure you will serve me well."

It was hot inside, so Flavius went to a small open window to breathe in some air. Such was the heat outside that it did not refresh him. Looking out of the window, he saw legionaries drilling in the square and heard a commotion coming from the workshop area. Some off-duty soldiers were sitting in a corner of the square playing dice. Laughter rose up from one of them as the dice rolled in his favour.

Flavius moved away from the window and sighed with relief as Gebhard carefully removed his helmet and arm greaves, then unbuckled and removed the body armour which covered his upper body, the two individual belts crossed over at the back and front which held his sword and dagger and the apron of metal disks, riveted to leather straps, which hung from these belts, then lastly the protective leg greaves. All were carefully placed to one side.

Flavius flexed his aching muscles, glad to be rid of the weight of his armour. He felt hot and very dirty. The sooner he went to the baths the better.

Gebhard led him to the bath house, then returned to his master's quarters. The bath house was empty, except for the slave in charge of the premises, who bowed low as he greeted him. Flavius was relieved. He would not have to make the effort of conversing with anyone. All he wanted to do was relax and ease the pain of his tired muscles.

The fawning slave took him to the dressing room, where he quickly discarded his sweat and travel-stained garments. As he entered the steam room, the stifling air made him catch his breath. He began to sweat profusely. He lay on a marble table and another skilled slave used a strigil to scrape the dust and dirt off his weary body. When this had been completed Flavius entered the tepidarium and dropped into the gently heated water. He swam around for a while, then floated on his back and let the warmth take the tension from his shoulders.

Although Flavius came from a pampered background, he had always taken great care of his taut, toned body. There wasn't an ounce of spare flesh on him. He loved all forms of exercise, regularly taking part in sporting contests, wrestling and running being his favourite pastimes. His parents attended and gave many banquets, but in their presence he would always eat and drink frugally. His handsome, aristocratic looks and firm, athletic build made him a favourite with Rome's most beautiful and overindulged women. He had toyed with the affections of several daughters of knights and senators who had been only too willing to indulge in sexual activity with him, especially the delectable Marcia, daughter of Senator Marcus Virilis. He would miss her. They had met in secret when the widowed Senator had been absent from the house. He had bribed the door porter of the villa and a female slave to let him enter into Marcia's bedroom, where she eagerly awaited him. Their moments together had been filled with lustful lovemaking – until the day Virilis had returned unexpectedly from the Senate and caught them in the throes of passion. Flavius had been unceremoniously thrown out of the house by surly household slaves and the bribed slaves had been executed. A shame, but it was just bad luck. In any case, with the money his father had given to Virilis, the slaves would soon be replaced. At this moment, Flavius was more concerned with how his life had changed. Here he was in the overpowering heat of Jerusalem at this forbidding fortress.

He suddenly remembered the invitation of Quintus Maximus and got out of the relaxing water. He moved on to the frigidarium and plunged into cold water, which closed his open pores and invigorated his mind and body. The slave dried him with a rough towel, then massaged his glowing body with sweet smelling oils. The slave then shaved off his chin stubble.

Flavius was feeling totally relaxed now. Conscious of the time, he roused himself and ordered the slave to dress him in clean undergarments and a fresh tunic. He slipped on his military sandals and the slave laced the loops of leather across his feet and ankles. A quick comb of his black, wavy hair and he was ready to dine with Quintus Maximus.

CHAPTER THREE

A powerfully-built man stood on the rooftop of the small house staring into the distance, his large, strong hands – fisherman's hands – gripping the top of the low wall surrounding the roof. He sighed as he breathed in the cool evening air. Somewhere nearby a dog began to bark, a call taken up by other animals grateful that for a few brief hours, Jerusalem would be free of the stifling heat of the day. The fragrant smell of olive groves drifted on the breeze. The olive trees grew abundantly on the slopes of the Mount of Olives and in the garden called Gethsemane – a place so beautiful, yet a place which held such bad memories; memories that, even now, made the man shudder.

The man, whose name was Peter, reflected on how his life had changed these past few years. He remembered his humble beginnings when he had worked alongside his brother Andrew as a fisherman in Galilee, and how on one momentous day they had been called to follow a new master, one who would change their lives forever. He had said they would now be 'fishers of men'. The Master had chosen ten other men to follow Him, naming the twelve as His Disciples.

Suddenly alerted by the all too familiar sound of iron-shod feet tramping up the dusty street towards the house, Peter edged away from the low rooftop wall, not wanting to draw attention to himself. A Roman patrol was making its habitual search of the ancient, winding city streets making sure all was in order. He breathed a sigh of relief as they passed by without stopping. As the sound of the Roman legionaries' boots and clanking body armour faded into the distance, he ventured back to the edge of the roof and gazed at the streets spread out below him. Shadows were beginning to creep along them, heralding the coming night. He saw tired workers wending their way home to their houses in those streets before night fell and danger lurked in every shadow. Some of the workers were strangers; others were converts who had joined the Disciples in the new religion, a religion which had been at odds with the Jewish authorities from its very beginnings, leading to the Master's cruel death. He swallowed hard. So much had happened since the Lord Jesus had been crucified. He and the other Disciples had been in despair, fearful for their lives, but the prophetic words Jesus had said to them, words they had not understood at the time, had come true: "After three days I will rise again."

Soon after His resurrection from the dead, the Lord Jesus had visited them: in the upper room of this house, on the road to Emmaus and on the shore of the Sea of Tiberius. It was on that shore that Jesus had asked him three times: 'Simon, son of John, do you love me more than all else?' His answer had been 'Yes, Lord. You know that I love you.' Jesus had looked straight at him and said: 'Then feed my sheep'. Why had Jesus called him Simon? Some time before, He had renamed him Peter, 'The Rock on which He would build His church'. Had Jesus meant that he was no longer fit to be that 'Rock'? He had been mortified.

After that day, the Disciples had been led to the Hill of Olivet, where they had witnessed the ascension of the Lord Jesus into Heaven, with His promise that they would receive the gift of the Holy Spirit and the instruction: 'You will bear witness for me in Jerusalem, all over Judaea, Samaria and to the ends of the earth'. Since that day, Peter and the other Disciples had gained new courage, vowing that whatever dangers threatened them, the work the Master had begun would continue. Peter had become their leader. A replacement was chosen to fill the place left by Judas Iscariot, the suicide, who had betrayed Jesus to the authorities. Two names had been put forward: Joseph and Matthias, both of whom had known Jesus in His lifetime on earth. Lots had been drawn and Matthias had been chosen.

A few days after the Lord's ascension into Heaven, as they sat together in the upper room of this house, tongues of fire had appeared above their heads, and the promised Holy

Spirit, like a whirlwind, had penetrated their very being, strengthening them and giving them courage to go out and spread the Word. From that moment on, they had told and re-told the story of the risen Lord Jesus and had performed miracles in His name. As a consequence, they had been constantly hounded by the authorities – to no avail.

The listening crowds had not been deterred; rather they had grown. At the time, Peter had wondered how they would cope with feeding the poor amongst them as well as telling everybody about the Lord. It was finally decided that seven Deacons would be chosen to help them in their work. One of those chosen was Stephen from Alexandria, a member of the Synagogue of Libertines, a Synagogue made up of Jews from Cyrene, Alexandria, Cilicia and Asia. Stephen had proved himself a worthy preacher, working many miracles amongst the people. He had become very popular with the public, but not with the Temple authorities - or Saul of Tarsus!

Peter felt a light touch on his arm. Turning his head, he saw a young man of some seventeen summers looking up at him.

"Peter…" his voice was hesitant, as though he was afraid to break into the elder man's thoughts. "Mother sent me to tell you supper's almost ready."

Peter suddenly realised how hungry he was. "I'm ready for the evening meal, John Mark. Come, we mustn't keep your mother waiting."

The young man hesitated. "We have a visitor tonight."

"Oh? Who is it?"

"My Uncle Barnabas."

The answer startled Peter. "Barnabas? But isn't he a friend of Saul of Tarsus? What's he doing here?"

"I don't know, but he says he's come in peace. Peter, I don't think he means us any harm."

"We shall see," Peter said sternly.

Peter followed the young man down the outside stairs, to the others waiting in the room below. John Mark entered the room but Peter stood in the doorway, his large frame almost filling it. He looked around warily. The other Disciples and some of the Deacons were seated around the room. He watched as John Mark exchanged smiles with his friend, Stephen, and sat down beside him, while Mary, John Mark's mother and owner of the house, stood stirring a large cauldron of vegetable broth hanging over the fire. Peter saw the slim form of Barnabas, Mary's brother, seated near her. Peter and Barnabas' eyes locked.

As Barnabas slowly got to his feet, the Disciples watched him closely, ready to act at any sudden violent movement from him against their leader.

"Peter..." Barnabas smiled hesitantly, unsure of Peter's reaction. Peter stood his ground. "Peter, I know it's hard for you to trust a friend of Saul, but I swear to you I have come here alone tonight, with no desire to harm you." He cast his eyes quickly around the room and saw the look of distrust from all who sat there, including his sister. "Any of you."

A burly man stood up and moved towards him threateningly.

"Thomas! Let him speak." Peter commanded as he entered the room and stood facing Barnabas. "What do you want?"

Barnabas looked up at Peter, who stood a full head taller than him. His voice didn't waver as he said "I want to join you."

The reply stunned them all. Mary stopped stirring the broth. Some of the Disciples jumped up, protesting. Peter held up his hand for silence.

Barnabas continued: "I've seen the miracles you've performed, heard the stories you've told, watched your bravery when you've been in great danger. For many weeks I have lain sleepless night after night turning these things over in my mind. Whoever this Jesus was – is – you are so convinced that He is the Messiah, the Chosen One of God that you are willing to lay down your lives for Him. I want to know more about Him. Then later, maybe you will let me help you in your work."

Peter stood silent for a moment, looking at the bemused faces of the others, then said: "You all know that Barnabas is a friend of Saul of Tarsus…"

Saul of Tarsus! Peter frowned as the man's arrogant face flashed before him and his harsh, accusing voice filled his ears. Why did Saul hate the Lord's followers so much? It was soul-destroying hatred. When he and the others had preached in their favourite place, the Beautiful Gate, the entrance to the Holiest place in all Israel, Saul would be in the forefront of the Temple Guard glaring at them malevolently, but he was always careful not to upset the watching supporters – he knew he could not risk the wrath of Rome if a riot broke out. The Fortress Antonia, the Roman Headquarters in the city, overlooked the Temple, so everything that happened within the Temple area could be seen by the patrolling soldiers above.

"So, do we let Barnabas join us?" said Peter.

Some agreed, but the majority shook their heads in disapproval. Arguments began to break out.

Andrew stood up. "If Barnabas has been sent by Saul to spy on us, he will have led the Temple guards here." There was a hush as he said the words. "They may be outside now, waiting to arrest us. We might all be sent back to prison, or worse."

"I remember the awful time we were in prison before," said John, his voice trembling. "If the Angel of the Lord had not appeared to us, miraculously opened the prison doors and set us free, then I dread to think what would have happened to us."

John's brother, James, joined in. "I was scared, but I'll never forget the look on the priests' faces when they saw us walking through the Temple courtyard the next day."

"And promptly arrested us again," Peter said soberly. "If it hadn't been for the Pharisee Gamaliel, the Sanhedrin would have condemned us to death." He shook his head "I still don't understand why he interceded for us."

"Nor I, but I'm glad that he did." John frowned. "Gamaliel may not speak up for us again. Respected as he is, he could place himself in great danger if he keeps arguing against the High Priests."

Peter turned to Stephen "You have said that lately, Saul seems to be always where you are preaching, watching you, making comments, Barnabas by his side. Knowing the danger of prison, or death, do you think it is safe to let Barnabas join us?"

Stephen looked at the suspicious faces of these people he had come to know and love, and smiled. "I know the problems we all face, Peter, but I won't stop telling people the story of Jesus, either in the market place or the temple precinct. You said yourself, that whatever the danger we face, the Good News must not be allowed to wither and die."

Peter nodded "Yes, I did say that, but the question now is, can we trust Barnabas?"

"All I know, Peter, is, yes I've seen Barnabas with Saul on several occasions at the Temple, but although Saul constantly rants at me, Barnabas has never uttered a word, he's always hung back, hesitant to join in the condemnations."

Peter weighed this statement up in his mind. Was Barnabas' hesitancy because of Mary? How much had he known about his sister's involvement with the group? Was it because of the fear of questioning his orthodox beliefs? Or fear of displeasing God by condemning the men who preached about His Son?

The murmurings grew louder amongst the Disciples. Peter raised his voice to cut across the arguments raging back and forth.

"We obviously cannot agree, so we must pray to the Lord for guidance," he said. He bowed his head, and the others, silent now, followed suit. In the brief silence that followed a quiet, inner voice spoke to Peter: *Trust this man, let him become my Disciple.*

Barnabas sat anxiously awaiting their decision, an earnest look on his face. The gathering raised their heads.

Peter spoke up. "The Lord has said to me we must welcome Barnabas."

Andrew, John and James murmured uneasily amongst themselves, while the rest of the Disciples cast a worried look in Peter's direction. Barnabas grabbed Peter's extended hand and clasped it with his own in gratitude and relief. "Thank you. I will sell my possessions and share the proceeds with you all."

"We don't want your money," Thomas snarled. Some agreed with him. Ignoring them, Peter turned to Mary, who was tasting the broth and nodding in satisfaction. "Ah, I think the food is ready," he said. He called to her "Mary, let's try your delicious broth." He pointed to the table. "Come, Barnabas, sit and eat with us." He led the would-be convert to the table laid ready for the evening meal and they sat down. Slowly the others joined them.

After Mary had laid out bread then ladled the broth into their bowls, she sat down at the table next to Barnabas.

Peter said, "Let us pray." All of the gathering bowed their heads. Peter picked up the bread and intoned a bitter-sweet remembrance of Jesus' words as He had blessed and broken the unleavened bread at the last supper they had all shared. Words that would stay with him forever.

"As our dear Lord commanded, we break this bread in remembrance of Him. On the night he was betrayed, He took bread, broke it and gave it to us, saying: 'Take, eat, this is my body broken for you...do this in remembrance of me'. He put down the bread and held up his cup of watered wine. "Then as Jesus poured the wine into a cup and passed it amongst us, he said: 'Drink from it, all of you. For this is my blood, the blood of the covenant shed for you and for many for the forgiveness of sins.'

Peter frowned. Betrayal - forgiveness - it brought back the shameful memory of his three denials of Jesus before His crucifixion. He constantly fought to remove the remembrance of his defiance as Jesus had warned him that he would deny Him: 'Lord, I will never deny you.' but a few hours later he had done exactly that. The crowing cockerel still haunted his dreams.

Peter closed his eyes and shook his head, willing the vision to vanish. But he had been forgiven by the Lord Jesus. He had told him so when, on the shore of the Sea of Tiberias that day, He had said 'Follow me'.

He had tried so hard to pray for forgiveness for Judas and now Saul. How could he not forgive them? Had not the Lord forgiven him?

He looked around at the raised faces of his friends and

saw their harsh, accusing looks. Then he said sternly, "If the Lord commands that we accept Barnabas as one of us, then who are we to argue against that command?"

The harsh faces took on a guilty look.

"I know I speak for myself and the others" a shame-faced John said quietly, "when I say that we are all sorry for doubting you, Barnabas. Welcome."

Peter smiled, then broke off a piece of the bread and passed the rest of it to Barnabas, who took some and then passed it along the table to the others. Soon those who shared the Lord's work were all eating heartily.

CHAPTER FOUR

After a simple but delicious meal of roasted lamb, freshly-baked bread and palm dates, Quintus asked Flavius to bring him up to date with all the latest news from Rome. When Flavius had finished, Quintus wondered why the young tribune had not mentioned the downfall of Sejanus and the Emperor's bloodthirsty revenge on his supporters.

Quintus was a professional soldier, and to his mind such men as Sejanus were guilty of the foulest treason to the Emperor and the people. He himself had trod carefully for the past nine years, knowing that Pilate had been Sejanus' man. Now, here was Pilate's relative sitting in front of him. What if he had been sent by the Emperor to check up on Pilate – and on him? He'd done his best to keep the Fortress running smoothly, he knew there was no cause for complaint, and yet... Keeping a neutral expression, he filled Flavius' wine goblet and smiled as Flavius sipped it and grimaced.

"I know." Quintus didn't apologise for the poor quality of the wine. "But you see, Tribune, the Jews don't furnish us with their best vintage. We are the hated conquerors, the enemy. They cannot beat us in battle, so I think they are slowly trying to poison us."

Flavius' face held a sour expression. "They may succeed, Commander."

Quintus became serious. "I think I should tell you something about these people so you know what you will have to deal with. Firstly, they call themselves the Chosen Ones of God. According to them there is only one God. They call him Jehovah."

"Only one god?" Flavius looked puzzled.

"Yes, it seems strange to us Tribune. We are used to many gods, including household deities. I come from a military background; my family have always worshipped Mars. Which deity does the Silvanus household honour?"

"Our family choice is the goddess Fortuna, the patroness of good fortune and luck."

Quintus was tempted to say "You're going to need all the luck you can get here," but he kept his thoughts to himself. Instead he said: "Did you see the massive structure below the fortress?"

Flavius nodded. "Yes sir. It's very impressive."

"That's the temple built to supposedly house the God of the Jews. The archives say that when Pompey the Great invaded and subdued Jerusalem some seventy years ago, he went to the Temple precinct. Several Jewish priests tried to stop him from entering the Temple. He had them killed, then marched into the building. He saw a room half-hidden by a veil, cut through the veil with his sword and entered the most sacred part of the building, the inner sanctum. If he expected to find the treasure trove of Israel in there, he was disappointed. There were no pots of gold, nor any sign of a godlike statue. Just some rolled-up scrolls, a large seven branched candelabra and a few vessels."

Quintus could see the bemused expression on Flavius' face, so he explained further. "A temple with no statues does sound ridiculous. But you see the Jews believe their God does not permit them to have statues or images as aids to worship. It is against His Law. The building is a symbol of His unseen power. Pompey took the scrolls out to those priests who had survived and was about to destroy them, when, hearing their piteous wails, he relented and gave the scrolls to them. Lucky for him that he did, for they contained the Sacred Laws of the Jews, said to have been dictated by their God Himself to one of their greatest Prophets. These laws and commandments have been kept by the Jews for centuries. Sickeningly grateful, the priests returned the scrolls to the temple, where they remain today."

He offered Flavius more wine, and Flavius reluctantly let him pour some into his goblet. Quintus poured more for himself, drank deeply then continued.

"As I have come to know, the Jews are a very religious race. Now there's a new sect – the Nazarenes – whose followers claim their founder rose from the dead."

Flavius almost choked on his wine. "Nobody can come back from the dead!"

"I agree, but they say he was what they call the Messiah, the Son of this God." Quintus laughed bitterly. "This place crawls with would-be Messiahs. For a long time, the Jews have thought that a great warrior will be sent by their God to deliver them from their enemies – they're still waiting."

"This one's dead then?"

"He was crucified about two, three years back."

"So, He was an enemy of the state."

"Governor Pilate thought the Nazarene was just another deluded Galilean trouble-maker. At the Nazarene's trial, he had the man flogged and would have let him go. To the Governor it was an internal religious affair, something we try to keep out of, but the priests brought in an extra charge of sedition against the accused. They said he called himself the King of the Jews."

Flavius was astounded. "King of the Jews? The Jews have been subject to Rome for years."

"Exactly, but the Governor was in a precarious situation – the Nazarene was popular with the mob, and if he ordered the death sentence he feared reprisals from the Nazarene's supporters. On the other hand if he didn't convict him then the priests would complain to the Emperor. You can imagine what the Emperor's view of a governor who freed a self-made King in Rome's territories would be. The priests knew this and stirred up the mob against the Nazarene."

"At Passover the Jews are allowed to be merciful to a condemned man – they chose Barabbas, a terrorist who had robbed and murdered his way across the country. It was not in Rome's interest to have Barabbas back out there rampaging across the countryside and slaughtering our soldiers, but knowing this Law and wishing to avoid a riot, Governor Pilate had no choice but to free him. Eventually, seeing the situation was beginning to get out of hand, he washed his hands of the whole affair and handed the Nazarene over to the people to let them decide on the Nazarene's fate."

The memory still frustrated Quintus. He'd always thought it curious that a man like Pilate, the Emperor's political spokesman, could be swayed by religious fanatics who would stop at nothing to have a man destroyed if it got in the way of their own ambitions. But he decided that this was not the time to test Flavius' loyalties and kept his thoughts to himself.

Flavius nodded. "Yes, I can see it must have been a very difficult decision to make. If you forgive me sir, this episode seems to have made an impression on you."

"I stood behind Governor Pilate at the trial in the Praetorium. It was a strange trial. The Nazarene hardly said anything in his defence. Although something he did say seemed to disturb the Governor, because I saw his expression change." He took another mouthful of wine

"I had to draw up the execution detail for the Nazarene and two robbers who were also to be crucified. I put Chief Centurion Sextus in charge, you will meet him tomorrow. I'm glad I chose him, because he is not easily intimidated. His report spoke of crowds lining the streets as the procession of the condemned went by. Several times he had to have the mob pushed back to clear the way to the place of execution the Jews call Golgotha." He rubbed his chin "I remember the storm too – there was some damage done to the Temple. It unnerved a lot of people, including one of the other centurions on duty at the crucifixions."

"Commander, this troublemaker, this Nazarene, was dealt with, so I'm a little confused as to why his followers are being allowed to continue to openly preach their sedition in his name. With what you've told me about the religious confrontations here, I don't understand why they haven't been arrested."

"Another complexity. Their offence is purely a religious one. As I have already said, Governor Pilate does not have to intervene. The priests have the power to see to that. They did arrest them, but they walked free." He shrugged. "Don't ask me how, all I know is they too are popular with the mob." Quintus brought his fist down hard on the table. "They continue to spread their ridiculous stories despite knowing that if they cause trouble in the city the consequences will be dire for them."

Flavius was bewildered. "You'd think after what happened to their leader they would have learnt."

Quintus shook his head. "The longer I've spent in this scorpion-infested, accursed land, the more I've despaired of ever bringing these stiff-necked, arrogant people to heel. Religious fanatics like them and murderers like Barabbas are problems that won't go away. This city and the surrounding countryside are full of thieves and cutthroats. The latest successor to Barabbas is a felon called Eleazar ben-Ezra. Only a few weeks ago yet another Cavalry patrol was ambushed, the men slaughtered and their weapons and horses stolen. The details of the ambush point to him and his gang being responsible."

He ran his hand through his short, greying hair. "Then there are those who call themselves Zealots. They look on themselves as patriots – freedom fighters." He sneered as he said the word. "To us they are no more than terrorists. They've killed more of our men than I care to think about."

Quintus could see he had Flavius' full attention.

"They come mostly from the region of Galilee to the north of here. They, along with ben-Ezra, cause us a great deal of trouble in this city too, especially at Festival times. The Jews have an interminable number of religious holidays. The worst as far as we are concerned is the Feast of The Passover. No soldier has leave at that time – in fact the guards are doubled in and around the porticoes of the Temple and the Fortress. The Governor has to be in residence too"

Flavius began to feel uneasy at the thought of the danger he could be facing in this city. He decided to change the subject and ask a question that had been bothering him.

"May I ask sir, why are there no Legion standards on view outside of this fortress?"

Quintus looked warily at Flavius. If he had been sent from Rome to test him, this would be the time for the young Tribune to show his hand. He refilled his wine cup, offering to do the same for Flavius, who politely refused. "I wondered when you would ask me that." Quintus gulped down his wine, obviously uncomfortable at the question. He placed the wine cup heavily onto the table, splashing some of the contents onto the polished surface.

"When the Governor first arrived in Judaea, he ordered our troops to bring the Legion standards into Jerusalem. As they had the likeness of the Emperor on them, the Jews felt that their holy city had been desecrated by idolatrous symbols and demanded they be removed."

Flavius was horrified. "Demanded?"

"Governor Pilate had to bow to their wishes then too – to keep the peace and stop an uprising."

A response didn't come and Quintus relaxed slightly but decided to keep his guard up.

Flavius sat forward, intrigued. "The Jews seems a very touchy race, sir."

"Let's just say it doesn't take much to upset them." He paused. "I hope you never have to witness a revolt here. It's not pleasant – even for a hardened soldier."

Quintus' face was grim as he remembered the last

uprising. When Pilate had built an aqueduct, he'd used sacred money taken from the Temple treasury. The riot that followed that act was still fresh in his memory. As Commander, he'd been forced to put the garrison on full alert and send out two cohorts of legionaries in full battledress to quell it. By nightfall the streets had been awash with blood. He'd lost some good soldiers, but many more Jews died that day.

Then there was the occasion when a group of Galileans, pilgrims who had come to Jerusalem from Galilee to offer sacrifice at the Temple, were massacred on Pilate's order. He remembered the uproar that day, for people said that the Galileans' blood had mingled with the blood of the sacrificed animals that were ready to be offered to their god. He decided not to speak of those two events to Flavius.

"That's why the Governor was forced to react the way he did when asked to condemn the Nazarene," said Quintus.

"But if Governor Pilate saved Jerusalem from another riot, surely he did the right thing?"

"I think so." Quintus sat down heavily. "Well, Tribune, do you have any more questions?"

"Yes, sir, I'd like to know why the Jews hate us so much. We've given them better roads and clean water through our aqueduct systems."

"Yes, we have – but Tribune, these people conveniently forget about all the good things Rome has done for them. I came to this country nine years ago with the Governor and I have a great admiration for him. His is a tough job, most of the time he's walking on eggshells."

He had to choose his words carefully; he did not dare tell the truth. The truth was that Pilate was not popular. In the eyes of the Jews he had made too many mistakes. He had served as Governor for nine years – longer than any other Procurator. Perhaps it was time he moved on – or returned to Rome. Perhaps it was time they both did.

Flavius smiled. "My mother was pleased for him when she heard he was to be awarded a Governorship. They were quite close in their younger days. When I was a child he was good to me."

Quintus shifted uncomfortably in his seat. "I think you will see a difference in your relative from the man you once knew; this country has a habit of changing people – I know how much I have changed." His mind returned to the day when as a young, keen officer he'd arrived in Judaea as part of the Governor's entourage. How proud he'd felt to have been given second in command of the Jerusalem Garrison. Over the years he had become more and more disillusioned. The bitter memories of his sometimes brutal, blood-soaked climb to promotion as Commander after the untimely death of his superior still haunted him. He suppressed a shudder, then looked directly at Flavius. "I hope this has helped to explain what you will face in this country, Tribune?"

Flavius smiled. "Your information has been most useful, Commander. It seems my choice of army post may be even more difficult than I imagined."

Quintus stood up, moved round the table and stood

closer to Flavius. "Governor Pilate's here in Jerusalem now, entertaining an envoy of King Aretas of Nabatea. Rome has a treaty with that country and this diplomat is of great importance to us, but I'm sure, when he knows you are here, the Governor will want to speak with you."

"I look forward to meeting him, sir."

"Until then... you have a free day tomorrow. I suggest you take a tour of the garrison, I'll get Chief Centurion Sextus to escort you, then later you can familiarise yourself with the city, see the problems for yourself. I have just the man to guide you. He'll bring you some civilian clothes... a merchant disguise will be best, I think." He saw Flavius' quizzical look. "I don't want my new Tribune knifed in the back." Quintus crossed the room towards the door, signalling an end to the evening.

Flavius rose from his chair. "Thank you, sir for a very pleasant meal and for your useful information."

The Commander's face broke into a smile. He could get to like this ambitious young man after all. "Thank you for patiently listening to my remembrances. I hope they will help you whilst you are in Judaea."

"They will, sir. I found them most enlightening and I'm sure they will help me to understand the Jews more."

Quintus' smile faded. "Don't try to understand the Jews Tribune, you'll fail. Be back here early tomorrow afternoon, your guide will be waiting for you."

Quintus acknowledged Flavius' salute with a brief wave of his hand. "Oh, and Tribune, try to keep out of trouble –

and keep away from the brothels. If a knife doesn't finish you off, disease will." He smiled grimly, then opened the door to let Flavius out.

Flavius saluted again and left the room, pondering on the Commander's revelations. The Commander said that his relative had changed. It was no wonder if what the Commander had told him had faced Pilate these past nine years. When the Commander had spoken of Pilate's difficult position, he had thought it best not to add that his mother's initial pleasure at Pilate's promotion had faded and she was now very concerned for him, given who had arranged the position.

Her words rang in his ears: "Be careful of what you say and do at all times, Flavius, my cousin was Sejanus' man. He holds his position as Governor only because he had gained favour with the monster who would have ruled Rome above the Emperor. Now Sejanus has gone, Pilate is here on sufferance. If Tiberius has cause to remove him, or worse, he will not hesitate to do so." She had added solemnly, "Or anyone else associated with him."

He didn't like the sound of this Eleazar ben-Ezra character either, or of the Zealots with all their murderous hatred. With all of this political tension, these criminal factions, as well as religious fanatics running amok causing unrest amongst the Jews, he wondered what he had got himself into.

CHAPTER FIVE

The morning sun had not yet reached its full power as Saul of Tarsus strode through the quiet, shaded courtyard of the temple precinct where his tutor, the eminent Pharisee Gamaliel, sat with his students. Saul had never felt such anger. His face was blood red, his body rigid with tension. He swept past Gamaliel without acknowledging his teacher.

Gamaliel saw the look of anger and hatred on the young man's face. He dismissed his pupils, got up and followed Saul.

"Saul – what has angered you so?"

Saul stopped and turned at the sound of the Rabbi's voice. His eyes burned and his voice was tight as he looked at Gamaliel, who he knew was respected as the greatest Pharisee of them all.

"I'm sorry, Rabbi, but it's the Nazarenes."

A brief smile crossed Gamaliel's face "So that's what the followers of Jesus of Nazareth are known as these days."

Saul clenched his fists. "I want to put an end to those accursed blasphemers and the poisonous lies they are spreading. It's an insult to the Lord God and to our faith."

Gamaliel studied his most accomplished student and saw the zealous fire in his eyes. He considered Saul's statement for a moment, sighed heavily, then spoke.

"Saul, Saul, you have such zeal, but you must use it in the right way. I will repeat to you what I told the High Priests: beware, for if these men are sent from God and you attack them, you risk the wrath of the Lord. If, however, they are blasphemers, then the Most High will punish them for their wickedness. Leave it to Him to decide. Remember, 'Vengeance is mine says the Lord'. Or have you forgotten your lessons so soon?"

Those words cut Saul to the quick. He was speechless as the Rabbi, considered the most learned in the Sanhedrin, shook his head, turned and slowly walked away.

He seethed inwardly. Let the old man show compassion for these followers of the crucified criminal Jesus of Nazareth. He could find none in his heart. He would make it his business to harry them, be a thorn in their side. He would begin by destroying that conceited young upstart, Stephen of Alexandria, the cause of his present anger.

Yesterday, he had walked to the market place and witnessed Stephen telling his lies to the crowd. He had looked at the faces of the mob as they stood transfixed, their gaze never leaving the handsome, animated face of the young Alexandrian. It was obvious these uneducated people were believing every false, blasphemous word they heard. He had noted that some Greeks were amongst the crowd, and sometimes Stephen had turned to them and spoken to them in their own language.

Saul had felt disgust to see the mob gasp as Stephen reached the climax of his preaching: the death and resurrection of Jesus of Nazareth. When he had finished speaking, many of the crowd had surged towards Stephen, clamouring to hear more. He had walked away, anger consuming him. It was obvious this insidious cult would continue to grow unless somebody put a stop to it. That somebody would be him. Without Gamaliel's knowledge, he had already visited the High Priest and begged for permission to follow Stephen's every move, arrest him and hand him over to the Council. Permission had been quickly given. Now, one day soon, he would trap him and destroy him. He would destroy them all.

After a restless night, Flavius went to the farrier to make sure the young groom had taken Saturn to him as ordered. When he arrived, the farrier was in the process of replacing the worn horseshoes. Satisfied, he walked to the cookhouse for breakfast. He could have had his food served to him by his personal slave, but he felt hot and confined in his room. He preferred to meet some of his junior officers, watch the rank and file at work and play and get to know the men who would be serving under him.

After breakfast he went to the parade ground and watched the men go through their drill paces. As he watched, a burly centurion approached him and saluted.

"Tribune. Sir."

Flavius looked into the weather-beaten, hard face of a man he guessed to be in his late thirties.

"I am Justus Sextus, sir, Chief Centurion of the 1st Century of the 3rd Cohort. The Commander asked me to escort you around the fortress."

"Then lead on, Centurion Justus Sextus."

The centurion saluted and led the way.

After visits to the men's quarters, the bath house, which Flavius was already familiar with, and the gymnasium, where two off-duty officers were throwing a large medicine ball back and forth. When they saw Flavius and Sextus they stopped briefly to acknowledge them, then carried on with their exercise. The gymnasium was a good size and had several pieces of fitness equipment. Flavius made a mental note that he would visit it, when time allowed, to keep up his physical training. Then it was on to inspect the kitchens, hospital and workshops. Sextus took him to the Principia, to the chapel where the Legion's Standards were kept. Two guards of the 1st Century of the 3rd Cohort stood at attention outside the room. They saluted as their senior officers approached.

"Stand easy, lads." Sextus' voice was brisk but friendly.

"Open the door, I want to show our new Tribune our sacred treasures."

The guards opened the door and the two officers entered the room. Sextus closed the door behind him. They walked to the far end of the room, where the standards were proudly arrayed. Flavius looked at the legion standard with interest. The standard was fixed to a highly-polished pole topped by a spearhead. At the base of the pole there was a smaller spearhead shape for planting in the ground in times of war. Above this, small silver handles were fixed to the pole with which to pull the standard out of the ground. Sextus was delighted to see the look of interest on the new Tribune's face. He proudly puffed out his chest as he explained what it meant to the cohorts stationed in Jerusalem.

"These days the bulk of the Tenth is in Syria where the Eagle stays unless the whole Legion is on the move. This standard is venerated by the cohorts of the Tenth when we are serving away from home." He moved closer to the flag and pointed out the legends woven into the red material.

"You will see, Tribune, the bull, the sign of the zodiac dedicated to Venus, the goddess favoured by Julius Caesar."

Flavius nodded. Every Roman schoolboy had been taught about the Legion used and made famous by Julius Caesar in his many victories.

"Here is the likeness of Neptune, and d'you see this trireme?" the Centurion continued. He pointed to the ship embroidered onto the flag. "The trireme represents the

Tenth's involvement in the war between Octavian, soon to become the Divine Emperor Augustus, and Mark Antony. We've also managed to accumulate during our illustrious history a dolphin and a boar."

Flavius was impressed. "The Tenth does indeed have a great deal to be proud of. I'm honoured to be part of this Legion."

A crooked smile spread along Sextus' craggy face. "That's good to hear, sir. Now, if I can show you the rest of the standards."

He went on to point out to Flavius the standards of the centuries stationed at the fortress. After, Sextus took Flavius to see the Treasury where the pay chests were kept. These chests held the soldiers' wages and money they had paid into their funeral club.

The tour ended and Sextus escorted Flavius back to his house. As they passed by the stalls, they heard murmuring. Flavius looked into one of the empty stalls and there, slumped against the far wall, were two legionaries. He called Sextus, who strode into the stall.

Sextus grimaced as he saw a flagon lying on the straw between the men. He picked up the flagon. His face reddened as he smelt what was left of the wine inside. He brought down his vine cane across their bare legs and bellowed, "Get up you drunken bastards!"

The violence of the blow brought cries of surprise and pain. It took seconds for the men to understand that they had been caught and as realisation set in, they struggled to their feet. Barely able to stand, they held on to the wall, swaying.

The angry Centurion put his scowling face close to the two quaking legionaries. His voice came as a hiss. "Don't move!"

Sextus went outside, leaving Flavius glaring at the men. Flavius heard Sextus shouting orders and very soon he returned, followed by four legionaries. "Hold these useless pieces of shit!" he snapped. At his command, the legionaries grabbed hold of the drunken men. Sextus leaned towards them threateningly. "If I had my way I'd cut your balls off and nail them to the fortress gate," he roared.

Flavius narrowed his eyes at the miscreants and growled "If my horse had been in these stalls and hurt because of you, I'd hold you down while the Centurion did it."

Sextus turned to face the guards and spat out, "Take these drunken fucks to the cells. I'll be along in a minute!"

Flavius cast a glance at the nervous faces of the errant legionaries as they were dragged out, the realisation of the serious trouble they were in obviously having a sobering effect. Sextus didn't seem the kind of man to let their drunken escapade pass without some punishment. He wondered what form it would take.

"Thank you, Centurion. I think I've seen enough. You had better go and sort this mess out," said Flavius.

"Sir. I'm sorry sir, and relieved your horse was not involved." Sextus saluted him and made his way to the guardhouse to deal with the miscreants.

CHAPTER SIX

Saul watched Stephen as he stood in the Temple Precinct near Solomon's Gate. His attention was suddenly diverted as he saw Barnabas approaching. He waved, but Barnabas didn't see him. Instead he went straight to Stephen, who greeted him warmly. Saul was startled. Could it be that his friend had joined the blasphemers? It certainly appeared so. No wonder he had neglected his studies lately.

A small crowd gathered around Stephen, waiting for the charismatic young preacher to speak. Stephen recognised some of them as regular listeners, but others were new to him. One of the newcomers tried to shout him down when he spoke about Jesus. Other listeners told the man to be quiet.

Stephen held up his hand and the crowd fell silent.

"My dear friends, I know that for some of you it is

difficult to understand and accept the things I have told you concerning Jesus of Nazareth and all He has done, but I stand here now and proclaim to you that the ancient prophecies have been fulfilled – a new age has begun. Jesus of Nazareth is the long-awaited Messiah."

The same man began to heckle him again, and Stephen stopped.

"How can Jesus of Nazareth be the Messiah?" said the man. "He was crucified years ago."

Stephen smiled as the murmurs began again. "You are right, my friend – but if you remember that, then you too must have seen Him or heard about Him and the great things He did before His crucifixion."

A second man's voice piped up. "I can remember when he came into Jerusalem on a donkey, of all creatures." the speaker turned to his companions and they all laughed. "Just before Passover it was."

Then another voice: "Was that when he caused all that trouble at the Temple with the merchants and the money changers?"

"Yes, that was it," the second voice replied. "I was there. I can still remember it. There'd never been anything like it before. He called the merchants robbers, overturned the tables of the money-changers and set the sacrificial animals free. It was chaos." He looked around for agreement from his fellows. "Mind you, He was right. The Priests have stood by for years while we've been robbed blind. I thought he was very brave to do such a thing."

"No wonder the authorities had the false prophet crucified," the first man put in sarcastically. An argument broke out between the first man and the second, then other members of the crowd joined in. Stephen sensed trouble looming and tried to defuse the situation.

"I ask you, friends, to listen to the rest of the story – and believe that I speak the truth. Jesus, born of the House of David, was crucified by the Romans, but He died in accordance with the Scriptures – bearing all of our sins upon his own shoulders. He suffered willingly in order to deliver us from this present evil age. Yet it was not the end – for three days after the crucifixion, God raised Him from the dead and exalted Him to sit on His right hand as the Son of God and Lord of the living and the dead."

Stephen studied the confused and openly hostile faces before him, drew in a sharp breath, then delivered his final hammer blow: "Now He has given His Holy Spirit to His followers as an assurance of His Lordship and as a foretaste of His return to be the Judge and Saviour of men at the Last Day." He lifted his face heavenwards and prayed out loud: "Lord Jesus, I pray that your Holy Spirit will enter the hearts of those who do not believe in you, so they may come to know you and bear witness to your Truth. Have mercy on them, o Lord."

A furious row erupted within the crowd. Some jeered and uttered curses at Stephen, some loudly called on Jehovah to send down thunderbolts on the blasphemer's head, and some, obviously overcome by Stephen's powerful words, bowed their heads in prayer. He heard some of the prayers being addressed to Jesus, the Lord, and knew he must speak more with those who were praying, because they were ripe for harvest and must be gathered in. As the unbelievers walked away, still laughing and jeering, he walked over to the new converts and began to speak quietly to them.

"Would you be willing to come with me to meet some of those who actually knew Jesus?" he asked.

At first they were hesitant, but they finally agreed to go with Stephen. Followed by Barnabas, he led them in the direction of the Pool of Siloam, where he knew some of the Disciples would be tending the sick.

As Stephen left with the would-be converts, four men who had stood at the back of the crowd listening to Stephen pushed back the hoods on their cloaks and turned to face each other, their faces filled with fury. Saul saw them standing huddled together deep in conversation.

Suddenly, one of them raised his voice in anger.

"Now we have heard for ourselves that the complaints from our congregation about Stephen are true. We must put a stop to his blasphemy. He's a disgrace, a rabble-rouser. Look how he stirred up the crowd. He cannot go unpunished."

The others agreed with his complaints. Hearing this, Saul approached them.

"I couldn't help overhearing – were you speaking about Stephen of Alexandria?"

The man looked at him. "And if I was, what's it to you? Who are you?" he asked haughtily.

Saul pulled himself up proudly "My name is Saul of Tarsus. I am a pupil of Pharisee Gamaliel." He could see they were impressed.

The man became more deferential. "We are members of the Synagogue of the Libertines. I am an Elder."

Saul nodded. "I have some influence with the Temple authorities, so perhaps I could be of some assistance to you. You see, friends, I happen to know the High Priests too are concerned about Stephen's blasphemous talk. They think he is a troublemaker. Mark my words, Stephen will cause nothing but trouble to all Jews who befriend him, especially those from outside Jerusalem – like yourselves."

Hearing that, they readily agreed to let him help them. He continued to stir up their anger and soon found witnesses amongst them willing to speak against the Alexandrian. When he finally suggested they should go with him to the High Priest, taking their complaints with them, they were eager to obey. Smiling, he promised them he would verify everything they said.

Annas, the High Priest, was delighted to grant the men from the Synagogue of the Libertines permission to take hold of Stephen and bring him to the Sanhedrin for trial; it would be better if his own people arrested him and took the blame off himself. He cautioned them to take him when he was away from the crowd; after all, he thought to himself, the ploy had worked when Jesus of Nazareth had been arrested.

As the four complainants left the temple area and made their way back to the Synagogue of Libertines, they suddenly saw Stephen come from out of a quiet side street. They couldn't believe their luck and hurried after him, grabbing him from behind. Taken by surprise, Stephen struggled with his captors, but there were too many of them. He could do nothing to stop them dragging him to the council chamber. When he was told, Annas was taken aback by the speed of the arrest, but he soon gathered the Sanhedrin together in the council chamber to begin the trial.

Stephen shook his head as one by one the witnesses gave their false statements against him. Annas and Caiaphas stared at the young Alexandrian standing so upright before them, a stance they took as defiance. Annas' voice was clipped as he said: "Are these witnesses speaking the truth?"

Stephen met his gaze, shook his head then looked around the chamber at the hostile faces watching his every move and waiting for words that would condemn him. Then he addressed them. He began by retelling the story of Abraham and the history of the Patriarchs, the story of the giving of the Ten Commandments by God to Moses and the Tent of Testimony made in the desert during the Hebrews' forty years of wanderings, of how Joshua brought the Tent of Testimony to this new land given to them by God.

"There it was until the time of David, who asked God to allow him to build a dwelling place for Him, but it was David's son, Solomon, who built Him a house. The temple rebuilt by Herod, you now have charge of. However, the Most High does not live in houses made by men."

Saul stood at the back of the council chamber glaring at the young man before him, not believing what he had just heard. He looked at the High Priest, who had leaned forward, his hands tightly gripping his chair in anger.

It was the previous High Priest, Caiaphas, the man who had condemned Jesus of Nazareth, who spoke.

"Stephen of Alexandria, you dare to stand before the council and lecture us on the sacred words of scripture? You speak of Moses to us, the religious leaders of this nation? You tell us that God does not acknowledge this magnificent house built for Him? Is it not enough that having already been accused of blasphemy by the elders of the Synagogue of Libertines, you now insult the Holy Temple and its priests?"

Those same elders who had brought Stephen to the High Priest looked at each other, aghast at Stephen's effrontery. Stephen raised himself up.

"The prophet says, 'Heaven is my throne, and earth is my footstool. What house will you build me?' says the Lord. 'Where is my place of rest? Did I not make all these things?'

Stephen looked around the room at the gaping, malevolent faces of the members of the council.

"You stiff-necked men, why do you always resist the Holy Spirit? As your fathers did, so too do you. Which of the prophets did your fathers not persecute? Those who came before the Just One have been killed. You have become betrayers and murderers. You have received the law by the disposition of angels – but you have not kept it!"

A gasp went up from the members of the synagogue and some members of the council rose from their seats, shouting and waving their fists at Stephen. Annas called out in a loud voice, "Members of the Sanhedrin, sit down! Remember where you are. I demand that order be restored, now!" The council members reluctantly sat down.

Stephen knew he had gone too far, but there was no going back now. He had tried so hard to get them to listen to his message of the risen Lord Jesus, but he could see their hearts were set against it – and against him. He looked up towards Heaven and a smile spread across his face. "Behold, I see the Heavens opened. I can see the glory of God – and Jesus, the Son of Man, standing on His right hand".

At that final statement, the whole council rose up and put their hands over their ears to shut out Stephen's voice. They cried out with one voice: "Blasphemy! Stone him! He must die!"

Annas rose up from his seat, his face contorted with anger as he tore his robe. He shouted above the clamour, "I've not heard such blasphemy since Jesus of Nazareth stood before us. Will these lies never end? Every week I'm hearing that more and more misguided people are joining this new sect begun by Him. I got rid of the original troublemaker, and I'll put a stop to those who spread His heresy". He made no attempt this time to stop the council members as they rushed upon Stephen, grabbing at his clothes and punching him.

Saul smiled a satisfied smile. At last, that irritating voice would be silenced. The members of the congregation of the Synagogue of Libertines had played their part well. He would go to the stoning pit outside the city walls and witness for himself the death of Stephen of Alexandria. He laughed as the angry members of the council continued to punch and kick Stephen. One grabbed hold of a handful of Stephen's hair and yanked it until hair and roots came out in a clump.

Annas and Caiaphas sat watching, ignoring the barbarity unleashed before them.

Flavius went to the baths to bathe and soothe away his temper. There he met with the Decurion Julius. Flavius judged the young officer to be at least three years younger than himself, very young to be a Decurion. When Flavius questioned him on this, Julius' reply was filled with pride.

"Yes, sir, I am the youngest Decurion to serve with the Legion Tenth Fretensis."

Flavius' voice held approval. "You must have worked hard to reach this position."

"I have worked very hard, Tribune. I gained this position purely on merit."

Flavius nodded. He was intrigued. He must indeed have gained the position on merit, for he did not think Julius came from a particularly auspicious background, although the family name of Cornelia was one of the more distinguished ancient family names. Given the lower rank of Julius, perhaps he was descended from another branch of the family.

"Tell me something about yourself, Decurion, your background and family."

Feeling slightly uncomfortable, but not wishing to refuse a senior officer, Julius complied with the request.

"I was born in Caesarea. My father is a Centurion at the garrison there. His name is Lucius Cornelius Vittelius. He's a *princeps* – one of the senior *primi ordines*, who, as you know, Tribune, outrank all other centurions in the legions." He saw the impressed look on the senior officer's face. "He's been in the east for over twenty years. We have a house near the coast. My father returns there every time he has leave." His face wore a look of admiration as he spoke of his father. "He's a most remarkable man."

"You don't mention your mother," Flavius gently prompted.

A look of sadness passed across the young man's face. "My mother died five years ago, a typhus epidemic brought ashore by sailors visiting Caesarea. I was fifteen and my sister, Julia Cornelia, was only eleven years old. My father's legion was on duty in Syria, so he didn't know of my mother's grave illness. I was sent to stay with friends and so escaped the worst of it. My sister should have gone with me, but the day we were due to leave, she too fell ill. She had to stay behind with our mother and those devoted servants who volunteered to look after them." He rubbed his forehead, visibly distressed by these painful memories.

Flavius spoke gently. "Did your sister die too?"

"No. By some miracle of the gods, she recovered."

Flavius had heard of this before. Some people came through the most virulent epidemics barely touched by the experience, whilst others died in excruciating agony. He wondered why the gods favoured some more than others.

"My father has never really recovered from my mother's death. He puts on a brave face for the outside world, but he can't hide the sadness in his eyes. He mistakenly feels that if he'd been there he might have saved her. To ease his despair and loneliness he's turned more and more to philosophy."

"That's a strange choice for a veteran soldier," Flavius mused.

"If it gives him some comfort, then I'm glad." Julius slicked back his short, dark hair. "When I told him I too wished to join the army, he said he felt very proud and, although I knew my going would add to his loneliness, he didn't try to stop me fulfilling my ambition."

"You love your father very much, don't you Julius?" Flavius looked into Julius' deep-set eyes.

"Yes, I'm not ashamed to admit it, Tribune."

Flavius felt a pang of guilt. If only he could feel the same way about his father.

"One day I hope to serve at the garrison in Caesarea," Julius continued. "Then I can be closer to my family." He looked straight at Flavius. "If you are ever in that area sir, perhaps you could visit my father, that is, if you don't consider a centurion to be beneath you." He hesitated, hoping he had not insulted his superior officer.

Flavius smiled, seeing the Decurion's discomfort. He knew, even with his limited experience, that the *primi ordines* were the backbone of the legions.

"I would be honoured to meet him, Decurion. It's men such as your father who've made the Empire so powerful and victorious."

Julius smiled, relieved.

A legionary appeared and stopped before Flavius. He saluted and said "Tribune, sir, the Commander requests your immediate presence."

Flavius nodded in acceptance and the legionary saluted and walked away. Flavius guessed that the guide who would show him around Jerusalem had arrived. He took his leave of Julius and hurriedly dressed himself.

As he made his way to the Commander's office his attention was drawn by loud cries. He looked across to the parade ground and saw a squadron of soldiers standing silently watching as two half-naked men strapped to a rough wooden frame were flogged by two burly soldiers. Moving closer, Flavius saw that it was the two drunken legionaries. Looking on was a stern-faced Sextus. The men cried out in agony each time the whip connected with their backs, and Flavius shivered. So this was the punishment meted out by the Chief Centurion.

The flogging finished, Sextus ordered the men to be released. They collapsed in agony and shock onto the hard ground. They were then taken to the hospital, where medical orderlies would tend the raw wounds on their lacerated backs.

Sextus voice rang out to the watching parade. "Men of the First Century, let this be a warning to you all! I will not tolerate drunkenness or any dereliction of duty. You two" – he pointed to two men in the front line – "Clean that mess up." He pointed to the blood-spattered frame and floor surrounding it. "The rest of you, go back to your duties. Parade dismissed!"

Sextus saw Flavius standing there. He walked over to him and saluted. "Tribune, I hope you are satisfied with the punishment meted out. This is how I deal with any kind of insubordination. Sometimes it takes a hard lesson to keep the cohort in line. I think I got through to them today."

Flavius narrowed his eyes. "Yes, Centurion, I think you did." With that he walked away.

Flavius entered the Commander's office. Quintus was looking out of the window, his expression grim after watching the floggings. He turned as he realised Flavius was standing there.

"Sextus is a good centurion, although sometimes a little harsh I think, but he carried out the punishments with my full permission. In this country we cannot afford to be lax or lose sight of what we have to deal with." He walked over to his desk and sat down. "Stand at ease, Tribune, your guide to the city is here."

As if on cue, the guide was shown into the office. He stood beside Flavius. Half turning, Flavius studied the man, who was thick set and dressed in a plain, homespun, grey robe. In his hand he held a matching robe and a spare ochre-coloured head cloth with a plaited cord dangling from it. His hair was greying at the temples, his expression hard and alert. Undoubtedly of Greek origin, Flavius decided. An auxiliary, or a civilian paid by the army to carry out non-military duties.

"This is Philo, your guide." The Commander's voice was clipped.

Philo inclined his head briefly to Flavius. "Tribune." Flavius acknowledged him with a similar nod.

"Show him what he needs to see, no more," Quintus ordered the guide. Then to Flavius, "Philo will take care of you, but you must do as he says and remember what I told you last night – stay away from trouble. Here's what you'll wear." He pointed to the garments Philo held. On Quintus' order, Philo handed the garments over to Flavius. Quintus continued, "Go back to your quarters and put these on. Philo will wait at the gate for you. There are still a few hours before dusk. I want you back here before nightfall."

"Yes, Commander."

Flavius took the rough garments and returned to his quarters. Dismissing Gebhard, he took his uniform off and slipped the tunic over his head, pulling a face as the coarse grey wool chafed his skin. Removing his hobnailed military boots, he pulled on a pair of plain leather boots. He covered his head with the cloth and secured it with the plaited cord. He wondered how his spoilt, overdressed women friends in Rome would react if they could see him now.

Satisfied that his disguise was complete, he slid a dagger inside his boot – just in case – then joined Philo. The two men left the fortress on foot and descended to the City below.

CHAPTER SEVEN

Flavius was looking forward to seeing the city. The Commander trusted Philo to be a suitable escort, so he was happy with that choice. He was eager to see some of the points of interest in the city. But there was one place he wanted to visit first.

"I wish to see the Temple," he said. He wanted a closer look at the magnificent white stone building, whose gold inlaid façade gleamed in the late afternoon sunshine. Set above a series of terraced, colonnaded and walled courts, the whole area was enclosed by a massive defence wall.

Philo was unhappy about this request, but seeing the look on the Tribune's face, he nodded, then led Flavius to a gateway. They entered a large courtyard. Flavius looked around and saw a great deal of activity, for this was where the merchant and money-changing stalls were kept. Flavius wrinkled his nose at the pungent animal smell. Part of the courtyard was filled with cages of doves and enclosures of sheep and oxen. The noise was indescribable as merchants invited pilgrims to buy their wares and frightened beasts bellowed their protests.

"The animals are for sacrifice to their god," Philo explained. "The poorer people buy a dove, the rich a sheep or a bullock. The priests then slaughter the beasts on behalf of the people."

So, thought Flavius, animal sacrifice was the same here as in Rome – a blood token to appease the deity. His attention was turned to a stall where a richly-dressed man was arguing with a merchant.

"The merchant is a money changer." Philo saw Flavius' bemused expression, so he explained further. "When Jews from outside Israel come to the temple in order to buy an animal for sacrifice, or to pay their annual dues, they are not allowed to use foreign money here, so they have to change their money into shekels, temple currency. It is, of course, often abused by the merchants and the visitors are usually short-changed."

Flavius smiled wryly. "Merchants are the same all over the world."

He moved deeper into the courtyard and would have entered the next gateway had Philo not roughly grabbed his arm, forcing him to stop. "No sir. We can't go in there," he said.

"Why?" Flavius wrenched his arm out of the Greek's strong grip, angry at the man's insolence.

Philo led him further along the dividing wall. He stopped and pointed to a stone inscription in Greek. Flavius knew enough of that classical language to understand what the inscription said. He read it out loud: "No stranger may enter within the balustrade or embankment round the temple. Anyone caught doing so will bear the responsibility for his own ensuing death."

"You see, sir," said Philo, keeping his voice low, "on the other side of this wall lies the Court of Women and beyond that the sanctuary area, the holiest place in all Israel. The sacred writings of the Jews, handed down over the centuries, are kept there. Some believe that their god lives there."

Flavius remembered what Quintus Maximus had said about Pompey the Great.

"The inscription must be taken seriously, sir. A few months ago, a drunken legionary foolishly went in there and a dozen spears immediately cut him down. Quintus Maximus could do nothing, for he knows only too well that the law of the temple must not be broken."

Flavius decided he'd seen enough. "Let's get out of here." Philo nodded in agreement.

As the two men walked towards the first gateway, a sudden commotion stopped them. They turned and saw a crowd of people rushing towards them. They were dragging a young man along with them. Philo tried to pull Flavius out of the way as the mob surged past. He was too late; such was the press of people that they could not escape and were caught up in the flowing tide of humanity. They were pushed through the gateway out into the street and onwards until they found themselves outside the city walls.

The young man was dragged to the top of a pit and roughly thrown down into it. The mob, screaming abuse and accusations, spread around the edge of the pit in order to get a good view.

"Come away, sir," Philo urged Flavius. "This is no place for us".

But Flavius was curious to know what was going to happen to the young man. Philo reluctantly positioned himself beside Flavius in order to protect him from the crowd.

"What are they going to do to him?" Flavius asked.

Philo replied grimly "Stone him to death."

"They're allowed to execute a man without Rome's consent?"

"Yes – if it's to do with local religious matters. Governor Pilate doesn't get involved unless there's a threat to the State."

Exactly what the Commander had said, Flavius thought as he looked at the young man in the pit. What he saw astonished him. He wasn't begging for mercy or hurling insults and obscenities at his tormentors; rather he stood quietly, his eyes raised to the sky. His lips were moving but Flavius couldn't hear what he was saying above the baying of the mob.

On the opposite side of the pit stood a thin-faced man, his eyes burning with zeal – and something else. Some of the mob took off their coats and piled them up at his feet. He lifted his hand and shouted "Stone him!"

A heavy-set man bent down and chose a large, jagged edged stone, weighed it in his hand, then threw it with all his might. Flavius winced as the stone caught the condemned man a glancing blow on the shoulder. The impact knocked him off his feet. This acted as a signal to the others. With fierce cries they too began to hurl stones as fast as they could. Blood began to poor from the condemned man's wounds, which incited the mob to a greater frenzy. In a brief respite Flavius heard him cry out "Lord Jesus, receive my spirit!"

This remark made the thin-faced man shout vehemently, "Kill the blasphemer!"

The mob continued to throw more stones until the battered and bloodied man sank to his knees. With one last effort he raised his eyes heavenwards and said in slow, painful gasps, "Lord, do not hold this sin against them."

Flavius stared. Surely his eyes were playing tricks? He thought he saw a bright light surrounding the dying man's head. He blinked and it was gone. Another barrage of stones brutally connected with the prisoner. He keeled over and Flavius knew that he was dead.

He looked across at the thin-faced man and saw his vengeful smile. The man returned his stare, and for a moment their eyes met. Flavius instinctively disliked the man. He was curious to know who he and the dead man were. He turned to a woman next to him and asked her.

"He is Saul of Tarsus," came the reply. "He's been ordered by the High Priest to put an end to the blasphemers."

"What do you mean, blasphemers?"

She studied his face, then said, "You must be a stranger in Jerusalem if you don't know what's been happening."

"I'm a merchant. I've only just arrived in Jerusalem. Who's the dead man?"

Her voice was full of venom. "He was one of the accursed Nazarenes. They've been spreading wicked lies about a carpenter from Nazareth who they claim was the Messiah. Messiah indeed!" She spat on the floor, narrowly missing his feet.

Nazarenes – that was the sect the Commander had told Flavius about.

"That one there." She pointed to the dead man whose body lay half-buried under the mound of stones. "He was the worst of them all."

"What was his name?" Flavius tried to sound disinterested.

"Stephen, a Jew from Alexandria. It would have been better for us all if he'd stayed there."

Better for him too, Flavius thought.

He felt a light touch on his arm. It was Philo.

"I think we should leave now. We must not attract too much attention."

Flavius agreed. He'd seen enough blood spilt for one

day. Besides, a strong wind was blowing up – and he was thirsty.

"I need a drink. I need to wash the stench of death out of my mouth."

Philo nodded. "I know just the place."

The two men hurriedly left the bleak place of execution. They made their way through the busy shop and stall-lined streets, but Flavius was not really interested in the scenes of everyday life taking place all around him. His thoughts were still at the pit of death. Why were his nerves so on edge? He'd seen men die before, in the arena and judicially. Yet, there was something different about this execution. The look on the man's face, such peaceful acceptance, almost joy as the stones had torn into his flesh, the light that had surrounded his head. Flavius knew he hadn't imagined it. Who was this 'Lord Jesus' he'd cried out to? Whoever he was, he hadn't helped his follower.

He pulled himself up. Why worry? It had nothing to do with him.

They entered the bazaar area and Flavius turned his attention to the many things on offer. Stalls and shops displayed clothes and materials in exotic colours, some fine and costly, others of a more coarse fabric. The smell of spices from all over the Empire filled the air. Flavius was fascinated by a cobbler working at his last, fashioning leather into boots and shoes.

He and Philo stopped to look at some pottery and immediately the craftsman began enticing them to view his fine wares. Flavius admired a vase, but did not purchase it. As they moved away, the man cursed. Philo spoke firmly to the man in his own language, and the man shrugged sheepishly, then turned to another customer.

Philo hurriedly caught up with his companion. They suddenly found themselves in the poorer part of the market place. Philo grew uneasy.

"We have wandered too far. I think we should turn back now. The tavern lies this way." He turned and pointed left to a street leading off the main thoroughfare, but before they could reach it, an old man appeared from out of a dark doorway and stood before them. He was dressed in a filthy, tattered robe. Some of his grey, matted hair hung down from under a greasy turban. His beard was straggly, and bits of food were lodged in the corners of his mouth. The old man held up a gnarled hand; his index finger was missing. He spoke in a whining voice: "You want to buy a young girl for a few hours?"

Flavius stepped back from the odious creature. "No" he said firmly and tried to push past him. But the man was stronger than he looked and did not budge from his spot.

"Take a look first." Before Flavius could reply, he clapped his hands and a young girl appeared in the doorway. She wore a dirt-encrusted, faded cloak. The old man hissed at her and she opened the cloak to reveal a totally naked body beneath.

"I promise you, she will fulfil your every desire." He rubbed his filthy hands together. "She's yours for only two tetra drachma." Imagining Flavius' silence to be ignorance of the Greek currency, he pressed on. "Two shekels – eight denarii." His voice grew insistent.

Flavius saw the barely formed buds that later would become breasts. "She's only a child," he said.

"My granddaughter is ten years old. I assure you, stranger, she is a ripe, juicy olive waiting to be harvested."

His leer disgusted the young Roman. "You would sell your own granddaughter?"

The old man smiled, showing black stumps for teeth.

Flavius looked at her again. "Cover yourself up girl," he said. She did so reluctantly, a petulant look on her face.

Flavius reached into the pocket of his robe and pulled out a small leather pouch. He took a number of coins from it and put them into the child's hands.

"Here's enough money to help you. Is there anyone else you can stay with?"

The petulant look had vanished. She stared incredulously at the small fortune she held in her hands.

"Listen to me, girl." Flavius' voice was gentle but firm "Get away from here as fast as you can." He turned on the old man and said threateningly "Get out of my sight before I have you arrested."

Flavius walked away, but was stopped in his tracks by a shout from Philo. "Look out sir!"

Flavius spun round and saw the old man coming towards him, a gleaming knife in his hand. He leapt into action, quickly overpowering the old man and wrenching the knife from his hand, then threw him to the floor. He lay there winded as the Roman and Greek hurriedly left the scene.

The old beggar's thoughts were in a whirl. The young man had been dressed as a merchant, but no trader he knew of could handle himself like that. The other one had called him 'sir'. Something wasn't right here. He must report this to ben-Ezra.

"Anna!" he called to his granddaughter, who had remained rooted to the spot. "Anna, come here and help me." He worried about what she would do. Would she run? She had money of her own now, given to her by the stranger. Would she abandon him? Surely she wouldn't be so cruel; after all he had looked after her for most of her life; her parents having long ago been executed by Rome's decree. He breathed a sigh of relief when she said "Yes grandfather" and helped him up.

Once on his feet, he grabbed her by the shoulders. "You're not going to keep all that money. I want my share."

She clutched it in her hand, not wishing to give it up. He shook her roughly then slapped her hard across her small, pinched face.

"Give me the money." Still she hesitated. "Give it to me!"

Reluctantly she gave it to him. He counted it, then put it gleefully into his own pouch.

"But you have taken it all. That's not fair, it was given to me." He raised his fist to her and she flinched. "Well it's mine now," he sneered. She knew it was useless to protest any further.

"Now, listen to me Anna, I need you to take a message to our leader. This is what you must say…"

He spoke hurriedly and urgently to her, then, having reassured himself that she had learnt the report by heart, he watched as she ran off in the opposite direction. He stood smirking. He would have his revenge on the stranger. Nobody treated old Simon like that.

John Mark felt sick. As he ran, his heart hammered against his rib cage; he thought his lungs would burst, but he had to get back to the others, tell them the terrible news.

Before entering his house, he looked over his shoulder to make sure he'd not been followed. Satisfied that he hadn't, he ran to the door and plunged through it.

Inside, his mother was sitting talking with her brother, Barnabas. She stopped abruptly and stood up as she saw her distraught son. He ran to her and dropped to his knees before her. With tears streaming down his face he tried to speak, but his voice came out as a sob.

"John Mark, whatever's the matter?" Mary laid a consoling hand on her son's head. Her heart was heavy as he raised his tear stained eyes to meet hers.

"Oh mother, they've killed Stephen."

Barnabas rose slowly from his seat, shaking his head in bewilderment.

"But I was with him only this morning."

"Mother gave me some food to take to you and Stephen. When I arrived at the Temple precinct, Stephen wasn't there. I looked around for you, but you weren't there either." He wiped away tears, then continued. "Suddenly, a great shout went up and I saw the people in the temple courtyard look around nervously then quickly disperse. Then I saw Saul of Tarsus – he was with some of the priests and Elders of the Temple. They were shouting for Stephen to be stoned. A mob began to form. With Saul leading the mob, they took hold of Stephen and forcibly dragged him away."

"I'd gone to meet Peter in another part of the city. If only I'd waited!" Barnabas was mortified.

"You could have done nothing except get yourself arrested too." Mary's voice shook with emotion.

John Mark continued his tragic tale.

"I followed the mob at a distance. I could see the top of Stephen's bloodstained head as they pulled and pushed him along. They were moving so fast, I struggled to keep up with them. I had to know what they were going to do to him." He stopped as a great sob shook his chest.

As John Mark told the terrible story of his friend's death, Mary tenderly stroked her son's bowed head, trying vainly to calm him. To die like that... she could not suppress a shudder. Stephen had been like a second son to her. "Gather your faithful servant into your loving arms, Lord," she whispered, choking back her tears.

Grim-faced, Barnabas began to pace the room agitatedly.

"Has the Lord forsaken us?" John Mark's voice rose pitifully.

"Hush now." Mary tried desperately to soothe him. "We must put our trust in Him."

"Stephen trusted Him and He didn't save him. He let him die a hideous death."

Barnabas stopped pacing. "You said that Saul of Tarsus was there?"

"Yes. He was the leader of the mob, urging them on at the stoning pit."

Barnabas sat down heavily. "Then the persecution he threatened has begun." He put his head in his hands. "We must pray that the others come home safely."

Some members of the Sanhedrin, including Gamaliel, were still in the Council Chamber as Saul arrived and stood before the High Priests. "Lord High Priests, the blasphemer Stephen is dead," he announced.

"At last!" Caiaphas's voice held a note of relief. On seeing Saul's frown, he said "Is there something else you wish to tell us?"

Saul took a deep breath. "May I speak plainly, my Lords?" Caiaphas nodded. "There is still work to do. There are many friends of Stephen in Jerusalem who will continue to spread their lies if something isn't done about them – and soon. If they cause trouble…"

Saul stood agitated as Caiaphas turned to Annas. He could not hear what was being said as the two spoke quietly together. He hoped his words would prompt them to act. He knew they were eager to rid the city of troublemakers before Rome intervened, with disastrous consequences.

"Saul of Tarsus, you have our full authority to seek out the blasphemers and throw them into prison," said Caiaphas. A wave of elation swept through Saul.

Annas added: "Go into the houses and shops of those you know to be guilty and arrest them, their wives and their children."

At last Saul was satisfied. With a broad smile on his face, he bowed "It shall be done, my lords." Turning towards Gamaliel, he fixed the old man with a mocking smile, then hurriedly left the council chamber. There was much to be done and time was short.

When the other Disciples were gathered together, they prayed for their murdered friend. Peter looked around the room at his sorrowful friends.

"Just before nightfall, before the gates of Jerusalem are closed, some of us will slip out of the city and hide until it's dark, then we'll go to the pit and recover Stephen's body."

The response was immediate. Cries of: "No!" sounded around the room, for they were afraid of being caught. But Peter would not be swayed. "The least we can do is give him a decent burial. Would you leave him for the wild beasts to devour?"

The protests stopped. Peter continued.

"Once we have buried him, we will go to our converts in Bethpage. It's only a short distance from here. We'll stay there until morning and when the gates are opened, we can mingle with the workmen and visitors and re-enter the city safely."

There followed a general discussion, but in a short while it was decided that a small group of Disciples, led by Peter himself, would leave the safety of Mary's house and slip through the city gates. They hoped to pass the guards easily, for they would be swallowed up in the mass of people hurrying home before the gates locked them in, or out, of the city for the night.

CHAPTER EIGHT

"What's wrong with this tavern?" Flavius had stopped outside a run-down looking inn.

"Not this one, sir." Philo's voice held a note of concern

"Why not?"

"This is not the one I had in mind, sir."

"Well, I'm thirsty and I need a drink after seeing that stoning, and then that old beggar. I insist we go in here."

Philo tried to protest, but Flavius would not be swayed. He reluctantly agreed and led Flavius through the door. Flavius wrinkled his nose in distaste. The inn smelt of rancid oil, stale wine and unwashed human flesh. Though it was dimly lit, Flavius could make out most of the other customers. They included working men and merchants, local and foreign – but no Romans. He asked Philo why this should be.

"Because they'd have their throats cut, or be poisoned. Romans are not welcome here."

Flavius took another look at some of the men who sat at the grubby tables and those who stood in groups, talking in hushed voices. He began to realise the wisdom of the Commander's orders, for dressed like this, he and Philo blended in with their surroundings.

A richly-dressed man entered and sat down at a table nearest the open space in the centre of the inn. As he took in the richness of the man's clothes, Flavius thought the newcomer looked distinctly out of place in these surroundings. He was dressed in a white djeleba with three-quarter length sleeves. A white head cloth, fixed with a white band edged with gold, covered his hair. His beard was brown, etched with grey.

Standing close behind him stood a huge, swarthy slave. He was dressed in a plain red-dyed sleeveless tunic which strained across his massive chest and accentuated his bulging biceps. An ornately-decorated scabbard holding a large, curved sword hung from a wide leather belt around his waist. Crossing his chest was a thick leather strap; it was attached to another decorated scabbard holding a similar sword, which hung across his back. His lower face was framed by a neatly-clipped beard the length of his chin and his oiled dark hair gleamed in the torchlight. His feet up to his shins were encased in brown leather boots.

Flavius was overwhelmed by curiosity. "Who are those men? What are they doing in a place like this?"

"The one in white is known as the Sheikh – the owner of the largest caravan to visit Jerusalem. He is a Nabatean and comes here every year at this time. The silks and perfumes he carries are quickly purchased by Herod Antipas, the Tetrarch of Galilee. His wife, Herodias, will tolerate no other merchant except the Sheikh. He's often been a guest at Herod's Jerusalem palace. As for this place – perhaps he's come to see the beautiful girl who dances here."

Flavius couldn't take his eyes off the slave. What a magnificent sight he would make in the arena. He was more powerfully built than any gladiator Flavius had ever seen.

Philo followed his stare. "His name is Drubaal – he's the Sheikh's personal bodyguard. Outside there will be four Nabatean guards keeping watch to make sure the Sheikh is safe."

Flavius was about to ask Philo how he knew so much about the rich merchant and the dancing girl when a sudden clash of cymbals reverberated around the room. All talking stopped. An atmosphere of expectancy filled the air. Then a drum began to beat out a steady rhythm. It was joined by more drums and the high-pitched sound of reed instruments. The musicians were half-hidden behind a beaded curtain which hung in the doorway leading to the back of the tavern.

A beautiful girl emerged through the curtain. Her skirts were made of peacock blue silk which hung in folds, flowing from her narrow hips down to her ankles. A heavy golden coin and jewel-encrusted girdle encircled her hips. Above her slim waist, her full breasts were barely covered by circlets of gold attached to bands of the same blue silk. Around her neck she wore a gold amulet in the shape of the inverted palm of a hand. Dark eyes smouldered above a veil which hid the lower part of her face. Her hair, the colour of jet, flowed down her smooth back.

She moved slowly and provocatively into the centre of the room. The beautiful encrusted girdle shimmered as she swayed in time to the exotic music. She began to dance. Her hips gyrated and the silver anklets clasped around her slim ankles jangled as the dance grew faster.

Flavius sat entranced. He had never seen so voluptuous a woman. He leaned towards Philo. "Is this the dancing girl you spoke of?"

"Yes. Her name is Al-Maisan. She's the most famous and lusted-after dancing girl in Jerusalem."

"She is indeed very beautiful." Flavius felt desire begin to course through his body.

Philo leaned towards Flavius, keeping his voice low. "She danced before Herod, but Herodias was so jealous that she banned her forever from returning to the palace."

Flavius nodded, not taking his eyes off the girl who danced so sensually before him. He became aware that she was returning his look – and gradually moving towards him. She began to dance around him, so closely he could smell her perfume. His senses reeled.

To the sound of the ever faster hypnotic drum-beats and the skirl of the wind instruments, Al-Maisan danced off towards a group of tables, where some men sat leering lasciviously at her. One of the men sitting there made a grab for her, but she deftly whirled away from him and danced back into the centre of the room.

Whilst all other eyes were on the dancing girl, Philo was keeping watch on the entrance to the inn. He saw two men enter and sit at a table in the opposite corner; he thought he recognised one of them. Philo saw the late-comers begin to scan the room, their eyes eventually settling on him and the young man who sat beside him. Philo hurriedly looked away, his eyes returning to Al-Maisan, who was dancing faster and faster and causing the filmy material of her costume to flare out, revealing long, shapely legs.

The dance reached its frenzied climax and the girl sank gracefully to the floor, her bosom rising and falling with exertion. The show was over. Immediately a loud cry went up for more. The girl rose and bowed, then gathered up the coins the appreciative audience had thrown at her. She glanced at Flavius and smiled at him, then disappeared back through the beaded curtain.

Philo turned cautiously and saw that the two men were no longer watching them, but were engaged in a heated conversation.

"We must return to the garrison, Tribune"

"Not now. I want to meet the girl," Flavius protested.

"Please, sir. It will be dark soon. It's dangerous to stay

any longer. You heard the Commander's instruction. We must go. Now!"

Philo's agitated voice unnerved Flavius. Reluctantly, he nodded and followed Philo out of the inn.

Al-Maisan watched from behind the beaded curtain. She saw the handsome stranger and his companion leave, and saw the two men get up and follow them. She hurried across the room until she came to the Sheikh's table. He welcomed her as if he had invited her to join him. She spoke to him quietly but urgently, then quickly disappeared back through the curtained doorway.

The Sheikh immediately beckoned his bodyguard closer and whispered commands to him. The huge man nodded.

"Yes, master." Drubaal went outside and gave the guards the Sheikh's orders. "Two of you stay here, two of you go inside and keep watch over the master."

The guards obeyed. Satisfied, Drubaal disappeared into the night.

The two disguised merchants hurried through the darkening, winding streets. The market stalls had gone, the shops were closed and the streets were empty. Philo constantly looked over his shoulder. He knew they were being followed. Two men at first, then more; they were flitting in and out of the shadows. The man he'd recognised in the inn was Abraham bar Saraf, a known terrorist and murderer, and part of Eleazar ben-Ezra's gang.

He cursed his own stupidity. He should never have agreed to take the Tribune to that inn, should not have allowed him to stay and watch the dancing girl. He'd been ordered to return him safely to the garrison before nightfall, and he had disobeyed that order. If he came out of this alive, he would have to face the wrath of Quintus Maximus.

The assassins came at them suddenly from behind. Flavius, alerted by Philo's shout of warning, spun round, quickly drawing his concealed dagger ready to defend himself. He fought ferociously, slashing and stabbing at them. Soon two men lay dead at his feet.

Philo too was fighting for his life. As he plunged his dagger into his opponent's stomach, another assassin emerged from the shadows and hurled himself at Philo from behind. Flavius ran to help him, too late. Philo toppled forward, his throat slashed wide open.

The four remaining killers appeared and surrounded Flavius. There were too many; he could never fight them all. He waited for the death blow, but instead, one of the assassins fell mortally wounded at his feet. He felt a rush of air close by and a second attacker slumped to the ground, his neatly severed head rolling past his feet.

The ghost-like figure struck again and another man staggered forward screaming, blood pumping out of the void where once his arm had been. So great was the impact that the arm, with its hand still clutching the sword, fell several feet away. The assassin fell forward in a dead faint.

The survivor of the terrifying assault ran off as though Pluto, the god of the Underworld, were after him.

Relieved, Flavius watched him go, then turned to thank his mysterious saviour, wondering who could have wielded such a weapon of destruction. But there was no one there. He looked around, but could not see the weapon that had done so much damage. A chill ran down his spine. Who was the ghostly form that had intervened and saved his life?

He saw the prostrate form of Philo and knelt beside him, but Philo was dead. He cursed his selfish stupidity. If only he had listened to the Greek and not gone to that tavern, they would be safely back at the fort.

Abraham bar-Saraf had stayed hidden in the shadows. As Flavius leaned over the corpse, he crept forward, lifted his sword hilt and brought it crashing down onto Flavius' skull. Pain ripped through Flavius. Bright lights flashed before his eyes. The world whirled around him, then darkness engulfed him.

Abraham lifted his sword again ready to deliver the death blow, then pulled back. Somewhere in the distance he heard the sound of iron-shod feet and a voice issuing clipped commands. He saw fiery torches coming closer. Romans! He turned and ran, disappearing down the maze of winding alleyways.

Flavius was still unconscious when the Roman night patrol found him.

With Peter and some of the others out of the city to find Stephen and bury him, the rest of the Disciples were gathered together in Mary's house. Suddenly there came the frantic sound of someone knocking on the door.

"Who's there?" John moved towards the sturdy door.

"Philip. Let me in."

John hurriedly unbolted the door and Philip rushed into the room. The news he brought shook them to the core. "All over the city Stephen's fellow Greek-speaking followers, men, women and children are being arrested and thrown into the Temple prison." A groan went up from the Disciples. "The High Priest has also ordered Saul to arrest any Jews who have converted to what he calls the new, blasphemous religion. We are top of his list."

"How do you know this?" John's voice was earnest.

"I have just come from visiting one of our Jerusalem converts, Alexander. He told me. I asked him why he and his wife were hurriedly packing their belongings. He said they were leaving Jerusalem before they too were arrested."

John looked heavenwards. "Lord Jesus, help our brothers and sisters to prevail. Be with us all in our hour of need." As one they all intoned "Amen." This was followed by a brief silence as all present became lost in worried thought.

It was Philip who broke that silence. "If we want the good news of the Lord to survive and prosper, I think it's time we left Jerusalem, and took it to areas outside the city. I've been thinking for a while now about travelling to Samaria. I feel it's the right thing to do."

John thought deeply about Philip's statement. He frowned. "The journey will be dangerous, my friend."

Philip smiled. "Not if the Lord travels with me."

John returned the smile and nodded. "When do you intend leaving?"

"Tomorrow."

"So soon?" John was dumbfounded.

"The sooner the better. There's no time to waste"

"Peter and the others won't be back until tomorrow morning, will you see them before you leave?"

"I will wait until they return. I'd like to go with all of your blessings." He smiled at John.

"Good." John studied Philip's drawn face. "You've been out all day, have you eaten?"

Philip shook his head.

Mary gestured to a seat at the table. "Sit and eat Philip, you must be very hungry." She put some bread, goat's cheese and olives on the table, and a cup of watered wine. Philip sat and gulped down a large mouthful of the wine, then ate hungrily.

Peter and the others returned safely early the next morning. He was surprised by Philip's decision, but when Philip repeated his belief that all would be well if he was guided and protected by the Lord, Peter put his hand on his shoulder and said "Yes, you're right. If you truly believe that the Lord intends you to undertake this journey, then go with my blessing."

He embraced Philip warmly. One by one, the other Disciples offered him their good wishes and blessings.

CHAPTER NINE

Flavius was standing at the foot of a lush green hillside; all around him bloomed sweet-smelling flowers. He felt happy and contented. He climbed to the top of the hill, then descended to the valley below, but instead of beautiful flowers, he found himself ankle-deep in sun-bleached human bones. He waded through them until he came to a pit where a man's body lay half buried under a pile of stones. He walked into the pit and lifted the corpse's head. He screamed – for he was staring at his own likeness.

Flavius opened his eyes, then shut them quickly again, for the light sent waves of pain through his head. After a while he re-opened them. The pain was not so intense now. Slowly his vision began to clear. He was in bed, but he did not recognise his surroundings.

The door opened and Julius entered the room. He

smiled with relief; his senior officer was conscious again. He moved to the bedside, concerned, as he saw Flavius try to lift his head from the pillow but sink back gasping and sweating with the effort.

"No, don't try to move, sir."

"Where am I?"

"In the garrison hospital, sir."

"How did I get here?" Flavius couldn't remember anything.

Julius kept his voice even. "The Commander will answer all your questions when you are fully recovered, sir. For the moment you must rest. You have a severe head wound."

Flavius gently touched his head and winced. "How long have I been here?"

"Three days, Tribune."

"Three days?" Flavius was staggered by the young Decurion's reply.

"Yes sir."

As Julius spoke, a medical orderly walked towards Flavius. Seeing that his patient was awake, he ushered Julius out of the room. Then he began to examine his patient's wounds.

It was another two days before Flavius was fit enough to leave the hospital. The first thing he did was check on Saturn. The horse was calm and his coat shone with constant brushing. The room was immaculate, the stone slabs had been scrubbed clean and there was clean straw on the floor and fresh fodder and water in their containers.

Satisfied, Flavius spoke softly to Saturn. "I'm sorry I've neglected you, I promise I'll make it up to you," he murmured. Saturn nuzzled his hand.

Zeno appeared in the doorway. "I trust all is well, Tribune?"

"Yes, thank you, Zeno, and thank you for taking care of my horse whilst I was in hospital."

Zeno bowed. "I exercised him every day, Tribune."

"You've done well. Saturn is looking sleek and happy."

"I am glad. If I may be of further service..."

"Not now, Zeno. I have to see the Commander."

Zeno bowed again, then walked away. Flavius made his way to the commander's office, satisfied that Zeno was indeed a good groom. The Commander was relieved to see Flavius back on his feet, but his voice was grim as he said "You were lucky, Tribune. Unfortunately, Philo wasn't."

Flavius swayed, and then, with a great effort, steadied himself. Blurred images of the Greek guide flashed before him.

Quintus locked his steel grey eyes onto Flavius. "Can you remember anything at all about that night?"

Haltingly, Flavius recounted details of the scant memory he had of that fateful night. The Commander stood stony faced until Flavius had finished, then roared, "You gave money to a beggar, a prostitute?

Flavius replied sheepishly. "She was only a child, Commander."

Quintus shook his head in disbelief. "You say an old man was with her?"

Flavius nodded.

"Describe him."

Flavius tried to remember what the old man looked like, but his memory was hazy. He felt a wave of dizziness sweep over him and fought the urge to vomit. "I'm sorry, sir, I can't remember."

"It was undoubtedly he who betrayed you to the assassins. He must be part of ben-Ezra's gang. Do you know how long we've been trying to capture that brigand?"

The dizziness passed. Flavius looked down as Quintus kept up the tirade.

"And what in the name of Jupiter possessed Philo to take you to that inn?"

"I wanted a drink. I thought it was just an ordinary inn, sir."

"It isn't just any watering hole!" Quintus was almost shouting now. "Didn't Philo tell you we've had that place under surveillance for some time?"

"No sir." Flavius' head ached intolerably. He desperately wanted to escape the Commander's raised voice, to lie down and forget the pain and guilt he felt. Instead he said "But how did the beggar know we weren't merchants?"

"Because you made the mistake of throwing your money around – no merchant would do that. And you defended yourself too professionally. As a result of your stupidity Philo paid for your mistakes with his life. It almost cost you yours too. Had it not been for the Night Watch arriving, you too would most certainly have been killed."

Flavius wanted to know who had alerted them. Had it been the one who'd dispatched the assassins with the terrifying weapons? But Quintus would not be drawn. Instead he said: "The Governor is staying at Herod's Palace and he wants to see you. I've no doubt he will tell you more. Go and smarten yourself up and don't keep him waiting too long, he is not a patient man. Since you are new to Jerusalem I will provide you with a small escort to accompany you to the palace. That's all, Tribune!"

Flavius saluted the Commander and went out.

Quintus stared after him, murmuring irritably "I knew he would be trouble."

Flavius ordered Gebhard to dress him in a fresh tunic and his newly-cleaned armour. He frowned as he felt the weight of the polished helmet. Would this ache in his head never go? He picked up the pouch holding his mother's letters and went outside. Four legionaries were waiting for him. They marched two on either side of him as they made their way to Herod's Palace.

The magnificent palace, built by Herod the Great, was situated on an upper hill on the western side of the city. It was a short distance from the fortress and reached by crossing a viaduct linking the palace to the Temple area.

Flavius looked up at the three towers surrounding it. Like the Temple, the architecture and design were superb.

He entered the courtyard and approached one of the

palace guards. The guard was talking with another of Herod's soldiers and both were dressed in black with silver accoutrements; the first guard was obviously of higher rank. The guard looked him up and down, barely concealing the contempt on his face. Flavius sensed immediately that this was not a man who welcomed Romans in his country.

"I am Malachi, Captain of Herod's Guard," said the guard. "Who are you?"

Flavius felt his temper rising. How dare this Herodian guard speak to him in such a haughty way? With great effort he held his temper in check and replied calmly, "I am the Tribune Flavius Quinctilius Silvanus. The governor is expecting me."

Flavius stifled a smile as he saw the man's obvious discomfort. The guard's tone immediately changed to one of stiff deference.

"Tribune, please follow me."

Flavius ordered the legionary escort to wait for him in the courtyard, then followed Malachi into the palace and along a corridor. Shafts of sunlight from the latticed windows set high above the gaudily-painted walls illuminated the magnificent tessellated floor. Costly ornaments stood on marble shelves carved into recesses set all along the walls. They were flanked by carved columns. One shelf held a marble bust of the Emperor Augustus Caesar, who had been a personal friend of Herod the Great. Another held a bust of the present Emperor, Tiberius Caesar. A quick glance showed Flavius that the sculptor had somewhat flattered, but basically captured, the proud features of both Emperors.

Flavius had never been inside the Emperor's Palace on the Palatine Hill, set above the busy Forum in Rome, but his father had. He had listened in awe to his father's description of the palace, both externally and internally: the towering, beautifully-carved marble columns, the exquisite mosaic floors, the subtly-painted friezes adorning the walls, the classical sculptures and works of art from all corners of the Empire. He had imagined the Royal Family at leisure in the magnificent gardens with their sparkling fountains and fruit trees highlighting a stunningly beautiful backdrop. Surely a dwelling place fit for the gods. He had to be content with those imaginings now that Tiberias preferred his palace on the Island of Capri. The Emperor had a morbid dislike of Rome, its residents and the incessant plotting that went on in the city. Tiberias obviously felt safer on his island.

As Flavius followed the guard along the corridor, he thought Herod had tried to copy the interior of a classical Roman palace, but despite the many craftsmen's efforts, it lacked subtlety. Herod Antipas had once lived in Rome, so he had attempted to add some typical Roman features, but Flavius came to the conclusion that it was a pale imitation of the palace on the Palatine Hill.

Flavius had heard stories about Herod the Great's son, Antipas, and his family. Antipas was known to be weaker than his father, very superstitious, sly and untrustworthy.

His illicit love for his wife Herodias had driven him to steal her from her previous husband, his half-brother Philip, Tetrarch of Ituraea. This had caused further enmity with those Antipas ruled in Galilee and Peraea. Flavius thought it a romantic story, but wondered if that enmity had been worth it, for she was said to be a devious plotter with a cruel manner. Her daughter Salome's beauty, however, was legendary amongst both Jew and Roman alike. He hoped he might meet them, or catch a glimpse of them, during this visit to judge for himself what the truth was about this exotic family.

Malachi stopped before a heavy door guarded by two Roman soldiers standing at attention. Flavius stepped forward and announced himself to them. As the Romans saluted Flavius, Malachi turned and walked smartly away. One of the soldiers opened the door, then stood aside as Flavius stepped into a large room; the door closed quickly behind him. Compared to the extravagance of the corridor outside, the room was austere; it was empty, except for an ornate, backless wooden chair inlaid with ivory with X-shaped legs and low, curved arms. It was set on a raised dais at the far end of the room. He remembered Quintus' words: that Pilate had changed. He wondered how much.

A door secreted in the wall opened and suddenly Pilate was walking towards him. Flavius stood rigidly at attention and saluted the Governor. Flavius saw that the Commander had been right, for the man standing before him had indeed changed. Gone was the natural easy-going manner he remembered from his childhood; instead Pilate's expression was hard, his eyes haunted, and the lines around his mouth caused by constant tension, marred his once distinguished good looks.

"My dear boy." Pilate smiled, easing some of that tension and smoothing out those lines in his face. He saw Flavius' nervous expression. "Please stand at ease – after all, we are family."

Flavius visibly relaxed. "Thank you, sir."

"How is your dear mother? Well, I hope."

"She is very well, Lord Pilate."

"Good, good. And your father and brother?

"They too are well."

Pilate nodded. "Has young Marius decided on his future yet?"

Flavius kept his voice steady "He has yet to decide, sir."

"When he does I'm sure he'll make a success of his chosen career. I remember he was always very studious."

Flavius felt uncomfortable hearing the praise for his brother and changed the subject.

"May I ask after the health of Lady Claudia Procula?"

Pilate smiled at the mention of his wife. "She too is well, Flavius, although these days she doesn't travel with me so much. She prefers the fresh sea air of Caesarea to the heat and claustrophobic atmosphere of Jerusalem."

Flavius was disappointed. He liked the Lady Claudia. "I was hoping I might see her sir, it has been a long time."

"Yes it has, Flavius. Perhaps you can visit us at Caesarea some time – we'll see what we can do."

"Thank you, sir. I'd like that. I have some correspondence for you from my mother."

Flavius reached into the pouch and pulled out his mother's letters. He presented them to Pilate, who tucked them into the folds of his immaculately-folded toga.

"I'll read these later." He studied Flavius closely. "You are very pale, Flavius. I hope you have recovered from your little adventure?"

Flavius caught the hint of sarcasm in the Governor's voice. He was afraid he had made a bad start to his new career, one Pilate might not forget. He pulled himself up. "I think so, sir, apart from a headache," he said. He ran the back of his hand gently over his forehead. "With your permission, Governor Pilate, there are many questions I would like to ask."

"First, tell me what you can remember."

Flavius repeated all he could remember of that night's events. The Governor listened intently. When he'd finished, he looked grim.

"I'm sorry about Philo, he was a good man. Quintus Maximus is convinced that the beggar is a member of a gang of cutthroats, led by Eleazar ben-Ezra. Perhaps you'd like to tell me why you allowed yourself to be in that situation with the beggar in the first place?"

Flavius felt his face redden. So the Commander had already debriefed Pilate. The Governor knew everything. He must be honest now.

"Governor Pilate, I behaved irresponsibly. I am ignorant of the ways of the east. I let my guard down with the beggar and the girl. I wish we had never gone to that tavern. I deeply regret my actions. I take full responsibility for the death of Philo. I deserve whatever punishment you decide to give me for my stupidity, sir."

Pilate looked at him sternly. "I'm glad you found the courage to tell me the truth, Flavius, for, as I'm sure you had already guessed, the Commander had told me as much. We knew that sometimes members of the gang frequented that place, that's why we had it under surveillance. There is, however, someone here who can tell you more."

Pilate clapped his hands and a slave appeared through a side door. He spoke quietly to the slave who bowed then left the room.

The slave soon returned. Following him was a woman. Her body was enveloped in a long cloak, the voluminous hood hiding her face. She threw back the hood.

Pilate greeted her warmly and smiled as he saw the look of disbelief on Flavius' face.

"Tribune Flavius Quinctilius Silvanus, let me introduce you to Al-Maisan – or to use her correct name: the Princess Farrah Yasmin bint Hassan Al-Khareem."

Flavius stood motionless as his eyes took in the beautiful woman standing before him. As she moved towards him, the cloak opened to reveal her shapely body.

Her dress was modestly cut in white linen with thin strands of gold crossing her full bosom. Her long hair was carefully arranged on top of her head, held with gold pins. She looked every inch the Roman maiden, and more beautiful than he had ever thought possible.

"Tribune." Her honeyed voice brought him out of his reverie. "I am glad to see you alive and well."

Seeing his confused look, she smiled. "After you left the tavern that night, I overheard the conversation between the assassins saying they were going to follow you."

"But how did you know who we were?" Flavius asked, confused.

Pilate interrupted, "It is her business to know – the Princess works for Rome."

His words took Flavius completely by surprise.

Pilate continued "Quintus Maximus had told her a new Tribune from Rome was expected at the garrison and when she saw Philo with a stranger..." He saw the puzzled look on the young Tribune's face. "You see, the Princess and Philo were working together undercover, observing the movements of ben-Ezra's men. We installed the Princess there as a dancer, an art she performs magnificently." He took Farrah's hand and kissed it, and Flavius saw his look of deep admiration.

"I'm surprised Philo took you there," said Pilate.

"I'm sorry to say that he didn't want to, it was on my insistence we went inside, sir."

"His death is a great pity, but Tribune, you didn't know about his undercover work. Besides, we don't always know when ben- Ezra will return to Jerusalem, he covers his tracks well. But it was not he who attacked you that night, it was his second in command, Abraham bar-Saraf."

Flavius vaguely remembered the ghostly figure who had intervened. "That night someone saved my life. Do you know who it was?"

Farrah smiled. "That was Drubaal." Where had Flavius heard that name before? "He is the Sheikh's bodyguard. The Sheikh too acts in Rome's interests. When I voiced my concern to him, he sent Drubaal to protect you. It was he who saved your life."

Flavius remembered the Sheikh and the huge slave who had stood behind him with the strangely-shaped weapons across his back and waist. It seemed there was a network of foreign spies in Rome's pay.

"I am deeply grateful to him," he said.

"I will tell him. He will be happy to know you have recovered from your wounds. It will go some way to alleviating the distress he feels for not being able to save Philo." Her expression grew sad as she remembered the faithful Drubaal's pain and guilt at the loss of her fellow spy.

She turned her attention back to Pilate. "Do you require me to dance at the tavern tonight?"

Pilate shook his head. "No, I think you had better return to Bethany for the time being. Keep a low profile. I don't want you placed in any unnecessary danger. I will have it spread around that you are suffering from a fever and are too ill to dance."

She inclined her head. "As you command."

He returned her smile. "And now, Princess, Tribune, I have many affairs of state that I must attend to. A carpentum will be waiting outside Princess Farrah ready to take you back to Bethany."

Knowing that the audience was over, Farrah bowed and Flavius saluted the Governor. Pilate briefly returned the salute, took Farrah's hand and kissed it lightly, then disappeared back through the same secret door by which he had previously entered.

Flavius escorted Farrah outside to a different part of the courtyard, where the ornate carpentum waited. He knew for certain that Pilate held Farrah in high regard, for a carpentum was usually a means of travel for only high-born Roman women or for members of the Emperor's family.

Flavius couldn't contain his curiosity any longer. "The Governor called you Princess, yet you spy for Rome."

"I am a Princess of Nabataea. As you know, my country has an alliance with Rome. Besides" – she glanced away for a brief moment, a brief look of pain masking her lovely features – "I have a personal score to settle." Before she stepped into the vehicle, she turned to Flavius and looked up at him with large, almond shaped eyes.

"I am sure these revelations have come as a shock to you," she said.

He ran his hand through his hair and smiled. "Yes, they have."

"I would like to tell you more of my story and how my uncle and I came to spy for Rome – that is, if you wish to know?"

Flavius relished the fact that he had been given this new, unexpected chance of seeing this lovely woman again.

"I would very much like to know more about you," he replied.

Her dark eyes fixed on his. "I shall look forward to seeing you at my house in Bethany," she purred. "That is, when you have the time."

Flavius tried to keep his voice steady, but he could not control the surge of excitement that shot through him. He would make sure he found the time.

"The garrison doctor says I am not yet fit enough to resume my duties," he said.

A look of disappointment crossed her face.

"But I am sure I am well enough to come to Bethany – when you say, of course."

Her smile was radiant. "Tomorrow then. I will send someone to guide you."

Assisted by Flavius, she daintily stepped inside the two-wheeled covered carriage. The driver flicked the reins and the horse-drawn vehicle slowly moved out of the courtyard and down into the busy street below.

Flavius looked up at the sun. It was only mid-afternoon. He knew the hours would pass slowly until the next day came. Expectation coursing through him, he made his way back to the waiting legionaries.

CHAPTER TEN

In anticipation that he might further his blossoming friendship with the beautiful Farrah, Flavius rose early and went to the bathhouse, taking his own personal body slave, Gebhard, with him. After he'd left the steam room, Flavius lay on the marble table thinking of the day to come. The bathhouse slave scraped the dirt off his sweating body. When this was done, before he moved on to the next section of the bathhouse, Flavius dismissed the slave, who, with a questioning look on his face, bowed and left the room.

Flavius beckoned Gebhard forward. "When I've finished bathing, I want you to pay particular attention to the post bathing ritual," he said.

Gebhard bowed. "All is ready, Tribune."

Flavius nodded, then went into the tepidarium. After loosening up his muscles by swimming, he went on to the frigidarium, where Gebhard was waiting in the room outside. Newly invigorated, Flavius lay on the slab there as Gebhard vigorously massaged his body with expensive oils. The slave then shaved the stubble off his chin. He carefully barbered Flavius' hair, and in order to disguise Flavius' rank, dressed him in a clean, plain tunic.

Back in his quarters, Flavius paced up and down impatiently. Would the guide never come? His pacing was interrupted by a knock. Gebhard answered the door and stood back open-mouthed as a colossus entered the room. The visitor briefly inclined his head, then said, "Tribune Silvanus, my mistress awaits you." His deep, accented voice was surprisingly soft.

"Drubaal! How did you get in here?" Flavius was genuinely surprised to see the huge slave enter his room. Then he remembered; Drubaal was a spy in Rome's pay. That was how he had been able to pass the Guard unmolested and reach these quarters.

"If you will come with me, Tribune." said Drubaal.

Flavius fastened a large cloak across his broad shoulders and followed Drubaal out of the room to the covered wagon waiting in the courtyard. Flavius climbed onto the vehicle and sat beside the slave.

Drubaal looked at Flavius. "Pull your hood up, please Tribune. You mustn't be recognised or you will place my master and mistress in danger."

Flavius pulled the hood of his cloak over his head. Drubaal lifted his own hood and covered his long, dark hair. At his command, the horse pulling the wagon moved forward.

As they journeyed on, Flavius took the opportunity to thank Drubaal for saving his life. Without taking his eyes off the road, Drubaal nodded in reply. The only information Flavius could glean from the taciturn slave was that he had originated from Carthage. Flavius frowned. Carthage was known to all Romans as the "old enemy", the hated ones. Images from youthful studies flashed across his mind. The Punic Wars and the Carthaginian leader, Hannibal. Using a herd of war elephants, that warrior, with his army, had managed the seemingly impossible feat of crossing the mountains that lay far to the north of Rome. He had almost put an end to the Roman Republic. Flavius remembered his tutor explaining the many reasons why the invasion had ultimately failed: the victories of the great general Scipio Africanus and the political wrangling and war amongst the allies of Carthage, ending in the total annihilation of the city by the Romans, who sowed the earth with salt so that nothing might grow. Twenty-odd years later, an illustrious member of the Republican Senate, Gaius Gracchus, had established Carthage as the first Roman Colony outside Italy. Julius Caesar's efforts had seen it begin to prosper. It had become a city again as part of the Empire during the reign of the Divine Augustus.

Flavius wondered how much of this historical information was known by Drubaal, and if he did know, what his feelings were about his nation's treatment by

Rome. Flavius looked again at the proud profile and saw a high brow and eagle-beak nose – prominent Phoenician features. He also remembered learning about Phoenicia and had admired that warlike nation. The Phoenicians had founded Carthage centuries before, when Rome was emerging as a small settlement on the banks of the Tiber. So Drubaal had come from an ancient bloodline, yet now he was a slave. One day, he decided, he would ask him about his past.

Drubaal did not acknowledge the young officer's stare but kept his eyes on the road ahead. How he hated the Romans. If it had not been his master's wish that he should save the man seated beside him, he would have willingly left him to die. He scowled as he flicked the reins of the large bay horse pulling the wagon, increasing its speed.

Before long they reached the house, which was set in the wealthy suburb of Jerusalem. Standing alone on top of a hill, it looked like a typical upper-class Jewish home. They entered the spacious courtyard, where Drubaal pulled on the reins and the horse stopped. Flavius climbed down from the wagon. A stocky slave unhitched the horse and took it to the stables. The Sheikh's four guards, who were barracked in an outbuilding next to the stables, briefly stared at Flavius, but seeing him with Drubaal, they relaxed and carried on playing their board game of Mancala.

A young girl came out of the house and bowed before Flavius. He guessed that she was no more than sixteen years old. Her pretty face was framed by a headdress in traditional Jewish style and her slight body was dressed in a simple robe, belted at the waist.

"Please, follow me, Tribune," she said. He followed her into the house, where she ushered him into a room.

What he saw made him gasp. Exquisite silken hangings adorned the walls, and lamps of beaten gold hung from stands set at regular intervals around the room. One side of the room had floor to ceiling latticed windows; the top half of the latticework was open to let in air to cool the room from the encroaching heat. On the opposite side of the room, a doorway, covered by a beaded curtain, separated the room from another behind. In the centre of the room stood two silken couches set opposite each other. Small, ornate tables stood next to them. Close by cushions lay piled up on the floor. Expensive woven rugs were scattered around the room. It looked like the inside of a wealthy desert dweller's tent.

The slave girl bowed as her mistress entered the room.

"Welcome, Tribune." Farrah flashed him a dazzling smile showing even white teeth. Flavius was mesmerised by the vision standing before him. An ornate silver hair adornment held her beautiful thick hair away from her lovely features, causing the ebony waves to cascade down her back. She wore a flowing gown of vermillion silk. Silver filigree clasps fixed one on each shoulder caused the delicate fabric of the bodice to hang in folds across her bosom. Around her waist she wore a wide matching silver filigree belt. On her feet she wore dainty silver-threaded vermilion slippers.

Flavius wondered vainly if she had dressed so beautifully for his sake, but then he chided himself. She was a princess, and these clothes would be natural for someone of her standing. Of one thing he was sure: she was like a goddess come to earth in human form.

"Ruth." Farrah spoke to the slave girl without taking her eyes, skilfully darkened with kohl, off Flavius. "Inform my uncle that the Tribune has arrived,' she said. 'And please bring food and wine."

"Yes mistress." Ruth bowed, and casting a glance at the handsome Roman who was obviously entranced by her mistress' beauty, she stifled a girlish giggle and left the room.

"Please." Farrah gestured towards one of the couches. Flavius sat down on one, while she draped herself sensuously over the other. He smelt the same heady perfume she had worn when she had danced in the tavern.

Before he could speak, the sound of the beaded curtain being drawn to one side made him look up. He received another jolt of surprise, for standing in the doorway was the Sheikh. He walked over to Farrah, picked up her proffered hand and kissed it. Then, turning towards Flavius, he greeted him in the way of his people, by placing his fingers to his mouth and forehead.

Farrah smiled at the Tribune's obvious surprise. "Tribune, this is my uncle, Sheikh Ibrahim bin Yusuf Al-Khareem."

"I am happy to see you have recovered from your wounds," said the Sheikh.

"Only through the timely appearance of your bodyguard." Flavius recovered himself quickly and returned the Nabataean's smile, studying him closely. The older man was bare headed, allowing him to see his features clearly. His dark brown hair was etched with grey, matching his well-trimmed beard. He had thick, unruly eyebrows above a large hawk nose which dominated his weather beaten face.

"I understand the surprise on your face,' said the Sheikh. "My niece has told me that you come from an aristocratic Roman family. You are no doubt wondering why my niece and I are in Jerusalem spying... no, I do not like that word, I prefer gathering information... for Rome. My niece, I am sure, will tell you of her part in the saga in due course." He sat down on the heap of cushions on the floor and crossed his legs in Bedouin fashion. "For myself, I have the honour of being the Chief Minister for Trade and personal Emissary to His Majesty King Aretas, King of Nabatea. As you know, our King drew up an alliance with Rome some time ago. Apart from political expediency, our two countries share certain mutual interests. One of those interests is the capture and execution of cutthroats and brigands who interfere with the caravan trade routes. Our caravans, of which mine is the largest and most travelled, are a major source of wealth for Nabataea. As for Rome, we bring her the finest silks, spices and artefacts to be found in the Empire and beyond..."

They were interrupted by Ruth bringing in the refreshments. She set down dishes of sweetmeats and delicate pastries on the table, followed by a silver carafe of wine with matching wine cups. She bowed to her master and mistress and waited for further instructions.

Sheikh Ibrahim told Ruth to pour wine into their guest's cup. Flavius sipped it, and a look of delight crossed his face. It was superb. He commented on its rich, full flavour.

"But this wine is far superior compared to the local wines here."

Sheikh Ibrahim laughed. "It is made from the choicest grapes harvested from the vineyards of the Rhône Valley. Consignments are specially retained for me by one of my suppliers in Antioch. It is a particular favourite with Herod Antipas. Having sampled it, I too liked the taste and bought extra amphorae to store some for my own use. I'm glad you like it."

The conversation turned to commercial life in Rome and the many merchants who visited the Capital of the Empire. While he spoke, Flavius was conscious of Farrah's eyes upon him. From time to time he would return her look, but she would turn away coyly and look at her uncle, or concentrate upon a dainty sweetmeat on the table close by.

Their eyes met. "I have never been to Rome," Farrah purred. "What is it like?"

Flavius told her about the wonderful architecture of the state buildings and described the grandeur of the temples dedicated to the gods the Romans worshipped. He described the opulence of the Emperor's palace and the wealthy villas set in the suburbs and hills overlooking the city, including his family's residence. Farrah sat entranced by his descriptions. When he had finished, she said, "I hope one day I might visit this wondrous place."

Flavius hoped it would be he who would escort her to his homeland. Then, after gentle prompting from Farrah, he told them about his family and his hopes for a political career. The conversation flowed back and forth between the three of them, until suddenly Flavius put his hand to his head and grimaced with pain.

"Is something wrong, Tribune?" Ibrahim was concerned.

"It seems the doctor was right, I haven't recovered sufficiently from my wound. I'm sorry to appear rude, but perhaps I ought to return to the garrison."

"I will ask Drubaal to drive you back." The Sheikh called out and Drubaal came into the room and bowed.

"The Tribune is not feeling well. Escort him back to the Antonia."

Drubaal bowed again as the Sheikh looked at Flavius.

"I'm sorry you are not well, but I understand your head wound was rather serious. We hope you will return here and see us again soon."

"I would be delighted," Flavius replied. He said his goodbyes and left the house.

On the journey back to Jerusalem, Flavius thought his head would burst with pain. He left Drubaal and went straight to his quarters. He let himself be undressed by

Gebhard, then threw himself onto his bed. He was angry that his longed-for visit to see Farrah had turned out this way; he had been so looking forward to taking up his new duties and seeing the Princess again. With her name on his lips, he fell into a deep and troubled sleep.

It was several days later that Flavius received an invitation from Sheikh Ibrahim to visit his house again. Flavius replied, thanking him and saying when he would be free. Now that day had come. He waited impatiently for Drubaal to arrive. When he did, Flavius could hardly wait to begin the journey to see Farrah once more.

The Sheikh welcomed Flavius into his house. He looked at Flavius and smiled.

"I am relieved to see you looking so much better now. You quite frightened us the other day. My niece and I have been worried about you. That is the reason for my invitation to you to come and visit us, and here you are, looking healthy once more."

Farrah came into the room. Seeing Flavius standing there, her face lit up in a smile. "Tribune Silvanus, how lovely to see you."

Her smile and the thought that she had worried over him melted his heart. "Thank you. I'm glad to see you both again."

Ruth brought in refreshments and the Sheikh pointed to a couch. "Please sit down, Tribune. Will you drink some wine with us?"

Flavius remembered the gorgeous wine he had drunk on his last visit here. "It would be an honour, Sheikh Ibrahim."

The conversation flowed back and forth. Flavius tried to concentrate on what the Sheikh was saying, but was constantly aware of Farrah and the shy looks she was giving him. For his part, he was finding it increasingly difficult to stop himself smiling at her in return.

Time passed too quickly. Reluctantly, Flavius realised it was time for him to return to the fortress. After giving his thanks for the invitation and saying his farewells, he climbed up onto the cart, where Drubaal waited to take him back to Jerusalem.

On the journey to the Antonia, Flavius took the opportunity to ask Drubaal about his background. At first, the Carthaginian stayed silent then, at Flavius' insistent prompting, he said: "When I was a child, my father told me about our ancestors' illustrious history. He said that our original ancestor was a Phoenician warrior, one who helped to create Carthage. His wife came from a high-born Phoenician family. For generations, their descendants were wealthy and respected. Then... the *Romans* came."

Flavius flinched at the sound of contempt in Drubaal's voice.

Drubaal continued, "After the Roman general defeated Carthage and destroyed the city, there were some survivors, and my father said they included his legendary great-great grandfather and his wife, who escaped west into Algeria.

Their children and their children's children lived in peace for many years, until Julius Caesar and his army increased the conquest of North Africa. The descendants of those who had originally escaped were gradually recaptured. My great grandfather and his family were some of the unfortunates. They were condemned to slavery and put to work restoring the land now renamed New Carthage, to grow crops, rebuild the houses and construct Roman temples."

He hesitated for a moment, obviously trying to control his rising resentment. Then he took a deep breath and continued, "From that time on, my family have been slaves. My father once said that whatever might happen to me, I should never lose my pride. My mother and father both died in bondage in Rome's New Carthage." He sneered as he said the last words, and Flavius could feel his tension.

"As I grew older and stronger I was taken from my country and shipped to Tripolitania, where I was sold to a wealthy Roman official to work the fields on his large estate. He was a cruel man." Drubaal's hands tightened on the horse's reins, his knuckles turning white at the memory of those days. "I tried to escape many times. Each time I was recaptured, I suffered cruel beatings – the scars on my back bear testimony to that. Knowing I would never give up the attempt to escape and would never be tamed, the master ordered me to be crucified. Then he changed his mind, realising I was financially worth more to him alive than dead, so he sent me back to the slave market and put me up for auction."

Flavius was curious. "So how did you become the property of Sheikh Ibrahim?"

Drubaal bristled. "I am nobody's property, Tribune. Fortune was on my side that day. The owner of a gladiator school was impressed by my physique and put in a bid for me to train as a gladiator." Drubaal shuddered. To become a gladiator was an occupation he had always dreaded. "Sheikh Ibrahim was also at the auction. He increased the size of the bid and eventually won."

Drubaal's relief had been profound when the Sheikh had told him he wanted him as a personal bodyguard. "He has always treated me as a trusted servant, not as a slave," he told Flavius. He flicked the horse's reins, annoyed that he had been made to relive things he would rather forget. "You asked me about my life, Tribune, and I have told you."

The bitterness he felt towards the Romans had eaten away at his soul. Yet, now, after all that Rome had done to him, here he was escorting one of its hated citizens, one who had become friends with his much-loved master and the beautiful princess.

Flavius did not know how to react. He had never heard Drubaal speak so freely and knew he'd caused upset by making the Carthaginian recount his life story and reveal how much adversity he had faced. Yes, the goddess Fortuna had surely been on his side the day the Sheikh had successfully bid for him at that auction.

With both men lost in their thoughts, the rest of the journey passed in silence.

CHAPTER ELEVEN

It was time for the slave-girl Ruth and Boraz, a fellow servant, to make their weekly visit to Jerusalem to pick up fresh supplies. Ruth sat impatiently in the cart. Where was Boraz? She wished he would hurry, for she was eager to reach Jerusalem. Today was market day and provisions were needed from the marketplace, but she also had another destination in mind. She adjusted her head-square and made sure it was folded properly to make a sunshield for her eyes and neck.

As she tied the plaited cord holding it in place, Boraz appeared. The stocky Thracian climbed into the driving seat on the cart, clicked his tongue and at a sharp command, the horse moved off.

As they trotted along the Bethany road towards Jerusalem, Ruth noticed the old beggar standing by the roadside. He'd come to that spot many times over the past weeks and whenever Ruth saw him she tossed the old man a coin, an act which irritated Boraz.

"You should save your money, instead of wasting it on scum like that," he grumbled.

"He's one of life's unfortunates," Ruth countered, earning a contemptuous look from Boraz. She knew only too well what it was like to be poor and hungry. She had been orphaned at an early age and left to fend for herself on the streets of Jerusalem, until the day the Sheikh had found her hungry and wretched and taken her under his wing. For the past two years she had been the servant of his niece, the princess.

Ruth could see the walls of Jerusalem in the distance. She suppressed her excitement. Soon she would be with John Mark and her new-found friends. She had never been instructed about the faith and traditions of her people, but she had always stared open-mouthed at the grandeur of the Holy Temple. She was constantly overwhelmed by the wonderful architecture, excited by the crowds who thronged to its courtyards and moved by the beggars who sat near the Beautiful Gate. She always shivered when she looked at them, remembering her past life.

It was at the Temple that she had first met John Mark. He'd been standing in the gateway listening as two men talked about someone called Jesus. She had stopped to listen, enthralled by their stories. John Mark had glanced over to her and smiled. When the two men had finished talking, he'd walked over to her.

"I noticed how interested you were in my friends' stories," he said. His voice had been warm and friendly. "Would you like to meet them?"

She had nodded shyly and he had taken her to the two men and introduced her. They too had welcomed her. When she had spoken of her wish to hear more about this man called Jesus, John Mark had immediately invited her to his mother's house, where he and the friends of Jesus lived. She'd explained that she wasn't able to go with him that day, for she had to return to her mistress who lived in Bethany, but she would make time to hear more on her next visit. John Mark had smiled at her and said the men spoke regularly in the temple precinct, and that was where she would find them.

So, on her next trip to the city, after having made an excuse to Boraz that she must run a private errand for her mistress, she had made her way there and found John Mark waiting for her.

"I have been here every day, hoping you would come," he'd said softly. "Peter and John have almost finished talking. Will you come back with us to my mother's house today?"

At first she'd been embarrassed by the handsome young man's attention, but she told herself she had time, so why not? Mary had greeted her warmly and she had sat listening to the Disciples as they talked about their Master, who they called the Lord Jesus. She had asked questions about Him, which his friends had been only too glad to answer.

After that, she'd gone to the house as often as she could. On the last occasion she'd told them that she believed in the Lord Jesus and asked Peter if he would baptise her. Peter had been overjoyed and had baptised her there and then. Now she too was a member of the Lord's family.

She came out of her reverie as the walls of the city loomed before them. They entered through the gates into the teeming city and made their way slowly through the busy streets, which were filled with vehicles and pilgrims who had come to Jerusalem early in preparation for the Feast of Tabernacles, commemorating the forty years their ancestors had spent wandering in the wilderness after their Exodus from Egypt, when they had lived in temporary shelters. Water brought daily from the Pool of Siloam to the Temple would be poured over the altar and lights would be provided by large lamps lit nightly in the temple courtyard. The eighth and last day of the festival would be the greatest day, for all the people would assemble at the Temple. Because of her background, Ruth had not been brought up to respect and enjoy the great feast days, but she had willingly learned about them from John Mark and her new friends.

They reached the Palm Tree tavern, a favourite drinking place of Boraz.

"We'll leave the cart here," he said. "I'll see that the horses are rubbed down, fed and watered."

Ruth was relieved. If Boraz kept to his usual pattern, he would visit the tavern before they went to the marketplace.

That would give her chance to go to the dressmaker's first on her mistress's errand, then visit her friends.

True to form, that was exactly what Boraz did. "Meet me back here in two hours...and don't be late!" Boraz said gruffly.

Ruth left him there and quickly made her way to the dressmaker's, where she collected her mistress's new clothes. She then made her way to Mary's house and knocked on the door. Mary's voice called out warily, "Who's there?"

She answered and Mary unbolted and opened the door. Ruth went inside. She greeted Mary warmly and looked around the room.

"You're on your own, Mary. Where are the others?"

"Barnabas is visiting some new converts in the city, and Philip and some of the other Disciples have gone to take the good news about Jesus to people who live outside Jerusalem."

Ruth could not hide her disappointment. "Has John Mark gone with them?"

Mary caught the look. She liked Ruth and knew that her son did too. She'd noticed that every time he saw Ruth, his face would light up.

"No. John Mark has gone to Bethany with Peter, Andrew, James and John, to the house of Lazarus. They left at first light this morning. They've gone to fetch Mary, the Lord's mother. Mary's come to Jerusalem for the festival. She's staying with Lazarus and his sisters for a few days. They should be back soon."

Ruth was afraid to show how pleased she was that she would see John Mark, so she asked Mary about Lazarus. "Is Lazarus the man Jesus raised from the dead?"

"Yes, that's Lazarus. Unfortunately you won't see him, or his sisters Martha and Mary. I'm afraid they don't come into Jerusalem any more. Since the Lord raised him from the dead, Lazarus has become a marked man. Saul would love to parade Lazarus in front of the High Priests and the Sanhedrin and force him to tell them of the miracle whilst they laughed and jeered at his story. After Lazarus' resurrection, certain members of the Sanhedrin spread a rumour that Lazarus had not died at all, but that as Jesus' accomplice, he had agreed to make it look like Jesus had the power to raise people from the dead. It was all done to impress the public." Mary shook her head at the remembrance of that wicked rumour. "Between them, Saul and the Sanhedrin would find a way to silence Lazarus – forever."

"I marvelled at the story when John Mark told me about the Lord's great miracle, but I'm disappointed not to be able to see Lazarus." Ruth thought it would be wonderful, albeit a little scary, to actually speak to someone who had returned from the grave.

"I know you would like Lazarus – Mary and Martha too." She saw Ruth's agitation begin to grow and smiled. "I'm sure John Mark and the others won't be too long now," she said kindly. "I hope you can wait, I know it will please my son." She looked at Ruth and saw a blush spread across her face. She nodded, knowing now for certain that Ruth liked her son, and she was glad.

"I can stay for a little while. I must be careful, we have supplies to buy and Boraz will be angry with me if I'm late. I may never be able to come here and see you again."

Mary nodded in understanding. "Then please sit down, Ruth." Mary went to her cooking pot, which bubbled over the fire, and stirred the contents. "Would you like something to eat and drink?"

Ruth shook her head at Mary's kind offer. She put her parcel carefully onto a chair, took off her head scarf and placed it beside her, then smoothed her neatly-plaited hair. She watched as Mary prepared food for her guests and laid out the table with earthenware dishes and cups and two large platters. She placed fresh baked bread on one and dates and olives on the other.

As Mary worked, she said "It seems strange, Ruth, that as you live in Bethany you have never met Lazarus or his family."

"My master and mistress are private people. They have never mixed with the local residents."

Inquisitive, Mary asked her, "What's it like being a servant to a wealthy family?"

Ruth was happy to answer. "They are very good to me. I count myself lucky to have found such good, kind people to work for."

After a while, the Disciples returned. With them was an older woman whom Ruth had not seen before. Mary greeted her with great affection, then helped her to a seat near the fireplace.

As soon as John Mark saw Ruth, he smiled and stepped forward to greet her. Ruth returned his greeting and shyly smiled back at him. He took her across the room and introduced her to their guest. "Ruth, this is Mary, the mother of Jesus."

Ruth was taken aback. How should she address the mother of the Lord? She studied the older woman and saw that though her face was etched with deep lines of suffering, her eyes were smiling. When she spoke, her voice was gentle.

"John Mark tells me you have been baptised into the Faith," said Mary.

Ruth nodded, suddenly tongue-tied and nervous of who it was she was speaking to.

"Welcome, my daughter." Mary held out her hand and Ruth took it into her own. In awe, Ruth sank to her knees, for just a few inches away from her sat the mother of the Messiah, the Son of God.

Mary smiled at her and laid her hand upon Ruth's bowed head. A rush of emotion shot through Ruth.

"Come child, sit by me," said Mary. Ruth stood up, then hesitantly sat down in the proffered seat next to her. She saw Mary's intense gaze fixed on her. It was a look that seemed to penetrate her soul.

Mary patted her hand. "You have had a hard life, too hard for one so young."

Ruth was astonished. How could this woman know about her previous life, what she had been before the Sheikh had rescued her? How she had stolen money for food, even thought about selling her body? She could not lie to Mary. Tears formed in her eyes and she said, "But I have done wicked things. Why should the Lord choose me? I have..." She faltered, knowing that John Mark stood listening close by. She couldn't bear for him to hear about her degrading past, not now. Ashamed, she looked away from Mary and John Mark's gaze.

Mary's voice was as soothing balm to her troubled soul. "My child, whatever you did in the past, I'm sure it was only for your survival. The important thing is that you have repented of those sins and given your life over to my Son. You are on the threshold of a new beginning. You have been chosen by my Son to work for His great purpose. I pray that He will give you strength to face the days ahead."

Mary looked around the room at the other Disciples, who stood quietly by. "My Son said if a man has a hundred sheep and one of them has gone astray, does he not leave the ninety-nine and go into the mountains and seek the one that is lost? If he finds it, he rejoices more for finding that sheep than for all the others who did not stray."

There was a general murmur of agreement amongst the group.

"I remember him saying that as if it was only yesterday – when we were happy, before..."

Seeing Mary wipe away a tear, John moved to her side

and placed a consoling hand on her shoulder. As he had been dying on the cross, Jesus himself had placed her in his care. From that day on, John had looked upon Mary as his own mother.

Silence descended on the room as they became lost in their own thoughts and remembrances. It was Mary who broke the silence.

"Friends, these are indeed dark days – but we must not let our hearts be troubled, for I know that my Son has not abandoned us." A fleeting expression of pain crossed her face as she continued: "As I watched my Son die on the cross I thought my own life had come to an end."

Ruth caught her breath as she saw the pain in the elder woman's eyes. How she must have suffered to see her son die so cruelly! She shook off the uncomfortable feeling as Mary's expression changed and her voice rose in triumph.

"But death could not hold Him and three days later as we were seated in this very room, dejected and anxious for the future, Jesus suddenly appeared to us and showed us his wounds. He had risen from the grave. He had triumphed over death."

Cries of "Amen" filled the room.

Mary continued "A few weeks later when He took us to Bethany, He promised the gift of the Holy Spirit would be sent to us – and there, we saw Him taken up to Heaven in the midst of a great cloud. That gift was given to us here in this same room." She smiled at the memory and the lines on her face smoothed out. "I forgot my anguish then, and oh, how great was my joy."

She looked at the faces of those around her, faces showing great emotion at the memory of all that had happened. "Do you think my son would have suffered the cruellest of deaths for nothing? Do you think He would break His promise to you? Remember, Jesus told us He would be with us always, yes, even until the end of the world. Believe this – and have faith, for whatever God has planned for us all, I know it will be part of His divine will."

Ruth shivered as Mary's eyes met hers again, but she did not understand why. Then Mary spoke again.

"My dear friends, what I am trying to say is this: my Son always knew that His life was in danger but He never gave up, never ran away from the great task His Father had created Him for. Do you remember His words as He spoke to the multitude on the mountainside? 'Blessed are those who have suffered persecution for the cause of right; the Kingdom of Heaven is theirs – and how blest you are when you suffer insults and persecution for my sake. Accept it with gladness and joy, for great will be your reward in Heaven, for this is how the Prophets were persecuted in days gone by.' She took a deep breath "He accepted His Father's will, even though it meant His death – but remember, the torturous crown of thorns gave way to a shining crown of gold."

Mary grew silent, lost in her own thoughts.

Peter and Andrew walked across to James and John. Peter spoke hurriedly to them. All nodded in agreement. Peter went to Jesus' mother and asked Mary to join him.

His face was grim as he said, "After speaking with the others, we are all in agreement that you, mother Mary, should return to Nazareth. It's too dangerous for you to go to the temple for the Festival, or to stay in Jerusalem with Saul of Tarsus on the rampage."

Mary knew that she too could be captured by Saul and imprisoned, or worse, put the others in danger. After a brief hesitation she agreed.

John Mark sat down next to a now scared Ruth. He saw her jump at the light touch of his hand on her arm. Ruth turned her head and looked at the handsome youth. Her heart turned over at his lopsided grin.

"Don't be afraid, Ruth," he told her. "I won't let any harm come to you."

Ruth tried not to let the fear show on her face as she wondered how this young man could possibly stop a frenzied mob from taking her. John Mark saw Ruth's wan smile. He squeezed her hand. "I was hoping you would return to us. I've missed you." His voice was soft.

Ruth blushed profusely, tongue-tied at his nearness. She lowered her eyes modestly. "I can only come to the city when I have to go to the market place."

"There's something I want to say to you," John Mark began. But Ruth suddenly stood up.

"Oh, I'm sorry but I have to go now, I had forgotten the time, Boraz will be waiting for me, I'll be in the most dreadful trouble if I'm late. Perhaps you can tell me the next time I visit."

Despite John Mark's protests, Ruth hurriedly said her goodbyes to Mary and the Disciples. When she came to Jesus's mother, she knelt down before her and bowed her head. Mary lifted her chin and looked deep into Ruth's eyes.

"My child, one day you may be asked to visit the ends of the known world for my Son's sake. It will be hard to keep faith sometimes, but remember my words today. He will never leave you, whatever happens."

Feeling a little uneasy, Ruth smiled. Having made her apology once more, she got up, put on her headscarf and picked up her parcel. Then, with a swish of her saffron-coloured skirts, she hurried out of the room and into the street.

John Mark went to the door and watched her run down the street, struggling to hold on to her parcel. As she reached the corner she turned and waved to him. He waved back and murmured wistfully to himself, "Don't wait too long before you return." He saw her hurriedly turn the corner and disappear from view. He was falling in love with the girl whose long dark hair and mischievous eyes had captivated him. It didn't matter to him that she had done bad things in her former life. As the Lord's Mother had said, she had done them to survive, and if she had forgiven her, could he do any less? All he cared about was that Ruth now believed in the Lord Jesus. He knew marriages amongst his people usually had to be arranged by the parents, and one did not always marry for love, rather love grew from marriage, but deep down, he knew that Ruth cared for him, as he did for her. He knew too that Ruth was an orphan and had no parent to speak for her, so he would discuss the matter with his mother and Peter. In any case, he was considered to be approaching manhood and Ruth was sixteen, and it was time to think about the future – about marriage. He'd wanted to say something to her today, but she couldn't wait and he didn't want her to get into trouble. He turned to go back into the house, deciding he would speak to Ruth about it the next time she visited.

Ruth hurried through the streets, her mind in confusion. Why had John Mark looked at her like that? Perhaps on her next visit he would tell her. She hoped she would be able to return to see him soon to find out the answer, because she knew now how deep her feeling was for him. If only she'd not had to leave so quickly to get back to Boraz. Boraz! "Oh, I hope I am not late," she gasped breathlessly as she ran towards the Palm Tree tavern.

Boraz was outside the tavern, pacing up and down impatiently. He turned and saw her hurrying towards him.

"Here you are at last!" He spoke irritably. "You're late, where have you been?

"I'm sorry." Ruth's voice faltered anxiously. "I was held up at the dressmakers – they were much busier than I expected." She hated telling lies, but her future with John Mark depended on it

"Get the baskets out of the cart, we still have provisions to buy."

Ruth obeyed. As Boraz spoke to her, she smelt on his breath the cheap wine he had been drinking. If the Sheikh smelt it, he would be dismissed; he'd been warned about his drinking before.

They headed off in the direction of the market place. Sometime later, all their provisions bought and loaded onto the cart, they were on their way back to Bethany. As they neared the turn-off in the road leading up to the house, the cart hit something hard and gave a sudden jolt.

Close by stood the beggar, Simon. When he saw Boraz and the girl, he called out: "Be careful sir, the road is dangerous, you might have an accident."

Boraz stopped the horse and jumped down from the cart to investigate. He soon found the reason for the jolt. A part of the road had crumbled away. Running a hand through his brown hair, he swore out loud. He walked round to inspect the rest of the cart.

"Perhaps a small reward for my information?" Simon held out a filthy hand with its missing finger.

Boraz growled his reply. "We damn near did have an accident, you old fool. If you think I'm giving you any money you can think again. You'll get nothing out of me, you filthy beggar." He spat on the floor, just missing the beggar's feet.

Simon shrugged, then, seeing some travellers coming towards him, he cried out a warning about the road to them and held out his hand for alms. The travellers thanked him for his warning and tossed him a few coins, which he scrabbled on the ground to collect.

Ruth was becoming agitated. "I hope no damage has been done, Boraz?" she called out to the angry servant. "My mistress will be worried if we are late."

Simon was immediately alert. 'My mistress'? He made a mental note to remember the name 'Boraz'.

Boraz shook his head. Satisfied that no permanent damage had been done to the cart, he scowled at Simon, climbed back up onto the cart and urged the horse to move on. Simon's eyes followed them and smiling, he patted the dagger hidden in his coat. When it had been quiet, he had taken the dagger and worked a bigger hole in the worn bit of road until it had crumbled away, leaving a hole large enough to do damage to the vehicles of unsuspecting travellers. By forewarning passing travellers of the danger, he had managed to earn himself a considerable sum of money.

He jingled the coins in his leather purse and grinned. It was only the beginning of the arrival of pilgrims on their way to Jerusalem for the Feast of Tabernacles. There could be a lot more where they had come from by the end of the day. He decided to wait around until sunset.

As the cart moved out of sight, Simon pulled his head covering forward to shield his eyes from the afternoon sun, then settled down to wait for his next gullible customer.

The next morning Andrew and James, John's brother, escorted Jesus' mother on the laborious journey back to Nazareth.

CHAPTER TWELVE

Philip eventually reached Samaria. He remembered when Jesus himself had travelled through Samaria on his way back to Galilee. He and the Disciples had stayed for a while in a place called Sychar. None of the Disciples had felt comfortable in Samaria, knowing the hostility between Samaritan and Jew.

When Philip and the other Disciples had returned from the town after buying food, they had been astonished to find Jesus sitting by a well talking with a Samaritan woman. Amazingly, that encounter had led to many local people believing in the Lord. They wouldn't know that Jesus had been crucified, so this, Philip thought, would be a good place to begin telling the news of that and the risen Jesus. He went into the town and began to preach in the local market place.

Some of the townspeople remembered Jesus and were sad to hear that He had been killed by the Romans. Their spirits soared as Philip told them the rest of the story. He converted many to the Master's cause by his powerful, moving, speeches. By night he stayed at a convert's house.

After a few days, Philip continued on his way, eventually reaching the city of Sebaste. He found a local marketplace, some way from the Roman forum, and began to preach. Some residents listened whilst others jeered, but Philip would not be deterred. Day after day he returned to the market place. Amongst the listeners stood a man who, Philip had noticed, had been there every day, listening avidly to his words. When Philip had finished his discourse, the man approached him.

"My name is Aaron, I am a potter," he said. "I am most interested in what you are saying." He saw Philip smile. "My wife and I would be honoured if you would lodge at our house."

Philip liked Aaron instantly, feeling that he was trustworthy and sincere. He readily agreed to go with him to his house.

The house, built of thick stone and whitewashed to keep out the heat, had stone steps leading up to the roof, which was pleasantly shaded by a tall palm tree growing close by. Aaron called out to his wife. She came bustling out to greet her husband, and stopped on seeing the stranger with him.

"This is Philip, he's come from Jerusalem," said Aaron. He saw the worried look on her face. The Jews were not always friendly to Samaritans. "It's alright, Deborah," Aaron reassured her. "He's a friend. I said he could stay with us for a while."

Although Deborah felt apprehensive about the stranger sharing her house, she put on a brave smile for her husband's sake and welcomed Philip into her home.

Philip thanked her warmly, then entered the house, Aaron following on behind. Philip looked round the spotlessly clean living room, then at the couple who stood by expectantly. He raised his hand and said "Peace be upon you and upon this house."

Aaron smiled. "Please sit down at the table and have something to eat with us," he said. Aaron motioned to Deborah to fetch some food and watered wine. She did so and placed them on the table. Philip sat down gratefully; he hadn't realised how tired, hungry and thirsty he was. He whispered a prayer over the repast, then began to eat and drink heartily, thanking his hosts for their kindness.

The next few days passed pleasantly. Philip would leave the house in the morning and go to the market place, where he continued to preach the Good News of the Risen Lord, praising God that more and more people were turning to the Lord Jesus. Each evening, Aaron would lock up his potter's shop on the other side of the market and go to meet Philip. Together they would wearily make their way back to the house, to be welcomed by Deborah with delicious home-cooked food and a much-needed cup of goat's milk or watered wine.

As they got to know Philip better, they trusted him enough to tell him something of their lives. One evening, after supper, Deborah told him about their son, Elijah, who had died of a fever two years before.

"He was only fourteen years old and we loved him very much. He was our joy, our life." She began to weep at the memory. Aaron saw his wife's distress. He put his arm around her and comforted her before taking up the sad tale.

"I was training him to join me in the business, he showed great promise..." Aaron shook his head, then looking straight at Philip, he confessed. "Any faith we had in God was destroyed the day Elijah died," he said. "All our lives we had worshipped Him, obeyed the rules He had given to our forefathers. We prayed constantly and asked Him, 'Why did you take our only son?' There was no answer to our prayers. We felt God had abandoned us – so we abandoned Him."

He swallowed hard, trying to stop the tears. "When I heard you preaching about God's Son, how God had raised Him from the grave, my bitter, closed heart stirred. Then when I saw the things that you did in the Lord Jesus' name – how you drove out the bad spirits from afflicted people, and healed the sick and the lame – I felt a sudden rush of hope... and shame, at how I, we, had railed against God." He looked at Deborah, then back at Philip, his face a mask of pain and regret. "We have prayed for forgiveness. Will God accept our prayers? Is it too late for us?"

Philip was much moved by Aaron's confession. "I cannot presume to know the mind of God, but the Master taught us that God's love and mercy are infinite to those who truly ask for His forgiveness and choose to follow His ways. This you have done. Surely He will have compassion on you. We have all of us made mistakes, but Jesus took the sins of us all on to his shoulders when he offered Himself up for torture and crucifixion. This was God's plan: that His Son should die to redeem the world, to bring wayward mankind back into His loving fold." Philip took Deborah's hands into his own. "I know that Jesus was raised from the dead by His Heavenly Father. I am convinced Jesus is with Him in Heaven – and I truly believe that your innocent son is there with Him too."

Deborah fell on her knees at Philip's feet and kissed them. "Thank you! Oh, thank you!"

Philip gently raised her head and looked into her tear-streaked face. "It is not me you should thank, I am only the messenger. It is the Lord your God you should thank. Pray to Him for strength and courage to go forward in your renewed belief."

All three then bowed their heads as Philip prayed for the new converts.

The next day, Philip had just finished preaching to the small group surrounding him when Aaron appeared, red-faced and out of breath. Breathing hard, he blurted out: "Please Philip, you must come with me."

Philip was surprised to see him. "Aaron, what is it?"

"There's a man called Simon, who I know practises magic. A little while ago, he bewitched a family who've bought their pottery from me for years. They changed overnight. Now they go around spreading the lie that he's a special one of God. I've just heard Simon himself telling people that he's been sent by God."

Philip bit his lip, trying to hold back his anger. "Take me to him."

The two men hurried into a poorer part of the city, where Simon was holding the crowd surrounding him in thrall. He performed magic tricks making objects disappear, then reappear again and taking coins from behind peoples' ears, all the while boasting about the marvellous things he could do. Philip stood amongst the crowd and heard some of them murmuring amongst themselves. "This is truly a great man," said one. "He must have been sent by God, for who else could perform such wonders?"

Philip had heard enough. He stepped forward and raised his voice. "Do not listen to this man!" he roared.

The crowd turned as one to see who had dared to challenge Simon. "This man has not been sent by God," Philip told them. "He has dazzled you with cunning and magic tricks. Listen to me." Philip then began to preach about the true Kingdom of God and the Good News of the risen Lord Jesus.

At first Simon glared at him, angry that the attention had been switched from him to this stranger. He was about to shout Philip down, but saw how he had gripped his audience with his inspired words and thought better of it. He looked on, scowling, as many of the crowd, both men and women, stepped forward to be baptised into the new faith.

Appearing to be overcome with sudden emotion, Simon too stepped forward. He looked straight at Philip. "Master, will you baptise me too?" he said.

Philip placed a hand on his shoulder and looked into Simon's eyes. "Do you repent of your actions?" Simon nodded quickly. "Will you stop your magic tricks and stop making people believe that you have been sent by God?"

Simon gasped at the intensity of Philip's gaze and he stepped back a pace in fear and awe. He knew he must not try to trick this man. "I will," he said. He looked down, afraid to meet Philip's eyes for fear of rejection.

Philip judged that Simon seemed sincere in his words. "Bow your head, Simon." Simon was clearly nervous, so he reassured him. When Simon was ready, Philip laid hands on his bowed head. "I baptise you in the name of the Father, and of the Son and of the Holy Spirit."

When the baptism was done, Philip smiled at Simon. "Come, friend, work with me. I will teach you."

"Work with you?" Simon was astonished, but he saw that Philip meant it, so he readily agreed. Aaron too was astonished at this turn of events. He followed, bemused, as Philip walked joyfully away with a humbled Simon.

From that day on, Philip taught Simon everything he knew. Simon followed Philip everywhere he went, marvelling at Philip's words, signs and miracles, all done in the name of the Lord Jesus.

CHAPTER THIRTEEN

Over the past few weeks, whenever he was free from his duties, Flavius visited the house in Bethany, accompanied by Drubaal. He looked forward to his visits, sharing conversation with the Sheikh and seeing Farrah. Farrah! He had never before experienced the feelings that flowed through him when he thought about her. He had to admit that the first time he had seen her at the tavern he'd been consumed by lust, but as their friendship had grown and he had got to know her, those feelings had changed – to what?

He must see her again – soon. He came to a decision; he wouldn't wait for an invitation to visit the Sheikh but would seek permission from Quintus to visit Bethany now, unannounced, on the pretence of checking on their safety.

Quintus gave his approval on the proviso that he would

be back before nightfall. "I was going to send a messenger to Sheikh Ibrahim to deliver these documents, but you may as well take them with you," he said.

Flavius took the documents, which were hidden in a leather tube sealed with wax, thanked the Commander, saluted and left the room.

Back in his quarters, Flavius put the documents in his saddlebag and ordered Gebhard to take off his armour and uniform and dress him in a plain tunic and a cloak. He covered his head with the cloak's hood then, for good measure, stuck a dagger in his waistband. Usually, Drubaal came for him and took him to the Sheikh's house, but today he would ride there alone on Saturn.

He fixed the saddlebag securely on Saturn's back and rode out of the garrison. It was early afternoon – there would be plenty of time to visit Bethany and get back before nightfall.

As he neared the turn in the road leading to Bethany, he saw an old beggar standing there. The man gave him a curious look as he rode past. When Flavius arrived at the house the Sheikh came out to the courtyard, his surprise evident.

"Tribune Silvanus – we weren't expecting to see you today. To what do we owe the pleasure of your visit?"

"I'm sorry for arriving unannounced, but Quintus Maximus asked me to bring you some documents." Flavius climbed down from his horse and lifted off his saddlebags.

Ibrahim raised an eyebrow. "And the Commander thought you would be the best man to do that?"

For a moment Flavius faltered, then said "He thought they were best brought to you by someone he could trust."

Ibrahim tried to hide his amusement as he saw Flavius' obvious embarrassment.

"Well you are welcome, Tribune. Were you followed? Did anyone see you come here?"

"I don't think so." Flavius remembered the old beggar he had seen by the roadside. Surely he would not pose any danger.

"I don't have to remind you that secrecy is of the utmost importance for the safety of my niece – and for me."

"I'm fully aware of that, Sheikh." Flavius grew serious. "If anything happened to either of you because of my carelessness, I would never forgive myself."

"Neither would Governor Pilate."

Flavius took note of the Sheikh's tone. What he said was true.

The elder man suddenly smiled as he turned his attention on Saturn. On seeing the noble stallion, he was impressed. "This is a fine horse," he said as he ran his hands over the stallion's flanks.

"My parents bought him for me as a present when I became a Tribune."

"They chose well. He undoubtedly has Arabian blood in him – I see that in the way he holds his head high and in his proud bearing. Arabian stallions are the finest in the world, but of course I am biased." He laughed.

"I know he was very expensive." Flavius smiled in return.

"Well, let's go into the house and you can give me the documents." Ibrahim called to Boraz, who came out from the stables. "Take care of the Tribune's horse."

Boraz bowed, then led Saturn to the stables as Flavius, carrying the saddlebags, followed Sheikh Ibrahim into the house. Hearing voices, Farrah came out of her room. A look of surprise lit up her face when she saw Flavius, followed by pleasure.

Flavius smiled at her in return; his eyes drank in her beauty. He never tired of looking at her and felt his heart leap when she smiled at him.

"Won't you sit down, Tribune?" Ibrahim pointed to the silken couch. "Ruth?" The young girl came scuttling in. "Bring refreshments; our guest must be parched from his journey."

Ruth bowed and went to do her master's bidding. Flavius thanked his host and sat down, placing the saddlebags at his feet. Farrah sat opposite him. He couldn't take his eyes off her. How lovely she looked in a flowing deep blue silk dress, with golden adornments, colours that contrasted beautifully with her dark hair.

Ibrahim's voice forced his attention away from Farrah. "You said there were some documents for me?"

Flavius quickly turned his attention away from the lovely woman and took the sealed tube out of his saddlebag and handed it to the Sheikh. Ruth returned with food and wine and laid them out on the table next to Flavius. Ibrahim bade Flavius eat and drink. Flavius gratefully did so; the ride to Bethany had made him hot and the dust from the road had stuck in his throat.

Ibrahim broke the seal on the tube, took out the documents and quickly read them. When he finished reading, his face was grim. He said abruptly: "I have received unexpected news. If you will excuse me, Tribune, I have things to do." He saw Farrah's quizzical look, but did not explain the reason for this surprise turn of events. Rather he said: "Perhaps, Farrah, you would like to show our guest the garden. It is quite beautiful at the moment." He smiled at Flavius. "I hope to see you before you leave Tribune Flavius." He turned and disappeared into his own room.

Flavius followed Farrah out into the garden, where they sat on a cushioned wooden bench under a small almond tree whose branches shaded them from the heat of the afternoon sun. The perfume of the beautiful white blossom mixed with Farrah's exotic scent made his senses reel. He wanted so much to hold her – to taste the sweetness of her lips. He sat silently watching her until Farrah, aware of his gaze, said shyly, "I am so glad to see you."

"And I you," he said warmly. With an effort, he checked his emotions. "I have been wondering – what does Al-Maisan mean?

Farrah smiled. "Al-Maisan means 'The Shining One'. It is our name for a bright star in the heavens."

He thought it a perfect description of her loveliness. "'The Shining One' – yes it describes you beautifully."

Seeing her embarrassed look, Flavius hoped he had not spoken out of turn and changed the subject quickly.

"Do you still dance at the tavern?"

"I haven't been there since the night you were attacked. The Governor thinks it better to stay away for a while and let things calm down. If ben-Ezra should..." She left the sentence unfinished, but a brief look of hatred crossed her face.

Flavius saw it. Why did ben-Ezra cause such strong feelings in her? He had to know what troubled her. "I have told you about my life in Rome; won't you tell me about yours and how you came to spy for Rome?"

At first Farrah hesitated, then, deciding she could trust the Roman, she began her story.

"My father was a distant relative of our King, Aretas. He was also the proud owner of the largest caravan in Petra, and Governor Pilate and Herod Antipas were some of his important customers. For many years he travelled throughout Arabia and Palestine delivering spices, silks and sometimes even precious stones. On one of his visits to Jericho, he was accompanied by his brother, my uncle Ibrahim and my elder brother Kadeem, who was as handsome and refined as the name suggests." Her face grew sad. "Uncle Ibrahim told me that my father delivered the costly goods, then, instead of returning to Petra with him, he decided to visit Governor Pilate, who was in Jerusalem for a Jewish festival at that time, to discuss a new business transaction with Rome. He wanted to take Kadeem with him, saying that as he was now a young man and would one day take over the family business, he should meet some of his future customers. My uncle argued against this, as the road from Jericho to Jerusalem is notorious for bandit attacks, but my father was determined. A compromise was reached when he agreed to be escorted by some of the armed caravan guards. My uncle took the proceedings from the sale of the caravan goods and turned towards Petra and home." She briefly paused. "As my father, brother and their escort began the rocky descent from Jericho to Jerusalem…"

Her expression changed to one of abject sadness and tears welled up in her eyes. Flavius was filled with compassion for her; whatever had happened had obviously deeply affected her. He spoke softly. "If it is too painful for you to continue I will understand," he said.

Farrah delicately wiped away her tears. "They reached a place the Jews call the Ascent of Blood – a name given for good reason. As they passed through this mountainous region, without warning, a band of robbers and cut-throats suddenly appeared, pouring out of the wadis, tributary gorges and caves that cleave the mountain wall. The armed guards put up a good fight, but they were outnumbered and no match for such savages. My father and brother were murdered, so too were the guards, except for one, who pretended to be dead. When the brigands rode off, although he was badly wounded, the guard managed to escape and eventually reach my uncle with the tragic news. Ibrahim wanted to find the bodies of my father and brother and bring them back to Petra, but the guard begged him not to as he too would surely die. Ibrahim reluctantly agreed, knowing the guard spoke the truth."

Flavius reached out and gently took her trembling hand.

"Please, 1 must finish my story. Ibrahim rode back to Petra, bowed down with grief, and told my mother the terrible news. On hearing the tragic story, she fell to the ground, wailing pitifully, tearing at her clothes and hair. She beat the earth with clenched fists, then looked heavenwards and screamed curses at those who had murdered her beloved husband and son.

"My mother was pregnant – the shock brought on early labour. In her anguish she would not let any of her women help her. Only I was permitted to stay with her and help her give birth. After hours of agony, my mother gave birth to a tiny scrap of a baby girl. My new sister did not live beyond one hour."

Farrah uttered a deep sigh. "This new tragedy caused my mother to lose all interest in things around her. She could not sleep and no matter how much I tried to coax her, she would not eat. She just continually cried out that she wanted to be reunited with my father and her lost children. She just gave up, worn out by grief. I watched helplessly as she gradually faded before my eyes, until she found peace in death."

Farrah was unable to hold back her grief any longer, and her tears flowed freely. She let Flavius gently wipe them away with his fingertips. Composing herself, she continued her story.

"My uncle appealed to King Aretas for troops to exact retribution from the murderers. But the king explained to my uncle that if he sent soldiers into that area, it would be seen as a declaration of war against the Jews and the Romans. Instead, he sent a diplomatic letter to Pilate asking him to use Roman justice to deal with the robbers."

"Is this why you came to Jerusalem?" Flavius asked gently.

"The king gave my uncle permission to take control of my father's caravan. Ibrahim took me under his wing. I decided to turn my back on Petra and all its hurtful memories and travel with him."

"How did you come to work for Pilate?"

She paused for a brief moment, then looked intently at Flavius. "I am happy to spy for him because I have such hatred towards ben-Ezra. Pilate also wanted the robber band brought to justice as they had murdered many Roman soldiers. He said their chief was a man called Eleazar ben-Ezra and it was his men who terrorised the road between Jericho and Jerusalem. He said it was he who had undoubtedly led the brigands that slaughtered my father and brother, he who broke my mother's heart and caused her death, he who ruined my life. I had always loved to dance and readily agreed to Pilate's request to perform as a dancer at the tavern, where it is known most of the criminals of Jerusalem drink, and some of them most certainly know ben-Ezra or members of his gang. Pilate asked me to report any suspicious people or conversations to Quintus Maximus – you see, I had made a vow that one day I would help to bring ben-Ezra to justice. My uncle pledged to help me."

"I too will help you." Flavius touched her face. "If you will allow it." He kissed her lightly on the lips, then quickly pulled back, concerned she might think he was taking advantage of her grief. "I'm sorry."

"Don't be." Farrah's expression told him his kiss had not been unwelcome.

She reached up, and taking the golden chain which held the gold inverted palm of a hand amulet from around her neck, she held it out to Flavius. "I want you to have this," she purred softly. She held up her hand at his protest. "Please, take it." She placed the chain over his head and settled the talisman around his neck, explaining its purpose. "It will guard you from the five forces of nature, fire, water, wind, lightning and earthquake – and the evil eye." She saw his look of disbelief and smiled. "My people believe it to be a powerful talisman. It will protect you."

"But what will protect you?" He asked, concerned.

She smiled coyly. "I hope you will protect me."

"I would give my life for you Farrah. I have loved you since the first time I saw you."

"Flavius!" She lifted her face to his, tilting her head

back, her lips slightly apart, her eyes shining as she looked at him through long, thick, eyelashes. She made no protest as he took her in his arms and kissed her again, this time slowly, deeply. Her mouth opened to him as a flower to the sun. As he crushed her to him, shockwaves ran through her; she felt her long dormant passion awaken and steadily rise to meet his.

It was a long time before Flavius released her. As he held her in his arms, her hair brushed his face. He could not resist running his hand through the thick, silken mass. He raised her face to his and saw the look of longing in her eyes. He bent his head ready to kiss her again, to taste the luscious lips he so desired – and stopped. He became aware that someone was watching them. He quickly pulled apart from her as he saw Ibrahim standing in the doorway.

A stern-faced Ibrahim clapped his hands and shouted for Boraz.

"Soon the evening will be drawing in, Tribune Silvanus," he said calmly. "I think it's time you returned to the garrison." He turned to Boraz, who stood patiently awaiting his master's command. "Boraz, fetch the Tribune's horse from the stable."

Boraz bowed and went to the stables. Flavius wondered how long the Sheikh had been watching them. Had he seen their kiss? Under Ibrahim's watchful gaze, an embarrassed Flavius reluctantly took his leave of Farrah.

Ibrahim followed him outside and drew him to one side. "Take care with my niece, Tribune. I will not stand by and let you hurt her." He cut off Flavius' protests "She has suffered enough. She has lost her father, my brother Hassan, her tormented mother, her brother and her scarce born baby sister. Since childhood, she had been destined to marry Abdul-Qawi, the son of a family friend, but with the loss of her father, there was no longer anyone to pay a dowry to Abdul's family. So he abandoned her." He uttered a curse under his breath. "It is for the gods to forgive him, for I never will." He looked intently at Flavius. "You must realise Tribune, her heart and mind are vulnerable."

Flavius wondered how any man could abandon this beautiful woman. "I give you my word, Sheikh Ibrahim, I will never harm your niece."

"I'll make sure you don't." His voice held a veiled threat. "Now, you had best be on your way, Tribune."

Flavius mounted Saturn and saluted Ibrahim. Then he gave Farrah a long, lingering look and shot her a dazzling smile. How beautiful she looked silhouetted against the late afternoon sunshine. He could still taste the sweetness of her lips, smell her perfume. He hoped the Sheikh would allow him to see her again. Raising his hand in farewell to Farrah, he turned Saturn and rode out of the courtyard towards the Jerusalem road.

Ibrahim had mixed feelings as he watched the Tribune ride away. He had unintentionally witnessed the couple embrace, had seen the smile Farrah had given the Tribune. It had been such a long time since he had seen Farrah so happy, and it did his heart good to see her smile again. Yet he was concerned that this handsome Roman might break his beloved niece's heart. Frowning, he turned to her.

"You have feelings for this Roman?" he asked gently.

Farrah looked down. "I…yes, uncle."

Ibrahim saw that the talisman she always wore was missing. "Where is your talisman?"

She looked up at him and said meekly "Was it not mine to give?"

He nodded in understanding. "Ah. You have given it to Flavius."

She looked away, embarrassed. "Yes."

"I see." He took her arm and gently led her into the house. He kept his own counsel but decided that from now on he would keep a watchful eye on the handsome young Roman.

As Flavius reached the turn in the road, he saw the old beggar involved in a heated argument with another man. Flavius pulled Saturn up and trotted over to them. He saw the man's furious expression.

"What's going on?" He asked in an authoritative voice.

The man turned to face him. "See that bad bit of road over there?" Flavius turned his head to look then nodded. "Well, I just stumbled over it and fell down. Instead of trying to help me, this filthy scum robbed me of my purse." He aimed a punch at the beggar.

Flavius knew it was really none of his business, but he detested thieves. He looked at Simon and spoke sternly. "Give this man back his purse."

"What's it to you?" Simon sneered in return.

Flavius pulled his hidden dagger from out of his waistband. "Give it back...now!"

Simon shrugged and grinned shiftily, showing blackened stumps for teeth. "All right, I'll give it back." He took the purse from out of his pocket and with a filthy hand, threw it back to its rightful owner.

Flavius noticed the missing finger. He tried to recall where he had seen that hand before, but his memory was still hazy.

"Where are you going, stranger?" Flavius asked the man.

"To Jerusalem for the Festival."

"Best be on your way then."

The man nodded his thanks and with a quick look of contempt at Simon, he turned and walked away.

Flavius glared at Simon. "You had better leave too. Go back to where you came from and don't let me catch you stealing again or I'll inform the authorities."

As Flavius leaned towards Simon, the golden amulet fell forward out of his loosely tied cloak.

Simon felt a surge of excitement as he saw it. Suddenly his attitude changed. "All right, sir. I'm going." Then he turned and shuffled away in the direction of Jerusalem.

Flavius watched the old beggar for a while. Then, clicking his tongue, he urged Saturn forward.

All the way back to Jerusalem, Simon smiled to himself. Thankfully the interfering man on the horse had not recognised him, but he had instantly recognised the young Roman as the one who had given his granddaughter money and tried to entice her to run away from him. The one he'd told Abraham bar-Saraf about. He was surprised the Roman was still alive – and even more surprised to see that gold amulet around his neck, for he recognised it as the same one he'd seen Al-Maisan wear when she danced at the tavern. What was the connection between the beautiful dancer and this Roman? Were they lovers?

Al-Maisan had not danced at the tavern since the night of the attack on the Roman. It had been said that she was ill. But now he wondered if that was the true reason. Then another thought occurred to him: the Roman had turned off the highway and taken the road to Bethany. That was the same route the hateful servant Boraz always took with his cart. The young girl with him had mentioned 'my mistress'. Could that be Al-Maisan? If so that meant she had to be living somewhere in Bethany. It was time to find out the real identity of this mysterious woman, and what her business was with Romans. His master would undoubtedly give him a reward for this information. He quickened his pace in anticipation.

On his way to tell the bandit chief his news, Simon bypassed Beggar's Alley, a place of stinking walkways and vermin-infested hovels, one of which belonged to him. Respectable people never ventured there for fear of their lives. Soldiers had often raided the place, but had never found ben-Ezra or any of his men there. They had always been warned in advance by Simon and had vanished by the time the soldiers had arrived.

Pilate and the troops at the Antonia did not know that ben-Ezra had already slipped into Jerusalem unnoticed and was staying at Sarah the prostitute's brothel, in a street not far from Beggar's Alley. But Simon knew. He also knew that the rest of ben-Ezra's men were hiding in the outlying regions of Jerusalem, waiting for his signal to move.

A while after Flavius returned to the Antonia, Quintus called all of his officers to a meeting. His expression was serious.

"As you know, the Jewish Feast of Tabernacles is approaching. Although it doesn't cause us as much trouble as the Passover, we still have to be on our guard – especially as my spies have informed me that ben-Ezra has recently been seen in the outlying countryside. I sent a patrol out to the area, but if he was there, he had left by the time the patrol reached it. He may infiltrate the mass of pilgrims coming to Jerusalem over the next few days and cause trouble in the city. I have been informed by Governor Pilate that he has asked the Legate in Syria for reinforcements," he added in a clipped voice. "They should be here soon."

He saw some of the veteran officers look quickly at each other. No doubt they felt insulted, as he did, that Pilate considered they were not up to the job. The officers looked back at him.

"Therefore, I have to tell you that all leave will be cancelled for the next nine days," he continued. "The garrison will be put on high alert and patrols increased throughout the city. Cavalry patrols will be sent out every day to scour the surrounding areas. If ben-Ezra dares to show his face, he will be arrested and most certainly made an example of to deter other criminals. Let's hope it's one of our patrols that finds him first, before the reinforcements arrive." There was a general murmur of approval at that. "If you have anything you need to do, then do it now. I want my officers wide awake in the morning and ready for any event. Is that clear?"

All officers, from Centurions to Tribunes, saluted and said as one: "Yes, sir."

"Good. See that your kit and your men's kit is clean and all weapons are sharp and ready for action. Gentlemen, you are dismissed."

The officers saluted again and filed out of the room.

"Not you, Tribune Silvanus." The Commander's voice was gruff.

Flavius stopped in his tracks, then turned to face the Commander, wondering what Quintus Maximus wanted with him.

"The Governor has ordered that you are to be part of his personal bodyguard during the Festival. You will report to him early the day after tomorrow to be told your duties." He saw the look on Flavius' face. "Do you have a problem with that, Tribune?

"Sir, I had hoped that I would be part of the Cavalry on their patrols."

"You have your orders." He saw Flavius' hesitation. "Get out of here Tribune, I don't have time to argue with you."

Crestfallen, Flavius saluted and marched smartly out of the room. He had hoped that as part of the Cavalry, he might see Farrah. Although he would have no physical contact with her, just to see her and know she was safe would be enough. But Pilate obviously had other ideas. Flavius's mood darkened. He hoped it was not Pilate's plan to keep him away from harm.

Flavius walked disconsolately back to his room and ordered Gebhard to start cleaning his armour.

Simon gave ben-Ezra his report.

"So, Al-Maisan has a Roman lover? You've done well, my friend." ben-Ezra patted him on the back.

Simon hinted at a reward for his information, but ben-Ezra dismissed his request with a wave of his powerful hand.

"You'll get your reward, old man, when that slut stands before me, begging for her life – and not before!"

Simon was bitterly disappointed, but he knew there was no point in arguing with the bandit leader. He would just have to be patient.

"We need to know exactly where the dancing girl lives." Ben-Ezra sat down and took a long drink from his wine cup, wiping the spilt droplets from his chin stubble with the back of his hand. "You say you can recognise the Roman and this servant, Boraz? Simon nodded. "Good. Then this is what you will do: you will continue to beg on the highway."

Simon stared at him. "What if the Roman should recognise me? He's already warned me off."

The bandit chief gave him a steely glare. "That's your problem. Just bring me the information I need – or it will be the worse for you."

Simon shuddered, knowing the cruel punishment ben-Ezra would inflict on him if he did not obey.

"I'll think of something, master".

"See that you do."

The bandit chief's attention was suddenly diverted by Sarah. She was looking at him intently, with one hand on a shapely hip, the other hand lingering on her heavy breast. She ran the tip of her tongue provocatively over her lips. He knew what she wanted and he would not disappoint her. He hadn't had a woman for days and needed to relieve his pent-up frustration. He had spent several days holed up with his men in their hideout outside Jerusalem. His woman, Rebecca, had not yet travelled from her home in Jericho, and the other women of his gang had stayed behind in their lair in the mountains. Without taking his eyes off Sarah, he said to Simon: "Get out, old man." He grinned, put down his wine cup and moved towards the waiting woman.

Simon quickly made for the door of the brothel. Before he entered the street, he heard Sarah's coarse laughter. He knew Sarah was said to be skilled in her art; perhaps, if he could give ben-Ezra the news he wanted, he might reward him by letting him have Sarah for a night. The thought of it made long suppressed desire run through his scrawny body. He had to think how he could find out where the dancing girl lived in Bethany to obtain this delight.

As he walked, Simon formed a plan. He'd wear a different coat and keep the hood up to hide his face, hoping it would be enough to stop him being recognised. He would take his granddaughter with him. The chances were that as the Roman had not recognised him from their first encounter, he wouldn't recognise the young girl either. If he saw the man Boraz, or the Roman, pass by, he'd tell his granddaughter to follow them – see where they went. She could run fast and being a child, who would suspect her? She would keep watch and if she saw Al-Maisan, she would tell him and he'd report straight back to ben-Ezra. Yes, it was a good plan.

Flavius lay stretched out on his sleeping couch staring into the darkness, his hands linked behind his head. He felt anger building up inside him. Why did the Jews have these incessant religious festivals? They put so many constraints on the garrison. Now, because of this upcoming festival, he didn't know when he would see Farrah again. His anger turned to burning desire as he remembered that final kiss when her mouth had eagerly responded to his, the lightning jolt when their tongues had met. He imagined her lying there naked next to him, her loosened hair spread over the couch like a luxurious mantle, his hands exploring her voluptuous body, her luscious mouth fixing on his waiting lips as she abandoned herself to unbridled passion. Lust coursed through his body...

No! He disciplined his erotic thoughts. How many times had he told Marcia and other women that he loved them, usually to pacify them as he satisfied his own lust? His feelings for Farrah were different. He knew now that for the first time he truly loved – and by her response to his advances in the garden, it seemed she too cared deeply for him. He touched the amulet fixed around his neck and smiled. He had forbidden Gebhard to remove it. She had placed it around his neck herself. He would wear it always.

His elation suddenly diminished as harsh realisation hit him. Farrah was forbidden fruit, the Princess of another land – in Pilate's pay. He was a member, albeit distant, of the Governor of Judaea's family and the son of an important senator. Farrah had not been given the rights and privileges of Roman citizenship. He frowned. Surely given the dangerous work she had done on behalf of Rome, this was unfair. Without citizenship, Princess or not, if they were to marry, they would be ostracised by the social elite in Rome; any future career prospects for him would be ruined. There would be no forgiveness this time – his father would disown him for bringing disgrace on the family.

He could take her as his mistress, nobody would mind that. It was common for soldiers to co-habit with the women of the country their legions were stationed in, although any children from that union would not be recognised as their legal heirs – or as Romans – but he would not, could not, dishonour Farrah in that way. He wanted to spend the rest of his life with her, as her husband.

In any case, as her guardian, would Sheikh Ibrahim allow his niece to marry a foreigner? He had caught the stern, suspicious look Ibrahim had given him when he'd seen them together in the garden; he was sure the Sheikh had witnessed their embrace. He had also noticed the way the Nabatean's body had tensed when he'd suggested, very politely but firmly, that perhaps it was time for him to return to the garrison. Then the Sheikh had told him of Farrah's abandonment by the uncaring Abdul. He knew it was a stark warning.

He suddenly grimaced. What if Ibrahim put in a complaint to Pilate? He knew that Pilate would never allow him to see Farrah again. He cursed his impetuosity, yet could not deny the overwhelming love he felt for her. She had been through so much; how could he ever abandon her?

With these dark thoughts churning through his mind, he groaned, turned on his side and closed his eyes, desperately trying to rid himself of the tormenting vision of her beautiful face and body.

CHAPTER FOURTEEN

The setting sun cast long shadows over the garden as Farrah sat dreaming. Was it only yesterday she had sat on this seat with Flavius? She shivered with delight at the memory of his kisses. She had never felt such happiness. Only one thing concerned her: what were the contents of the documents Flavius had given her uncle? Her uncle had obviously been disturbed by them. She decided she couldn't wait, she must go and ask him outright.

The Sheikh was sitting at the table checking some accounts. He looked up as Farrah approached him.

"Uncle Ibrahim, what was in the documents Flavius gave you?"

He placed the marked tokens he was counting onto the correct pile on the table, quickly adding their value to the amount written on papyrus by their side.

He gave a brief sigh. "I have been summoned by our King to return to Petra. The King's sealed letter addressed to me was with a communiqué he sent to Pilate. As the governor is in Jerusalem for the forthcoming Festival, Pilate passed it on to Quintus Maximus to be delivered here to me."

"But travelling to Petra is a long and dangerous journey. Must you go?"

"I am afraid I must. It is the King's command that I return."

Tears formed in Farrah's eyes. "I'm so afraid for you after...."

He stood up and went to her, comforting her. "Don't think about that now."

"I can't help it. Please tell me why the King needs you?"

"I don't yet know the full facts. All I can tell you is that it concerns a new trade route he wishes me to open. I shall be gone for several weeks." He saw her concerned look. "Don't worry, I shall not be travelling alone. One of our caravans is staying just outside Jerusalem now, complete with the usual armed guards. I will return to Petra with it when it has finished its business here. The second document was from Pilate. He has assured me that he's ordered troops from the Antonia to escort the caravan as far as the border." He smiled at her. "So with my four guards, the caravan guards and Pilate's soldiers, I will be very well guarded."

"What of me? Am I going with you?"

His smile faded. "Not this time, my child. It is better –

and safer – if you stay here. Boraz and Ruth will look after you, and Drubaal will protect you."

"Drubaal is not going with you?"

Ibrahim smiled. "Not this time. It is more important for him to be here with you. Pilate is also arranging with the Commander of the Antonia to have some soldiers sent here to ensure your safety."

"When will you be leaving?" Farrah looked earnestly at her uncle.

"The day after tomorrow."

"Oh." That was all Farrah could find to say.

The next day Ibrahim called Drubaal, the servants and guards to a meeting, where he explained the position to them. At first Drubaal had protested, dismayed at the prospect of the Sheikh travelling without him, but when Ibrahim impressed upon him the importance of protecting Farrah, the bodyguard bowed his head in obedience to his master's wishes. Ibrahim then sent Boraz and Ruth into Jerusalem to stock up on provisions before he left.

Simon, with his young granddaughter at his side, decided to abandon his usual begging spot on the Bethany Road, just in case the Roman came along again. Instead he moved further down the road to the other side of the turn-off to Bethany. He pulled the hood of his coat tightly around his face – and waited.

An hour passed by then, suddenly, he saw a cart he recognised. Sure enough, there was the surly driver with the young girl seated by his side. They were obviously going to Jerusalem. He would wait patiently for the cart to return.

It was some time later that the heavily-laden cart returned.

"Quickly" he ordered his granddaughter. "Follow them; you know what you have to do."

Needing no second telling, the young girl obeyed.

Simon passed the time begging in his usual fashion. The waiting seemed interminable. He was relieved when he saw his granddaughter in the distance running towards him. He waited impatiently while she got her breath back. When she recovered, she told him she had followed the cart to a house in Bethany. She described the house and its position to him.

"I peeped round the gate and looked into the courtyard. No one saw me, they were too busy unloading the cart. A foreign-looking man dressed in a white robe came out of the house and ordered the servants to take the goods into the house; then a beautiful lady came out and began speaking to him."

Simon could feel his excitement building. "What did she look like?"

His granddaughter gave a full description of Farrah to her agitated grandfather.

"Yes!" He cried out. "She is the one. Come, we must hurry back to Jerusalem and report this."

The smile was wiped off Simon's face when ben-Ezra ordered him to return to the Bethany Road the next day.

He was to send his granddaughter back to the dancing girl's house and keep watch on any movement there.

"One of Sarah's customers has told her there is a rumour that the Romans have been ordered to stay alert at the garrison and increase patrols in Jerusalem," said ben-Ezra, laughing. "It seems they're frightened I might cause trouble at the festival. The fools don't know I'm already in the city!" He laughed again, then grew serious. "It will work for me if the Roman scum are kept in Jerusalem. This time I don't care about the festival – I've got more important things to do."

The morning after, Flavius rode out from the Antonia. Leading his horse, he followed a legionary to the palace stables used by Pilate and his guards and watched as Saturn was installed there. He was satisfied by what he saw. The stables were a vast improvement on the cavalry block back at the fort. Saturn would be well looked after. He then followed the legionary to the governor's apartments and presented himself to Pilate.

"Ah, Tribune Silvanus," said Pilate.

Flavius saluted. "Sir."

"The legionary will show you to your quarters. Get yourself settled, then return to me here and we will discuss your duties."

Pilate signalled to the waiting legionary, who saluted, then asked Flavius to follow him.

Flavius' quarters were clean and comfortable. He

dropped his saddlebags, then returned to Pilate, wondering what his duties would be.

As Flavius was listening to Pilate's orders, Farrah was reluctantly saying goodbye to her uncle. He was mounted on his favourite bay horse with Drubaal, riding a fine brown horse, at his side. Trying not to let her fear for him show, she said "May the warrior God Al Qaum, he who guards the caravans, be with you on your journey."

"Do not fear for me, I know that he will." Ibrahim smiled at her. "Once I have reached the Antonia safely, Drubaal will return to you. There will be some Roman legionaries with him."

She waved goodbye as Ibrahim, flanked by Drubaal and the guards, rode out of the courtyard and onto the road leading to Jerusalem. No one noticed the innocent-looking young girl squatting on the dusty ground, playing knuckle-bones.

Simon watched as Ibrahim and his entourage rode down to the Bethany Road, then turned towards Jerusalem. He saw the armed foreign guards and recognised the wealthy merchant on the bay horse as the man known as the Sheikh, for he'd seen him at the tavern a few times. The heavily-muscled man on the big brown horse was the bodyguard, who never left his master's side. Simon wondered where they were going in such a hurry.

The answer arrived soon after as his granddaughter came running to him. She told him the farewell conversation she'd overheard between the Sheikh and Al-Maisan.

Simon was astounded "You're telling me that the Sheikh came from the same house as Al-Maisan?"

She nodded. "I heard her call him uncle."

"And the bodyguard?"

"The big man is going only as far as Jerusalem with the Sheikh and the guards, then he is returning to the house."

"So, the Sheikh is leaving Judaea with only two servants and the bodyguard left to protect Al-Maisan."

The girl nodded again, then added "I think some Romans will be there too."

Simon grimaced. "The chief won't like that news, but at least he'll be forewarned." He patted her on the head. "You've done well. We must return straight away to ben-Ezra with this news."

"So, what you're saying is the Sheikh is the dancing girl's uncle?"

Ben-Ezra roughly grabbed the young girl's arm and tears welled up in her eyes. "You'd better not be making this up girl, or you know what will happen," he hissed. She shook her head, too frightened to speak.

Not daring to intervene physically, Simon reassured ben-Ezra that his granddaughter was telling the truth. Ben-Ezra let go of the girl's arm. He paced around the room for a while, then turned back to her. "And there are only two servants left at the house with Al-Maisan – one of them a girl?" The girl nodded. "The servants will be easily dealt with. The bodyguard is another matter."

"The Sheikh said some Roman legionaries will be there too."

Ben-Ezra swore out loud. "They must both be in league with the Romans. How many legionaries?"

The girl shrugged. "He didn't say."

"Right! We'll just have to deal with them when the time comes."

Ben-Ezra hadn't reckoned on Romans being involved. He would have to change his plans. He began to pace again, trying to construct his thoughts, until a new plan began to form in his mind. He suddenly turned to Simon. "Take off your coat and give it to me."

Surprised, Simon did so. Wrinkling his nose in disgust, ben- Ezra took the coat and put it on. "It's a bit tight and I'm taller than you, but if I stoop I may just get away with it," he said. He pointed to the girl. "I want your granddaughter to accompany me out of the city. She'll return to you later when I've got safely past the gate guards." He turned to Sarah. "You, go to Joel, tell him what's happened. This is his current address." He beckoned her closer and spoke quietly so Simon couldn't hear. "When you have done that stay here – I need to know Pilate's movements around next Passover time. You have your source, you know how to get the information I need out of him."

Sarah smiled. "I can wheedle anything I want out of my young recruit."

Ben-Ezra grinned. "With your skills, I'm sure you can. When you have that information, tell Joel he will find a way to send me what I need to know. Tell him he must stay in Jerusalem to oversee things. And be ready when the time comes."

She nodded, bemused. When the time comes for what? She turned her attention back to ben-Ezra, who was still talking. "Keep an eye on the old man, Sarah. I don't want him spoiling my plan by getting caught by the Romans. At the first sign of torture he will crumple."

Simon bristled at the insult, but kept silent as ben-Ezra turned to his granddaughter.

"Girl!" the young girl approached him warily. "Come with me." He gripped her hand tightly so she couldn't run away.

"Where's my reward? You promised," Simon snivelled.

The bandit chief cast him a withering look. "I told you, you will get what you deserve when I have the woman." Dragging the girl behind him, ben-Ezra left the house.

Simon was alone with Sarah. He would wait no longer for her. Who was there to stop him? He lunged towards her, but she quickly dodged him, pulling out a small dagger from her waistband.

"Get away from me, you stinking bag of bones!" she snapped.

Seeing the dagger, Simon stopped in his tracks. "You wouldn't hurt old Simon now, would you?"

She was used to dealing with surly customers. As he

made another move towards her, she lashed out at his hand with the knife, slicing open his palm. She laughed as Simon howled in pain and backed away from her, whimpering. Sarah looked at him stonily as he tore a piece of cloth from his dirty tunic and wrapped it around the deep wound. She snarled. "If you come near me again, you dirty pig, I swear I will kill you."

Defeated, Simon retreated to his hovel, weeping tears of pain and frustration.

One of the three Roman guards standing at the gate leading out of the city curled his lip as he saw the old beggar and his young companion walking towards the gate. "It's that stinking old beggar and his granddaughter again," he grunted. He spat on the ground in distaste. "Didn't you get enough money this morning, you old goat?"

Ben-Ezra, dressed in the beggar's coat, stooped and kept his hood pulled well up over his face. He tried to pass by without looking up.

"I'm talking to you," The guard said angrily when ben-Ezra ignored him. "Come here. Look at me!"

"Let him go, he's harmless," another guard said. "Besides, he stinks. I can smell him from here."

The first guard laughed. "I suppose you're right. You don't know what you might catch if you go too near him."

Just then he caught sight of a beautiful young woman approaching them, and stopped laughing. Impatiently he waved ben-Ezra and the child out through the gate. "Fuck off! I don't want your stink lingering around, it'll put her off." Then, turning his attention to the young woman, he drew himself up, puffed out his chest and said to the other guards, "I'll deal with this one."

A third guard shook his head, looked at the second and laughed. "Any woman is fair game to him. He thinks he's Adonis."

Ben-Ezra heard the guards' laughter and silently thanked the lovely girl, whoever she was, for taking their attention off him. He heaved a sigh of relief as he and the girl passed through the gate. Still holding her hand in a vice-like grip, he waited until they were out of sight of the guards, then released the girl's hand. "Lose yourself amongst the people entering the city," he said. "I don't want you recognised by the guard. Then make your way back to your grandfather."

A group of pilgrims who had come up for the festival were approaching the city. She waited until they were nearer, then ran up to the leader of the group saying, "Can you help me please?"

The man looked at her. "What's the matter, child?"

Her voice held a tremulous note. "I don't know where my parents are, I lost sight of them as they went through the gate. I'm scared." She began to cry.

The man took pity on her. "Come with us, we'll help you find them."

She let him take her hand and entered the city with the group.

Ben-Ezra watched until she had successfully

disappeared through the city gate, then, satisfied his ruse had worked, he walked away. When he was safely out of sight of the Romans he threw off the odious coat, smiling at the chance to commit more murder and mayhem. He would fight the despised Romans until the end of his days.

He remembered the moment his thirst for vengeance had begun: it was on the day he had returned to his village in Galilee from his work as a jobbing builder in Tiberius, some three years before. The terrible things the Romans had done there would stay with him forever. They had swept through his village, burning it to the ground. Amongst the still smouldering ruins lay the bodies of women and children, some with Roman javelins piercing their bodies. One of the women was his mother. He'd knelt over her body and cried bitter tears. Why had they done this? He'd wondered at the time if they had been looking for Zealots, but the people of his village had never been involved with them. They had paid their taxes and led peaceful lives.

On the edge of the village he had seen a row of crosses and had gone to look. Amongst those who had been crucified were his father and brother. His father was dead, his brother barely alive. As he moved closer he had seen his brother's blistered lips move and heard his rasping voice plead: "Avenge us!"

Anger had consumed him. His heart had turned to stone that day, beginning a downward spiral into darkness, his body and his soul craving vengeance. With his best friend Joel, he had joined a group of Galileans who harboured the same desire: to destroy the enemy. Amongst them were Abraham bar-Saraf and Isaac. More and more recruits had been only too willing to join them. Eventually, he had become their leader. Together, they had robbed and murdered their way across the Province. Over the years he had killed dozens of legionaries without a second thought, foreigners too; anyone he thought was in league with Rome. He had become rich on the proceeds of stolen horses and personal items. He had also gathered a large supply of weapons taken off the dead and dying legionaries. These he planned to use – soon.

Anger still burned inside him, and it would not be quenched until all of the hated conquerors were either dead or had been driven out of his country. It seemed that the Sheikh and Al-Maisan were friends of the Romans. He would make them pay dearly for their collaboration.

Out of sight of the city walls, he detoured off the highway and made his way to the camp and his waiting men.

Making sure she was not followed, Sarah went to Joel's house. She knew he moved around the city, not staying in any one place too long, but ben-Ezra had given her Joel's present address.

"What do you want Sarah? Is the chief with you?" asked Joel.

She shook her head. "No. Ben-Ezra's left the city."

"You'd better come in." Joel quickly shut the door behind her. "Well?" he prompted.

"Ben-Ezra told me to come here with his instruction

that you are to stay in Jerusalem and oversee things, and be ready when the time comes." She shrugged. "Whatever that means."

He moved closer and put his arms around her waist "Nothing that concerns you, my lovely." He bent to kiss her, but she deftly wriggled out of his arms.

"We may both work for ben-Ezra, but I don't give my favours for free to the rest of his gang," she said.

Joel grinned. Sarah might be a lowly prostitute, but she was a proud and wise woman. He had thought himself in with a chance to bed her, but she was right: on ben-Ezra's orders she must only give her favours to paying customers, as all the money she earned was given to him.

Sarah looked at him slyly. "Perhaps I will tell ben-Ezra about you trying to kiss me. He's told me he trusts you. Should he, I wonder?"

"If you know what's good for you, you will stay silent about my... mistake." He emphasised the word 'mistake'. "Ben-Ezra has every right to trust me, we grew up together in the same village." He saw the look of shock on her face. She obviously didn't know. Why should she know of the connection between him and their leader? He went on, "We both lost our families when Roman legionaries attacked our village. I was tending our small olive grove when the attack came. I was helpless to do anything, so I just hid there and witnessed the atrocities they inflicted on our people." He looked away, still ashamed of his cowardice. "Our parents, brothers and sisters were good people who had faithfully attended the synagogue, as I did. Until the day they were murdered. I have neither attended a synagogue nor prayed since that day." His voice grew bitter. "Why should I pray to a God who has abandoned his so-called 'chosen people'? Where is His much-lauded mercy when we so desperately need it? He's left us to a cruel fate under vile conquerors. As for our religious authorities…" he curled his lip in disdain. "They are just as bad. They're no more than corrupt puppets whose strings are pulled by Rome." He drew himself up. "The only power I recognise is the power of fire, the sword and vengeance."

She stood listening to his tirade and despite herself, was moved by it. "I will stay silent," she said. Backing away from him, she opened the front door. "I'll bring you the information the chief needs when I have it. How you get it to him is your problem." She turned and quickly walked out into the street.

Joel smiled. So ben-Ezra was intent on carrying out his plan. Well, he knew what he had to do and he wouldn't let his friend down. He welcomed the chance to help bring the audacious, dangerous plan to fruition. The long-awaited day of retribution was coming.

Farrah ran out into the courtyard when Drubaal returned, hoping to see Flavius with him. But Drubaal was accompanied only by three cavalrymen she didn't know. She could not hide her disappointment.

Drubaal guessed that it was the young Tribune she'd hoped to see return with him.

"The Commander told your uncle the garrison is on full alert – for the Jewish Festival" he said, not wishing her to know that Quintus Maximus had also told the Sheikh that he was worried ben-Ezra might enter Jerusalem by hiding amongst the visiting pilgrims. He saw the look of concern on her face and tried to allay her fears. "But as it was for your safety, he would spare some of his men to patrol the grounds of the house. Further cavalry patrols will also ride out into the countryside around Jerusalem every day of the Festival. One will ride through Bethany."

"Very well," she said disconsolately, then called out, "Boraz!"

Boraz came out from the stables. He'd been cleaning them after the Sheikh's departure.

"Yes mistress?"

"Take Drubaal's horse and the cavalry horses to the stables. See that the horses have a rub down, food and water. Then make the soldiers a comfortable place in the outbuilding where my uncle's guards usually stay. They can take turns resting there."

Boraz nodded stiffly, trying hard to keep his annoyance in check. He knew his mistress was not to blame, but he'd worked hard to clean up the cart and covered wagon and clear out the mess in the stables made by his master's and the guards' horses, thinking the Sheikh's one remaining carthorse and Drubaal's horse would be easy to look after.

Now all his hard work would be ruined as they, together with the Romans' three horses, would surely make it dirty again. The Sheikh's guards hadn't been too tidy in the outbuilding either, so he would have to clean that up too. He grimaced as he led the horses into the stables.

Farrah called out again. "Ruth!"

The young servant girl came out of the house. "Yes mistress?"

"Bring watered wine and some food for the soldiers."

Ruth bowed, then went back into the house to carry out Farrah's orders. She soon returned with some bread, olives and watered wine for the men. The soldiers thanked Farrah for her consideration, then briefly acknowledged Ruth as they took the food and wine from her.

Farrah returned to the house and sat down, disappointed and forlorn. Why hadn't Flavius come? Quintus Maximus could not have told him that she was alone and vulnerable, for surely if he had known, he would be here now. The Festival would finish in five days' time; perhaps he would be allowed to come then. She sighed. Five days – an eternity!

For the rest of the day, knowing how upset her mistress was, Ruth tried to cheer her up by offering her sweetmeats and wine; she set out a delicious meal for Farrah, who refused to eat it. Later, Ruth bathed Farrah's body and massaged her with her favourite precious oils, hoping that it would soothe her mistress. But Farrah would not be soothed. Her disappointment over Flavius was too great and despite her uncle's assurances, her unease about his departure and anxiety for his safety on the perilous journey ahead made her nervous and fidgety.

Farrah retired to her room early, complaining of a headache, but sleep would not come. Apart from the worry over her uncle, she could not get Flavius out of her mind. Her imagination conjured up his strong, finely-chiselled features, smooth, lightly-tanned skin and large, dark brown eyes framed by long, thick lashes. She loved his black, wavy hair, cut short in military fashion, a style she was not used to, as her own countrymen wore their hair long and flowing in traditional style. Above all, she loved his smile. She sighed as she remembered his wide shoulders and muscular arms as he'd held her to him. His athletic build mirrored those of the Roman and Greek gods depicted in the drawings her uncle had shown her, drawings he had purchased on his travels across the Roman Empire.

She touched her lips, reliving the sweet pressure of his kisses. They had awoken something in her she had not known was there, and she shivered involuntarily as she remembered the waves of pleasure that had shot through her body. She had never experienced a man's arms around her, nor passion-filled lips on her own. Her relationship with her former betrothed, Abdul-Qawi, had been governed by strict tribal laws: whenever the couple had been in the same room, a senior member of one of their families had been present. The relationship would not be consummated until after the marriage ceremony had taken place. The 'bride price' had to be considered. A bride's lack of purity would dramatically decrease her value and sometimes lead to abandonment by her intended husband.

She had had no understanding of what consummation meant until, a few days before the intended wedding ceremony, her mother had told her about the marriage bed and what her husband would expect of her. At first, she had been shocked and a little afraid, but her mother had reassured her that after the first time, it would become pleasurable and she would welcome her husband's attentions. She stared into the darkness, bitter thoughts crowding her mind. There had been no marriage. She had kept herself pure and unsullied, her virginity intact, yet still, through no fault of her own, Abdul- Qawi had abandoned her. From that moment on, she had let her heart grow cold and had vowed that no man would possess her body – or her heart. But then she had seen Flavius at the tavern and felt an instant attraction to the handsome Roman, knowing instinctively that fate would make their paths cross again. How glad she was that she had sensed he was in danger and that Drubaal had saved his life.

Fate had been kind, and she had seen him many times since and had grown to love him, hoping that he would one day return her love. When they had been alone in the garden, his words and kisses and the declaration that he would give his life for her had proved that he did feel love for her. She knew now that she would break her vow. She would give herself willingly to only one man, and that man would be Flavius.

She hugged her pillow and whispered into the darkness, "Please Flavius, come to me soon!"

With the hope that she would see the man she desired so much, she gradually closed her eyes and drifted off to a happy, dream-filled sleep.

The next two days passed much like the days before. The soldiers patrolled the perimeter of the building and a squadron of cavalry searched the surrounding area, with nothing to report. Each night, Farrah slept easily, happy with the thought that it was another day closer to the end of the Festival.

CHAPTER FIFTEEN

Boraz lolled on a bale of straw, his back braced against the stable wall to steady himself. He put the empty wine jar down by his side, then reached for an unopened jar, opened it and poured some of its contents into his cup. In his master's absence, the Roman cavalrymen busy keeping watch in the grounds, the Princess safe in her bed with Drubaal in the house to protect her, he at last had the freedom to drink the jars of wine he'd stowed in a compartment under his seat on the cart, on that last trip to Jerusalem.

He drank deeply, the welcome feeling of oblivion beginning to creep over him again. His drinking was solace for a broken heart – the only way he knew how to blot out the love he felt for his mistress, an unrequited love. It eased the torture he felt every time he saw her; gave him respite from tormenting dreams of possessing her. He was just a lowly stable hand, a Thracian slave, purchased from the slave market in Damascus by the wealthy Sheikh because of his knowledge of horses. Why should she even look at him as a human being?

He had borne this secret burden for a long time, tolerating it only because he knew there was no man in her life other than her uncle. Then the Roman had come. Over the past few weeks it had become obvious to him that she'd given her heart to the Tribune. Waves of jealousy had washed over Boraz as he had seen the secret, lingering looks they exchanged, witnessed the closeness that seemed to be forming between them. He had spent many nights weeping with frustration and anger at the hopelessness of his situation.

He finished off the second jar of wine, then began a third. His head drooped onto his chest as he gradually fell into a drunken sleep. The half empty jar slipped through his fingers, hit the ground and shattered, spreading earthenware shards and wine over the stone floor. The remaining contents of his wine cup spilt down his legs as it too fell to the ground. Soon he was snoring loudly.

The attack was swift and deadly. The Romans patrolling the courtyard were taken completely by surprise as the first of ben-Ezra's men crept silently out of the darkness.

The need to relieve himself roused Boraz from his drunken stupor. He rose unsteadily to his feet and staggered outside to the courtyard, cursing at the disturbance to his dreams. He stared in disbelief as he saw the cut throats and mutilated bodies of the three Roman soldiers lying on the blood-soaked cobblestones. He shook his head from side to side, trying to clear his befuddled brain, looking around nervously in case the murderers were still there. He saw nothing, but knew he must tell Drubaal what had happened. He turned and walked quickly towards the house.

Abraham bar-Saraf came from out of the shadows. As silent as a ghost, he crept up behind Boraz with his razor-sharp knife and slashed the unsuspecting Thracian's throat with one swift, vicious movement. Eyes wide with shock, Boraz clutched his torn throat, gagging as his life's blood flowed through his fingers. He fell forward, hitting the ground heavily, and died in a pool of his own blood.

Farrah woke up with a start, feeling pressure on her hand. The room was pitch black. When her eyes adjusted to the darkness, she saw that it was Ruth who was pressing her hand.

"What is it, Ruth? Why are you disturbing me?" Farrah's voice held a note of irritation.

Ruth put her fingers to her lips and whispered: "Please, mistress, try to stay quiet."

"How dare you!" Farrah was incensed at the servant girl's audacity. She saw that Ruth was fully clothed "Why are you dressed?"

"I'm sorry, mistress, but didn't you hear the screams?"

"Screams? No. I was in a deep sleep."

"Drubaal fears we are in danger."

Farrah slipped out of bed and Ruth handed her a robe. Farrah put it on and went to the bedroom door. When she opened it, she saw the massive form of Drubaal, curved swords held out in front of him in readiness. He was in a half-crouching position, as if poised to spring at an unseen enemy. When he heard the door opening, he half turned, saw her and said in a low voice, "Mistress, stay in your room and keep the door closed. Do not open it until I call you."

When Farrah questioned him he said: "I heard screams, yet the soldiers have not come to report anything. Something is wrong. Please, stay in your room – find something to barricade the door."

Without further question, she closed her bedroom door. With Ruth's help she struggled to move a wooden chest and placed it in front of the door for extra protection in case anyone should be strong enough to get past Drubaal.

With the soldiers and the stable-hand out of the way, some of the assassins moved towards the house, leaving the rest guarding the courtyard in case any rescue attempt should be made. With a sudden rush, two of ben-Ezra's men crashed through the front door, with the remaining bandits, bar-Saraf and ben-Ezra following them. Ben-Ezra knew instinctively that the formidable Carthaginian would be inside protecting his mistress. He smiled cruelly as he saw Drubaal crouching ominously in front of a door. Then he ordered two of his men to kill him.

Drubaal stood his ground as the bandits rushed towards him. He dispatched them quickly with his deadly curved swords. Two more dead men soon joined them.

Infuriated, ben-Ezra shouted "Nathan, kill him!" A man who was almost as large as Drubaal stepped forward and began taunting him with insults. Two more bandits stood behind him. The big man laughed as he lunged at Drubaal, wounding his right arm with his sword.

Drubaal raised his right-hand sword, swung it in a semi-circle and decapitated his attacker. The severed head, mouth open in a grotesque grin, rolled across the floor. The second bandit slipped on the blood-soaked floor and crashed to the ground. Drubaal finished him off before he could regain his footing. The third retreated, disregarding ben-Ezra's threats that he would kill him for cowardice.

Angry at the failure of his men to overpower the Carthaginian, the bandit chief drew his sword and cursing, ordered the coward and one more of his gang to kill Drubaal. Both men moved towards Drubaal, separated and stopped. Drubaal looked from one to the other waiting for them to make a move. One of the men feigned an attack; Drubaal turned slightly ready to repel him.

Afraid of what the bandit chief might do to him if he failed again, the coward seized his chance. He leapt forward, aiming his dagger low, and slashed Drubaal across his thigh. As the man retreated, afraid of the fearsome weapons Drubaal wielded, the other man lunged at Drubaal slicing into his left arm leaving a deep wound;

but he was not quick enough to retreat and despite the pain, Drubaal lifted his sword high and brought it down onto his head, cleaving his skull in two. The force of the blow was so great that it damaged the sword. Before the Carthaginian could turn back again, bar-Saraf was upon him. With a triumphant cry he plunged his dagger deep into Drubaal's side.

Drubaal cried out involuntarily and his head began to swim. He felt an unaccustomed weakness as blood poured from his wounds. Pain from his wounded side, arms and thigh now overwhelmed him. He blinked, trying to focus, shaking his head from side to side in an effort to remain conscious. He knew he had to defend his mistress, who was trapped, helpless, on the other side of the door. He must not let the bandits kidnap, or worse, kill her, but he knew he was fighting a losing battle. His hands, grown numb through his arm injuries, dropped his swords; they clattered on the floor. His legs buckled and he dropped like a stone.

Moving forward, ben-Ezra stood over Drubaal and brought the hilt of his sword down viciously on his head. The bandit chief gloated as the huge form of the Carthaginian lay bleeding and unconscious on the floor.

Ben-Ezra's order was sharp. "You two men" – he pointed to two of his gang – "Move the slave out of the way." He watched as his men struggled to drag the massive form from the door, then he kicked the curved swords across the room. He put his hand on the door handle and tried to open it. It would only open a fraction. He braced himself and shoulder-charged the door.

Farrah and Ruth had heard the terrible struggle outside the bedroom door. Forgetting protocol, they were instinctively clinging to each other in fear. Ruth stifled a scream as the bedroom door crashed open and the chest was forced aside. Both women watched, horrified, as the bandit chief swaggered into the room. Ruth stepped in front of her mistress, but ben-Ezra threw her roughly aside. Farrah raised her head proudly and looked him squarely in the face. She would not allow this monster to see how scared she was.

He looked Farrah up and down contemptuously and said with a sneer "So, Al Maisan, all this time you've been working for the Romans! Well, no more. You belong to me now – and I'll make you pay, you slut!"

He raised his hand and struck her hard across her face. She bit back a cry, struggling bravely to hold back her tears.

Abraham bar-Saraf stepped forward, brandishing his blood-soaked dagger. "Shall I finish her off chief?"

"No. She's far too beautiful to die. I have a much better use for her." He walked around her staring at her curvaceous body, then abruptly said "Get dressed."

Farrah did not move. He pushed her roughly towards her clothes, laid out on a chair. "I said get dressed!"

Farrah looked at him defiantly, but he raised his hand to strike her again and she knew she had to obey. Deeply embarrassed, she took off her nightclothes and put on the clothes from the chair.

Leering lasciviously at her nakedness, he laughed at her discomfort, then suddenly snarled "Outside. Now!" He turned to bar-Saraf. "Bring the slave girl too. You can have the girl, Abraham. The dancer is mine."

"Rebecca won't like that." Bar-Saraf's voice held a warning note.

"I don't care what Rebecca likes."

The second-in-command smiled, showing uneven, dirty teeth. "All the same, chief, Rebecca won't take kindly to having a rival – especially one as beautiful as Al-Maisan."

"She'll do as she's told!" Eleazar ben-Ezra pushed Farrah towards the door as bar-Saraf dragged Ruth behind him.

Farrah stifled a cry when she saw Drubaal lying unconscious on the bloodstained floor. She struggled to go to him, but ben- Ezra pulled her away and dragged her outside into the courtyard.

Another bandit came out of the stables. "There's a covered wagon and a cart, five horses, three with the legion brand on them, one that looks like a thoroughbred and a carthorse. What do you want, chief?"

"Hitch up the carthorse to the covered wagon, leave the cart. We'll take the other horses with us." Ben-Ezra turned to his men. "Ransack the house, I want anything you can carry loaded on to the wagon – especially money and valuable items of jewellery."

The bandits needed no second bidding. They laughed greedily when they found a box containing money. They picked up some expensive looking ornaments and found Farrah's box of jewellery together with her costly silver, gold and jewelled hair adornments and belts. They proudly presented their haul to their chief, who nodded in satisfaction. "There's some expensive-looking garments in there too, shall we take them?"

"No. She'll have no need of them where she's going." He leered at Farrah. "Anyway, Zeke will find them difficult to sell. Just stick with what you've got there. Now let's get going."

The man ran back into the stables, soon returning with the hitched-up horse and wagon, as another brought out the remaining horses.

Farrah averted her eyes from the horrific sight of the mutilated corpses laying on the blood-soaked ground. She tried desperately not to heave as a dirty strip of material, brought by ben-Ezra to act as a gag, was forced between her teeth. A second strip was used to gag a struggling Ruth. The captives' hands and feet were bound by the two gang members who had moved Drubaal from the doorway. The two captives were then roughly lifted onto the seat of the wagon. The stolen goods were stacked in the wagon behind them.

As the flaps of the cover at the back were tied up, hiding the treasure from view, the bandit chief rubbed his hands with glee. "We can do a deal with old Zeke when we get to the camp. We should get a good price for this booty."

Four more men took hold of the reins of ben-Ezra's horse, the horses of their dead comrades, and the reins of the captured ones. Then ben-Ezra climbed up onto the wagon beside Farrah and Ruth.

"Shall we set fire to the house, chief?" One of the men asked.

"Don't be stupid. A fire will draw attention. Someone will alert the Romans."

"What if the Romans turn up now?" The coward shifted himself in his saddle.

Ben-Ezra dismissed the question. "Why should they? There's still three hours to sunrise. By the time they find out we'll be well away from here. Now, shut your mouth!" He looked over his shoulder and gave the order, "Mount up men". He ordered some of the others to ride in front of the wagon so that he and his precious cargo were protected to the front and rear. He leered at Farrah, then called out triumphantly, "We ride to join the others at the winter camp." Without a backward glance, the brigands rode out of the courtyard and onto the highway.

Secured on the wagon, unable to escape, Farrah and Ruth shivered with terror. They were wondering what lay in store for them at the bandits' winter camp.

The sun had been up for an hour when a squadron of Gallic light cavalry, some thirty strong, reached the outskirts of Bethany. Julius, as Decurion in charge, barked out the order: "Split up. Optio Marcus Valerius, take half of the company and search that side of Bethany." He pointed to the left. "The rest of you come with me. My orders are to check up on the Princess, make sure she is safe. We rendezvous back here in thirty minutes."

The Optio and his men steered their horses to the left and rode away as Decurion Julius led his men through the rest of the wealthy Jerusalem suburb and up to the lone house on the hillside.

Julius, followed by three of his cavalrymen, rode into the courtyard, the sight that greeted him turned his blood to ice.

The first bodies he saw were those of the Roman soldiers. Their throats had been cut and they had been disembowelled. He shuddered. He'd shared a joke with these men only yesterday when he'd last checked on the Princess. Now they lay dead, their blood-streaked faces fixed in masks of agony.

Staring at the horror before him, Francus, one of the young recruits, new to the Legions and not yet battle hardened, paled, swayed on his horse, leaned over and vomited onto the ground below. Aware that the others were looking at him, he wiped his mouth with the back of his hand, trying desperately to hold back his nausea.

Julius looked hard at the other men, daring them to comment. He did not reprimand the recruit; he remembered his own similar reaction the first time he'd seen terrible wounds inflicted in battle. He had never forgotten, nor forgiven, the humiliation he had suffered at the hands of his Decurion, Antonius, known throughout the Legion for his cruelty. When he became a Decurion himself, he vowed he would never treat any of his men that way.

"Steady, trooper" he said quietly "Remember your training."

Julius knew the young recruit would be grateful for his senior officer's understanding and would be loyal to him in battle. He watched satisfied as, with a great deal of effort, the trooper sat up straight and gradually let his strict training take over.

A few feet away from the dead soldiers lay the corpse of Boraz, his life-blood congealing on the ground around him. Julius was worried. He'd seen mutilations like this before. Some months before he had led a patrol sent out to find a squadron of legionaries who'd failed to return to the garrison. He had found them, or what was left of them, on the Jericho road. The bandit ben-Ezra and his gang had been blamed for that. It looked like they had done their dirty work here too.

Not sure if any of the perpetrators were still around, Julius quietly passed back the order for his remaining cavalrymen to enter the courtyard, ready to fight if necessary.

"You!" Julius pointed to one of his men. "Dismount and search the stables and any other outbuilding. Francus, hold his horse." The cavalryman saluted, then went off to carry out the search, leaving his mount with the young recruit, who had now regained some of his colour. Julius pointed to two others of his men. "Otto – Semporius – stay here, keep mounted. Be alert for any intruders." Julius dismounted and untied his flat oval shield from alongside his horse. He hefted it in his left hand and with his right hand drew his long cutting sword out of its leather scabbard. Handing the reins to Francus, he said "The rest of you, come with me." He signalled the rest of the cavalrymen to dismount and draw their weapons. Their horses too were left in the charge of Francus.

Julius crept warily up to the house, his men moving silently behind him. He saw the splintered front door hanging off its hinges and automatically tensed his muscles ready for action as he cautiously made his way inside. More bodies, one decapitated, lay scattered around. Then one of his men saw the inert body of Drubaal. He went to investigate.

"Decurion, sir!" he called to Julius "You'd better take a look. I think this one's still alive."

Julius moved across the room and crouched down to check. "It's the Carthaginian, the Sheikh's bodyguard". He was astonished to hear laboured breathing and to feel a weak pulse, for given the savage wounds inflicted on the man and the amount of blood he must have lost, it was a miracle he had survived. "Body of Jupiter!" Julius swore. "The man must be made of iron."

He looked at the curved swords laying close by Drubaal, one of which was badly damaged. He gave a sharp intake of breath as he saw the size of the blood-soaked blades. "By the gods, these would do some serious harm." He remembered the decapitated body and realised that one of these formidable weapons must have been the instrument of death.

He had to get the Sheikh's bodyguard back to the fortress, but how? He was so badly wounded that he had to be handled carefully. One of the soldiers who had searched the stables came in. "Look around for something – anything – we can use to get this man back to the fortress," Julius barked out.

The cavalryman stepped forward. "Sir, there's a cart and some harness in the stables and some sacking, but the cavalry horses and any others that may have been in there are gone."

Julius cursed loudly, but at least there was a cart and harness. "Right. Hitch up your horse to it. You will drive the cart back to the fortress."

Leading his horse, the soldier went back into the stables. He was soon back outside with his horse hitched up to the cart. He climbed up onto the driving seat.

"You three." Julius pointed to three of his men. "Carry out the injured man and lay him in the back of the cart. Bring the undamaged sword with you, leave the other one, it's of no use now."

It took all of the three men's strength to carry Drubaal out of the house and lift him as carefully as they could onto the cart. One returned to the house and brought out his sword, laying it on the cart away from the massive body.

Julius barked out further orders. "Cover him with the sacking. We must get him to the Antonia as soon as possible." He turned to Otto. "Otto, ride as quickly as you can to the fortress and tell the Duty Officer what's happened here. Tell him I'll give the Commander a full report when I return. Oh, and alert the garrison hospital."

Otto saluted, spurred his horse on and rode out of the courtyard. As the cart pulled away, Julius murmured a prayer to the gods for Drubaal's survival, for if he died, they would have lost a valuable witness.

Julius returned to the house. A worried frown furrowed his brow as he saw the battered bedroom door. He walked into the room and saw some beautiful and costly women's clothes haphazardly strewn across the bed. This was obviously the Princess's bedroom. The room, like the rest of the house, had been ransacked. Where was the Princess? If ben-Ezra and his gang of thieves and cut-throats were responsible for the carnage, and if they had kidnapped her, she would need the help of all the gods of her country as well as all the gods of Rome. He stepped outside and called the remainder of his men together.

"You two! He pointed to two of the men. "Stay here – question the local people, find out if they saw or heard anything. Threaten them if necessary. We need answers – and quickly! The rest of you will return with me to the rendezvous point and meet up with the others – I hope they haven't met with any trouble. If not, we'll return to Jerusalem."

The men did as ordered. Julius mounted his horse with a heavy heart. He knew he'd have to give Quintus Maximus a full report – and he knew only too well what the Commander's reaction would be.

CHAPTER SIXTEEN

Julius stood rigidly to attention as he nervously gave his report. He fixed his stare on the opposite wall, not daring to look at Quintus Maximus.

"By the gods!" Quintus roared "How did that bastard ben-Ezra know about the Princess? How did he discover where she lived? He was too clever for us. We were ready and waiting for him to come into Jerusalem, when all the time…" He let out a deep sigh. "He must have skirted around the city. Hades! How did we miss him?"

The Commander banged his fist on his desk in anger and frustration at being duped by the bandit chief. "Damn the Jews and their interminable religious festivals! If I'd not had to worry about what was going on in this foul city, I would have sent a whole squadron to stay at Bethany to protect the Princess! Well, it's too late now."

With a supreme effort, he recovered his composure and after a moment's hesitation, made his decision. "Decurion, you will order a detachment of your men back to Bethany to dispose of the bodies. In this heat the corpses will decompose quickly. We don't want an epidemic on our hands. When you have done that you will return here immediately and I will convey my orders to you." He ran his hand through his hair. "I now have the unpleasant duty of informing Governor Pilate. The gods only know what he will say." Quintus angrily waved Julius away. "You are dismissed!"

"Commander!" Julius brought his arm across his chest in salute, turned smartly on his heels and left the room.

Julius marched along the Via Praetoria, still bridling from the Commander's tirade and the degrading task he had just been given. His men! The courageous Gallic horsemen, some of the best in the Empire, reduced to handling rotting corpses! He would have to choose the men carefully. It would be those he knew would put up with the gruesome work without too much complaint.

Later, Julius marched in to see Quintus Maximus to tell him the bodies at Bethany had been safely disposed of. As he entered the room he stopped in his tracks. Standing next to the Commander was a man he recognised – a man who brought back bitter memories. He hoped the shock had not registered on his face. Quickly pulling himself together, he stood to attention and saluted.

"Come forward man." Quintus barked. "Decurion, I think you know Prefect Alae, Antonius."

"Yes sir."

Quintus continued: "As you know, Governor Pilate had requested reinforcements to help us find ben-Ezra, and now also to help in the search for the Princess. With the Legate's permission, the Prefect has come straight from the legion in Syria, along with a squadron of his North African Cavalry." Quintus tried hard to keep the annoyance out of his voice. He remembered Antonius from his time previously spent at the fortress. He had never liked the man.

He turned to Antonius. "There is a spare cavalry officer's house. You may use that, Prefect. As for your men and horses, there's room for them in the cavalry block."

"Sir, thank you sir." Antonius saluted.

"In the meantime, Decurion, I want you and your men to join with the Prefect's North African Cavalry. You will be under his direct command."

Julius kept his gaze steady, trying not to show his concern at having to take orders from a man he detested, a man he knew had nothing but contempt for him.

Quintus stared sternly at both men. "There will be no rivalry between your two squadrons, is that clear?" Both men quickly nodded. "Any sign of trouble between your men and I will come down hard on them. This is a well-run fortress. I intend to keep it that way. Is that understood?"

"Yes, sir," replied the two officers in unison.

"Good. Here are my orders: you will begin by searching the gorges and caverns along the road to Jericho. We know ben-Ezra and his assassins have been active there in the past. It's possible he'll return there now. If so, it's imperative you bring the Princess safely back here. You will kill his men – but I want ben-Ezra brought back alive, do you understand?" He turned and faced Julius. "Do you understand?"

"Yes sir."

"It will be done as you command, sir." Antonius' voice was gruff.

"See that it is! I want this brigand's death to be a spectacle that will turn the stomachs of even the toughest men. There are still several hours of daylight left, cover as much distance as you can. Now go!"

The two officers saluted, turned smartly and left the room. Once outside, Prefect Antonius looked Julius up and down and sneered. "So, Julius Cornelius Vittelius you made it to Decurion after all," he said. "I never thought you'd have the guts to see it through." He poked Julius' upper arm. "I'm glad to see you've developed some muscle. You've grown up a bit from the scrawny boy I trained."

Julius kept his gaze steady. He was several inches taller than the Prefect, though much lighter in build, for what Antonius lacked in height he more than made up for in body weight and muscle. He saw the tough veteran's battle-scarred arm and leg muscles bulging beneath his uniform. Julius controlled his rising anger and waited for the next jibe.

Antonius hawked and spat on the ground, just missing Julius' feet. Then he leaned forward until his face was so close that Julius could smell his sour breath.

"Listen, Decurion! You heard what the Commander said – you are under my direct command, so whether you catch ben-Ezra or I do, I want the glory for it. Is that understood?" He glared at Julius, daring him to argue.

Julius gritted his teeth and nodded.

"I'll give the bastard a good kicking, teach him a lesson – but I won't damage him too much. The Commander said he wants to make an example of him – and I'm going to make sure I'm present at his torture and execution." He laughed hoarsely. "Now, are you and your Gallic sons of whores ready to go?"

Julius bit back a reply at the insult to his men and said through gritted teeth, "I had to send four of my men to Bethany to dispose of the bodies there. They're at the baths getting cleaned up, shall I wait for them to return?"

"Don't bother. I won't need them. My cavalry will more than compensate for yours. Use what men you have left. We leave in ten minutes."

Julius saluted and returned to his men. He dreaded having to tell them that added to the insult of the task at Bethany, they would now have to join forces with Antonius. Quintus Maximus had called Antonius 'Prefect Alae'. Julius remembered Antonius as a sycophant to his superiors and a bully to those he considered beneath him, and he had no doubt that Antonius had fawned and bullied his way up to his new rank. Antonius had been born in Picenum, and Julius was convinced the Prefect knew that Rome-born officers and rankers looked down on him as a provincial upstart. This, however, had not stopped his boasting and surly manner.

What Antonius didn't know was that he was universally hated by all who served with or under him; that those same officers and rankers had nicknamed him 'The pig from Picenum.' Everyone at the Antonia had been glad when he had been posted to Syria. If only he had stayed there.

No rivalry between the squadrons, the Commander had said. Julius grimaced. There always had been and always would be rivalry between the North African and Gallic cavalrymen. It was notorious throughout the legions, if not the Empire. The North African cavalrymen rode without a bridle and wore no armour. They carried small shields, javelins or light spears and were famous for their speed and agility. They laughed at the Gallic horsemen for wearing scale armour or chain mail cuirasses and for carrying oval shields and long cutting swords as well as their javelins, calling them weaklings for being so protected. Julius had no doubt that Antonius would tell his men that the Gallic cavalry had been ordered to dispose of dead bodies. They would add humiliating comments with their usual insults. He drew in a deep breath, for he knew his men would feel the same as he, but, like it or not, they would have to obey the Commander's order.

The Gallic horsemen let out growls of disapproval on hearing the news, and Julius reluctantly had to speak sharply to them in order to keep discipline. "I dislike it as much as you," he told them sternly, "but we have to obey the Commander's orders. If I hear any man complain in front of the Prefect's men, or throw any insult at them, I will personally have that man flogged for insubordination. We will show Prefect Antonius that we are capable of doing a good job. Is that clear?"

The men reluctantly murmured agreement, then prepared to ride out to the Jericho road.

Flavius, standing behind Pilate, was paralysed with shock when he heard Quintus tell the Governor the terrible news about the events at Bethany. The blood drained from his face when the Commander said: "As for the Princess, she has disappeared. It's highly likely that ben-Ezra has kidnapped her and her servant, for their bodies have not been found amongst the others. Drubaal is in the fortress hospital. He's in a bad way, but the surgeon thinks he'll live."

"How could this happen?" Pilate was furious "Your lax legionaries deserve punishment for this dereliction of duty!"

"Sir, it's my mistake," said Quintus. "I take full responsibility. I did order the men to cancel their leave, but I told them to concentrate on ben-Ezra coming into Jerusalem. I sent those cavalrymen to the house to protect the Princess and a light cavalry patrol rode there first thing every morning. The assassins caught me unawares..." His voice trailed off as he saw the Governor's face darken.

"Not good enough!" Pilate's raised voice filled the room. "The Sheikh has returned to Nabatea on the King's business. What message do you suggest I send him?"

Quintus looked down at the ornate marble floor, trying desperately to think. Then he looked straight at Pilate. "Prefect Alae Antonius has arrived with his cavalry. I've just dispatched him and Decurion Vittelius with their squadrons to the caves and tributary gorges along the Jericho Road. If ben-Ezra and the Princess are there, they will bring them back to Jerusalem, I'm sure of it."

"And if they are not there?" Pilate's face was grim. "What then?"

"We'll keep on searching until we find them."

"Go back to the fortress, Commander, and wait for the Cavalry to return. In the meantime, put other search parties on standby. You must find Princess Farrah – at any cost."

Quintus saluted, turned smartly and left the Governor's residence.

Flavius felt sick with anxiety for Farrah. He wanted to ask Pilate if he could follow the Commander and ride out to look for her, but knew that he could not tell the Governor of Judaea, relative or not, of his love for the beautiful princess.

Pilate turned and looked up at the ashen-faced Tribune. He did not like what he saw.

"Are you all right, Flavius?"

Flavius had to think quickly. "The news is a terrible shock, Governor Pilate." He stared straight ahead, unable to look Pilate in the face. "In truth, sir, I don't feel too well. I think I may be going down with a fever."

Keeping a steady voice, Pilate said, "I know only too well how suddenly fevers can strike in this country, Flavius. I suggest you try to shake off the malady that disturbs you so."

Flavius saw Pilate's knowing look. Had the Governor guessed his secret? He hoped not. Flavius was angry with himself for not keeping a tight rein on his emotions. He hoped Pilate didn't know about his relationship with Farrah, but the Governor was no fool. Trying to keep a blank expression, he replied, "Yes, Governor Pilate."

Pilate watched as Flavius gave his salute, then walked towards the door. Who could blame him if he was upset by the Princess' disappearance? With beauty like hers, any man could fall under her spell – any man except the son of a Roman Senator, one who was destined for the Senate himself one day. He sighed. If he was right, and Princess Farrah was still alive, he would personally put a stop to any blossoming romance between them, for the diplomatic repercussions would prove difficult and certainly embarrassing for him and for Flavius' family.

Pilate came to a decision. He must take Flavius's mind off the Princess. He must take him away from this place.

"Flavius?"

Flavius turned to face him.

"The Festival will be over soon. I think you can return to the garrison now and resume your duties there. After all, ben-Ezra is no longer an immediate threat to the city. However, I may have need of you in the future. If so, I will send for you."

Pilate turned his attention to several scrolls which lay on his desk. Without looking up, he said "Take care Flavius. I don't want you to suffer any harm whilst in my care. After all, what would your dear mother say if I stood by and let something happen to you?"

Flavius knew the interview was over. He saluted and left the Governor's office, relieved that soon he would no longer be under any further scrutiny from Pilate. But once outside, he could no longer hide his fear for his lost love. What had become of her?

CHAPTER SEVENTEEN

Farrah felt despair wash over her. Her body was beginning to ache from the jolting of the wagon. Would they never reach their destination? She shivered at the remembrance of ben-Ezra's voice barking out orders, and the terror of being gagged and bound and bundled onto the wagon, a whimpering Ruth by her side. Try as she might, she could not wipe the memory from her mind of the horrific sight of the mutilated Roman guards; the blood-soaked corpse of Boraz – and the badly wounded Drubaal lying on the floor, blood seeping from his many wounds. Surely no man could survive such wounds? She desperately hoped that he had survived, that the Roman patrol had found him and taken him back to the Antonia.

The sun would soon be reaching its full height and the heat would become unbearable. Sweat was beginning to trickle down her back. How much longer would they have to travel? If she didn't have something to drink soon, she felt she would die of thirst before they reached their destination. She cast a sideways glance at Ruth, who sat slumped on the seat. She too was obviously suffering badly.

A group of tents appeared in the distance. She knew escape was impossible, but just to be able to have something to drink...

When they reached the tents, some of the occupants were sitting talking while their children played close by. An older man was repairing one of the tents. He stopped his work and moved towards the newcomers. Brigands, he thought. He singled out ben-Ezra and said bravely, "I am Joseph, leader of this group. What do you want from us? We don't have much money."

The bandit chief stared back at him, then spat on the ground.

"We're thirsty. Give us water from your supplies." His voice was threatening.

Joseph instructed three men to fetch water skins from their precious supplies and bring it to the brigands. Ben-Ezra and his men drank greedily. He ordered the travellers to bring more water for the horses. Joseph gave an enquiring look towards the two women seated on the cart.

Ben-Ezra followed his look. "Give them water when you've finished with the horses."

That being done, Joseph gave a cup of water to one of

ben-Ezra's men, who pulled down Farrah's gag and held it to her parched lips. Desperately in need of the water, Farrah drank deeply. Then the gag was put back in place.

Ruth turned her head away.

The brigand grew angry. "Think we'll let you die of thirst?" He roughly pulled down Ruth's gag, forced her head back and practically poured the contents down her throat. At first she spluttered, wasting some of the precious liquid as it ran down her dress, but then she swallowed more slowly until enough had been taken to quench her agonising thirst.

The bandit chief climbed down from the wagon and walked towards Joseph. Taking out his dagger, he put it to his throat. "Now, give us all of your money." The dagger bit into the terrified man's exposed flesh and a trickle of blood ran down his robe.

Shaking, Joseph told one of his group to go round to all the people and collect any money they possessed. The man needed no second telling. Within a short time, a small amount of money was placed at the feet of ben-Ezra.

"Put it on the wagon with the other things, Abraham."

Abraham bar-Saraf grinned as the men put it with the other stolen goods.

"Mercy!" Joseph wheezed to a smiling ben-Ezra. "Leave us something, I beg you. We are poor, how can we buy food, get water? Without this money we'll starve."

Ben-Ezra did not reply. He simply thrust the dagger into Joseph's throat, laughing cruelly as he watched him drop to the ground like a stone, blood pouring from his wound. He climbed back up onto the wagon, casting a threatening look at the horrified onlookers. "That's one mouth you won't have to feed," he said. He ordered his men to mount up and resume the journey.

Farrah looked back at the weeping travellers as they carried their stricken elder away and carefully placed him in one of the tents. She was filled with sympathy for them. They had given them water to save their lives and probably all the money they possessed, and this was how they had been repaid. Yes, they were poor; she could see their patched tent covers, their worn-out clothes. Unless they were helped, these desperate people would indeed starve. Was there no end to ben-Ezra's cruelty?

As they travelled onwards the terrain began to change, growing arid and rocky. Farrah didn't recognise her surroundings. Suddenly ben-Ezra called his men to a halt. He stopped the wagon and pulled out two more dirty strips of cloth from a bag at his side. "You will both be blindfolded for the final stage of the journey," he said. He put the cloth around the struggling Farrah's eyes and roughly tied it. He did the same to a weeping Ruth. Not being able to see made the situation worse. Fear overcame both of the women and they clung to each other for support.

Sometime later, ben-Ezra called out to one of his men, who brought his horse around to ride alongside the cart. "Reuben, you are new to us, your face isn't known to the Romans. I want you to ride to Beth Bassi and find Zeke, the horse dealer. When you find him, tell him we've arrived and that he must send his men to meet us at the usual place early tomorrow morning. They must also bring their own covered wagon. He'll know what to do."

"Yes chief."

"And Reuben, keep off the main highway, use the quieter tracks. Now, ride quickly. In a few hours the sun will start to go down."

Reuben nodded and rode off.

After an interminable time, they began to climb a steep incline; then the jolting finally stopped. The women's ears were filled with shouts of pleasure from the men. Farrah guessed that they had arrived at their destination. She breathed in. Fresh air had changed into musty dankness. She was roughly pulled to the ground and her blindfold removed.

Ruth was manhandled off the wagon and her blindfold too was removed. She stood close to her mistress, trembling.

Farrah looked around nervously; they were standing in the tunnel of a large cave. In front of them, the cave forked into two. The men took the wagon and horses and turned to the left. Farrah waited anxiously to see if she was supposed to go with them, but ben-Ezra grabbed hold of her and pushed her roughly to the right; Abraham, clutching a struggling Ruth, followed them.

As they went deeper into the cave, their surroundings grew darker. Abraham took a flaming torch from out of a sconce fixed to the cave wall. As they moved, their ghostly shadows danced on the dank walls. Farrah stumbled over some loose shale; ben-Ezra steadied her so she did not fall. Eventually the cave began to widen again and the sound of distant voices drifted down the rocky passageway. They turned a corner and suddenly the cave opened up into a large, brighter area. Inside were several men and women. They stopped what they were doing when they saw ben-Ezra standing in the entrance. Immediately a whoop of joy filled the air. Some of the men came to their chief, voicing their pleasure at seeing him, but the smiles disappeared from the faces of the women as they saw the beautiful woman at his side. They gave her sidelong disapproving glances and whispered amongst themselves. When Abraham appeared holding onto Ruth, one of the women threw down the garment she was repairing, gave him a murderous look and retreated into a corner, cursing softly. Another went to console her.

"It looks like you've upset Rachel, Abraham." Ben-Ezra laughed loudly.

Abraham grimaced. "She'll get over it, if she knows what's good for her!"

Farrah took in the sly, curious glances of the women. Although exhausted and dishevelled, with every bone in her body aching, she forced herself to stand straight and proud. She would not let these bandit whores see how afraid she was.

Then one of the women said so she could hear, "Wait until Rebecca finds out, then there'll be trouble." Another replied, "She'll be arriving from Jericho soon. It should be good sport to watch what happens when she gets here." The others sniggered. They were silenced by a curse from ben-Ezra.

Ben-Ezra and Abraham took Farrah and Ruth to another part of the cave system, stopping outside a series of large hollowed-out recesses. Ruth let out an anguished cry as she was parted from her mistress and dragged by Abraham into one of them.

Then Farrah was led into another recess. Alone with her captor, Farrah fought desperately to stifle the cold fear coursing through her as she saw his eyes take in her body, then travel up to her face. She looked back at him with contempt.

He resisted the urge to slap her. Instead he said coldly, "I would advise you not to mix with the other women, for your own safety." He smiled slyly. "Oh, and don't think about trying to escape. Even if you knew which way to go, the desert heat would finish you off – or the wild beasts that roam it." His laugh as he left her chilled her to the bone.

She looked around her prison. In one corner was a bale of straw with a rough cloth laid on top. This must be her bed. She wrinkled her nose in disgust. How long would she be kept prisoner in this terrible place? She sank onto the cold, stony floor and gave in to despair.

Ben-Ezra walked back into the main cave and called one of the men to him. "Isaac, are all the provisions here?" Isaac nodded.

"Is there enough to see us through the winter period?"

Isaac answered confidently, "We've been bringing supplies here for some time now. There's plenty of fodder for the horses. We have bundles of kindling for fires. There should be enough grain to make bread for weeks. We have stacks of baskets of salted meat and fish, several large amphorae of wine and, hopefully, enough water until the rains come."

Ben-Ezra nodded. "Let's hope they won't be too long in coming."

"I've already checked the channel we constructed from the top of the hill last year, there's been no damage done to it," Isaac went on. "The cistern we dug out is in good working order. The rainfall, when it comes, will collect in it with no problem."

"What about the weapons?"

"The Roman armour and weapons are here ready for you." Seeing ben-Ezra's questioning look, he added, "We made sure we weren't followed."

"Good. The weather is still good for hunting fresh meat and the salted foods can be stored until the weather turns. Reuben has ridden to Zeke to make arrangements for the horses. I want the horse that's harnessed to the wagon to remain here. Unhitch it and take it outside with mine to the hidden shelter under the rocky outcrop. Rebecca will be arriving on her own horse, and that too will go to the shelter. You were a farrier, you'll be responsible for the three horses. I'll inspect the provisions later."

Worn out with exhaustion and fear, Farrah lay on the stony ground. She sat up, alert, as she heard heavy footsteps coming down the tunnel, then stood up, readying herself for what might happen next.

Ben-Ezra appeared at the entrance to the cavern. He lounged against the wall, staring at her, then staggered into the room. As he lurched towards her, Farrah could see he'd been drinking. She backed away from him into a corner.

"You can't escape me," he hissed. Without warning, he lunged at her, forcing her to the ground. He punched her in the face, splitting her lip, as she tried to fight him. "You can scream and cry all you like" he snarled. "Your Roman lover can't save you. You belong to me now. You will learn to obey my will."

"Never!" she cried vehemently then spat in his face. He hit her again. The world rocked around her. She tried to recoil from him as he ripped open her dress and pawed at her breasts, but he was too strong for her. She stifled a scream as he brutally entered her. As pain racked her body, she silently called on Al-Uzza, the Mighty One and Goddess of Power, to strike him down. When it was over, he got up and lurched out of the cave without a word.

Left alone, she pulled her ripped dress around her and wept bitter tears of shame and pain. She had dreamed that her first time would be given freely, to the man she loved above all others. Instead, the cherished flower of her womanhood had been taken in a cruel act of rape. As his beloved face appeared before her, she cried out "Flavius!" Then, ashamed, she tried desperately to banish all thoughts of him and of their growing love for each other, so cruelly cut off before it could flourish. If she was ever free of this place and of her vile abductor, she knew she would never be able to face him. Her shame was too great.

Early the next morning, Abraham and some of the gang took the horse-drawn covered wagon filled with the treasures stolen from Farrah's house and all but two of the gangs' horses and led them out of the cave hideout. The horses, their reins tied together, were led down to the base of the hill to a remote track. There, they saw a group of men Abraham recognised as belonging to Zeke, the horse dealer. Zeke's men transferred the treasures from the covered wagon and put them into their own. Abraham then gave the leader of the group a bag of money.

"The chief says you must give this money to Zeke for his trouble and he is to sell the goods in the wagon to buy weapons for us," said Abraham. "There are also twenty-five horses here. Take care of these animals, we want them back fit and well fed. A messenger will come to your master when we're ready for their return."

Abraham stood, legs slightly apart, hands on hips, his dagger clearly on show hanging off the belt around his waist. The men who had accompanied him stood in similarly threatening poses. They continued to watch as the horse dealer's men carefully led their cart and horses away until they were out of sight, then they made their way back to their hideout.

The horse dealer, Japheth bar-Saraf, or Zeke as he was more commonly known to the Romans, the Beth Bassi townspeople and his clients, watched warily as his men brought the wagon and horses to him. So Eleazar ben-Ezra and Abraham, his own younger brother, had returned to the region for the winter. He hoped they'd brought him a rich supply of their ill-gotten gains. He inspected the covered wagon and rubbed his hands together gleefully. The wagon's contents were magnificent. They would fetch a good price when sold to the right dealer, enough to buy the weapons ben-Ezra needed. He knew just the dealer to supply those weapons. He could only hazard a guess as to where ben-Ezra had acquired such exquisite jewellery, along with those beautiful hair adornments, belts and costly ornaments, but he could see they had come from a wealthy household. He nodded, satisfied. All of these treasures were worth a small fortune, and they would earn him a healthy commission from the dealer.

He returned to the privacy of his trader's office, opened the bag of money and tipped the coins out onto a table. He counted out the coins and grinned, satisfied at the amount. "Very generous. Very generous indeed." Not bad for fulfilling the tasks required of him.

The bandits' horses were taken to his own property out in the countryside surrounding the area, away from his sale stock here in the centre of Beth Bassi. He didn't want the Romans eyeing them up, especially as he knew some of the horses had been stolen from them during ben-Ezra's raids.

Those horses would have to be rebranded. He didn't think anyone would question him about the new arrivals, but if anyone should ask, he would tell them he was keeping them for a special client who was away on business and would collect them when he returned. He would deliver the wagon tomorrow to the dealer, who he knew would be more than interested in its contents.

Japheth hated the Romans, but considered he was too old to travel up and down the countryside fighting them like Abraham. Besides, it was too dangerous. He didn't relish the idea of being skewered by a Roman sword, or nailed to a cross, things he worried might one day happen to his brother. Both he and Abraham had grown up despising the Romans for what they had done to their people. Abraham had always been a volatile hothead, a veritable zealot for the cause of freedom, whereas Japheth, had been considered the brains of the family. Using those brains, he had found another way to seek revenge for his forebears and the Romans' hated presence in his country, one that suited him very well.

The first thing he did was get as far away from Galilee as he could. He had always been good with horses and with money. For several years now he'd been building up a considerable business in horse dealership to wealthy residents of Judaea and by selling some of his stock to the Roman army. No one had guessed that he was related to the notorious bandit Abraham bar-Saraf, mainly because he had made sure that the two of them had never been seen together – and he had taken the precaution of changing his name to Ezekiel ben Judah, his trading name locally being Zeke.

So far it had all worked out fine. Romans! He laughed to himself. They thought themselves to be the masters of the world, yet they hadn't managed to work out how much he was overcharging them for the horses they purchased from him. Or if they had, perhaps money was no object to them. He liked to think that they knew he dealt in the finest horseflesh in the whole region. Whatever the reason, it didn't matter to him. No one had complained, and he had grown very rich.

He put the money in a safe place and returned outside to his stockyard, which was filled with quality stock. He was all smiles and ready to deal with his latest customer.

CHAPTER EIGHTEEN

The two squadrons rode out from Jerusalem to the 'Ascent of Blood', to caves they had not yet searched. The journey seemed interminable to the band of Roman horsemen as they made their way along the steep, winding, inhospitable road to Jericho. Antonius cursed at the column's slowness; the horses had to carefully pick their way across the rugged and rocky terrain to avoid stumbling.

Eventually the mixed cavalry unit reached the caves. Antonius instructed Julius to take his men and search the nearest cave, whilst he took his North African horsemen to search one a little further on. Aware that the assassins could be lying in wait for them, the Romans approached the caves as quietly as possible, in case of a surprise attack.

Inside the cave, Julius' nostrils were hit by a dank, musty smell; the air felt clammy and moisture clung to his face. He tried to wipe it away with the back of his hand, but the dampness persisted. The entrance was narrow and claustrophobic, but some daylight filtered through. Deeper in, visibility was poor so Julius stopped his men and instructed Francus to strike a flint. The young cavalryman reached down into his saddle bag and pulled out a C-shaped fire steel and a piece of flint. Otto unfastened a dormant torch strapped to his saddle and held it out towards Francus. Francus leaned forward and struck the flint against the fire steel several times, holding it close to the pitch-soaked torch. He leaned back quickly as the torch began to smoulder. Once it was ignited, Julius let his men grow accustomed to the surrounding area lit by the flickering light then instructed Otto to go to the front of the column to light the way ahead.

As the riders continued deeper into the cave, a horse whinnied as its hooves slipped on the wet, rocky floor. Julius stopped, turned in his saddle and hissed at its rider to get the animal under control. The rider quickly controlled his mount and the patrol resumed the search.

In the middle of the cave a chamber opened up. A chink of light from a gap high up in the rocks enabled Julius to see more clearly. He looked around and saw no sign of recent habitation. He turned his attention to a dark passageway leading off the chamber.

"Otto, ride forward and see what lies beyond this chamber."

Otto saluted, then rode off. The light from the torch

he carried threw up eerie shadows on the walls, which gradually diminished as he disappeared down the passageway. After a few moments, torchlight began to filter back down the narrow corridor and Otto reappeared. He saluted Julius.

"The cave beyond is filled with stagnant water left over from the last floods, Decurion. No one could have got past that."

Satisfied that the first cave was empty, Julius and his men rode out and continued the search in the next cave, which was also flooded, as was the next. It would be impossible for anyone to hide in them. Knowing that it must be late afternoon, Julius ordered his men back outside into the dwindling warmth of the lowering sun and waited for Antonius' return.

He did not have long to wait. A few moments later, Antonius and his men emerged out of the next series of caves. Julius saluted Antonius and reported his findings. "Sir, we've searched three of the caves on this side – there's no sign of ben-Ezra or his men."

"Right. My men have searched some of the others. No sign there, either."

"I don't think they've come here, Prefect."

Antonius snarled at Julius. "It's not your place to think, Decurion. Remember who's in charge here."

Antonius wiped the sweat from his face with the back of his hand. He was hot and frustrated by this seemingly wasted journey. He shaded his eyes and looked up at the hills surrounding them and saw the long shadows of dusk slowly begin to change the landscape. "We'd better return to Jerusalem now before night sets in, but we'll be back out here again early tomorrow and search the wadis," he said. "I won't rest until we've hunted down this stinking piece of shit. Get your men in order and prepare to ride."

Julius saluted and carried out his orders as Prefect Antonius shouted at his men "Come on, get in line!" Once in formation, the troopers, still tense and alert for any trouble, began their journey back to Jerusalem.

While the cavalry was out searching for Farrah, Flavius returned to the Antonia. He left Saturn with Zeno, reported to Quintus, then went back to his quarters.

A short time after, Antonius and Julius returned to the garrison. Quintus was angry that they had found no trace of the missing princess. He paced around the room "Where in Hades are they?"

"Permission to speak, sir?" All the way back from the Jericho Road, Julius had mulled over in his mind whether to tell his Commanding Officer his opinion and had decided that he should.

"What is it?" Quintus turned and looked at him.

"I don't think ben-Ezra and the Princess are in those caves, sir." He ignored a warning look from Antonius and continued. "We've searched them twice. May I suggest that going back to that area would be a waste of valuable time?"

"Why is that?" Quintus asked irritably.

"Because, sir, the caves my men and I have searched are mainly flooded and unfit for human habitation."

"I see. Is that the case, Prefect?

"The caves my men investigated were the same, sir. But there are still wadis to search. I'd planned to return there tomorrow to finish off the job."

"So, Decurion Vittelius, if you don't think they are in that area, then where do you think they are?" Quintus towered over Julius.

"I'm sorry, sir, I don't know."

"Then talk to me when you do!" He turned to Antonius. "Prefect, return to the area early tomorrow morning and search the wadis. Report to me tomorrow night when you return. If you still haven't found them you will scout out in another direction. The Judaean desert, or further south. You are dismissed."

The two men saluted their Commander and went outside.

Antonius waited until they were away from the Commander's office, then he rounded on Julius. His face was dark as thunder as he glared at the junior officer.

"I told you to keep your opinions to yourself, Decurion. Were you trying to show me up as incompetent?"

"No, Prefect, but I stand by my gut reaction. I still think it will be a waste of time going back to that area. I don't think we'll find ben-Ezra there."

"You don't think! You arrogant little bastard! It's for me to decide what to do next, not you!"

Flavius was settling Saturn back in his quarters. He stroked the magnificent animal's muzzle, then ran his hand over Saturn's strong shoulders, feeling the hard muscles beneath the smooth hair, muscles taut with longing to stretch themselves in hard riding.

He sighed. There would be no riding out to Bethany today. "Yes, I know you long to gallop freely my friend, but be patient, we will ride out together soon."

He was suddenly aware of a loud, angry voice outside. He left the room in time to see Antonius raise his fist and strike Julius full in the face. Caught unawares, Julius staggered under the impact and fell to the ground. Antonius drew back his iron-shod boot ready to connect with Julius' midriff.

"You there! What do you think you're doing?" shouted Flavius.

Antonius heard the sharp voice and put his foot down quickly.

"I said, what do you think you're doing?" Flavius' voice rose angrily at the sight of a senior officer attacking a junior officer, especially one he liked.

Neither man had seen Flavius approach. Antonius turned sharply ready to retaliate. When he saw a Senior Tribune standing glowering at him, his manner immediately changed. He stood to attention and saluted. "Tribune, sir! This Decurion has been insubordinate."

"I see." Flavius held the elder man's gaze. "And you are?"

"Prefect Alae Antonius, sir."

"Well, Prefect Alae Antonius, if that's the case, you know

full well there are certain procedures that must be followed – procedures that do not include personal assault, by you or anyone. Shall I accompany you to the Commander's office whilst you put in a complaint about this man – and tell him what I just witnessed?"

Antonius became flustered. "No sir, sorry sir. I got carried away, sir. It won't happen again."

"You're damn right it won't happen again. Now help the Decurion up."

Antonius leaned forward, grabbed Julius' arm and pulled him up roughly to a standing position.

"Are you alright, Decurion?" Flavius saw Julius shake his head, trying to focus. A vivid bruise was beginning to form around the young officer's eye.

"Yes, sir. Thank you, sir."

Flavius turned to Antonius. "Prefect Antonius, get back to the barracks and don't let me see you assault this man, or any junior officer, again. Is that clear?"

"Yes, sir."

"Now, get out of my sight."

Antonius saluted, turned and squaring his shoulders, marched off in the direction of his quarters.

Flavius turned to Julius. "Go along to the hospital and get an orderly to take a look at your eye. We'll speak later."

"Thank you, Tribune." Julius saluted and turned, stopping briefly as dizziness overcame him. He pulled himself up, not wishing to shame himself in front of the Tribune, shook his head and when his vision cleared, continued on his way.

Flavius watched as Julius walked unsteadily in the direction of the garrison hospital. He would have to keep an eye on Antonius. A bully was one thing he would not tolerate.

He walked to his quarters, let Gebhard take off his armour, then fell onto his bed.

"Shall I bring you some refreshment, Tribune?" Gebhard asked, his voice filled with concern.

"No. I wish to be left alone." He saw Gebhard hesitate. "I said leave me alone. Go and find something else to do."

Gebhard ignored the curt reply. He could see how stressed Flavius was and knew, given the mood the Tribune was in, that it would be better to obey. He bowed and left the room.

Flavius lay on his bunk staring up at the ceiling. He realised he'd been too sharp with Gebhard, who had only wished to serve him. Worry about Farrah had tied his stomach in knots. Where was she? Was she alive or dead? He prayed to all the gods that she was still alive and consoled himself by plotting his revenge against ben-Ezra.

CHAPTER NINETEEN

Adolfo was one of the scribes who worked for Pilate's chief scribe, Scribonius. He had been born and had spent his early youth in Lecce, an ancient trading centre set in the heel of Italy. Although not wealthy, his merchant father had made sure he was educated enough to help him with his business, so that one day he would perhaps succeed him. Adolfo had other ideas: he wanted to make his own way in the world. He was intelligent and a quick learner. Feeling stifled in Lecce, he had left home, despite his anxious parents' misgivings, and travelled to Rome to seek his fortune. He had quickly found his skills in mathematics and literacy in demand amongst the patrician families there.

In Rome, he had secured a position as tutor to the children of a prominent family. One of the family's friends was Pontius Pilate. Adolfo had impressed Pilate with his skills in teaching the family's young children. Pilate was then a rising star in the political world of Rome and Adolfo felt he was well favoured among the right people. When Pilate had offered him a position as scribe, he had jumped at the chance. Since then he had travelled with Pilate wherever he went, the culmination being Pilate's appointment as Governor of Judaea.

In Adolfo's own opinion he was an admirable scribe, far superior in his professionalism to some others who had ingratiated themselves with Pilate, and as a result had risen up in the world through their master's whim of the moment, whilst he had been ignored, even though he had been with the Governor for a long time. Lately he had become more and more frustrated by his low situation. How could he obtain the position he desired more than anything else in the world: to become Pilate's chief scribe?

Some days he would feel guilty as he remembered his past conduct in reporting certain secret incidents, at great risk to himself, to a soldier based in the Antonia. He had been given some money for his efforts, which he had added to his meagre savings, but his overall situation had not changed. Then the soldier had been transferred elsewhere and the money had stopped. Adolfo had heaved a sigh of relief; he had not been caught, but he would have to think of some other way to fulfil his dream of gaining wealth and position. Putting these thoughts aside, he would carry on scribing Pilate's latest edict, which Scribonius had laid before him.

Adolfo was on his way back to the Antonia after paying his usual monthly visit to the papyrus merchant to order more scrolls to be delivered to Scribonius. Jerusalem was exceedingly busy with people bustling to and fro. To avoid the crowds, he decided to take a short cut down an alleyway.

A cold stab of fear shot through him as a man came up behind him, overtook him and blocked his way. Was the man going to rob him – perhaps murder him?

The man spoke. "Adolfo. How are you? Don't you remember me?"

Adolfo studied the man's face, half hidden by a hood. He froze, his memory suddenly jolted. It was a man he had hoped never to see again. "You!" he gasped in surprise. "What are you doing here?"

The man smiled. "That's of no consequence."

"How did you know I was still in the city?"

"I've been watching you for days, I've got to know your routine. I followed you from Pilate's residence."

"What do you want with me?"

"All in good time, my friend." He briefly looked Adolfo up and down then said slyly: "I see you are still a menial of Scribonius. After all these years I thought you would have risen by now."

Adolfo stood up straight and looked the man in the eye. "What's that to you?"

The man's voice was placating. "In recognition of things you have done for me in the past, quite successfully may I add, I'd like to give you another chance to rise higher than you could ever have dreamed of."

Adolfo was wary. "How?"

"All I ask is that from time to time, you find a way to slip certain communications I will give you amongst the dispatches Pilate sends to Rome, specifically to..." He leaned forward and whispered a name in Adolfo's ear. He laughed softly as he saw the shock on Adolfo's face. Looking intently at the scribe, he said smoothly, "I assure you, if you are careful you will not face any danger, and think what rewards there will be for you if you are successful." The man could see Adolfo was interested and pressed on. "What is it you most desire, Adolfo?"

"Wealth – and to be Pilate's chief scribe."

"My master has the power to bring that about, to change your life. I guarantee he will look after you if you do as I propose. Think of it, Adolfo, you could be a rich man, in charge of your own staff. No more being subservient to Scribonius."

Adolfo thought for a moment. It seemed a simple task, as long as he was careful. What satisfaction it would give him to rule over others the way he had been ruled over these past years. He knew he was worth more than Pilate and Scribonius would ever allow. "What will happen to Scribonius?" he asked.

"Don't worry about him. He'll be taken care of. Now, what do you say to my generous offer?"

Perhaps, Adolfo mused, this man could, after all, help

him to reach his goal. The temptation was too much for him. "Your master will assure my safety if I'm caught?"

"I've just told you that he will."

"Then I'll do it. When shall I start?"

The man nodded, satisfied. "When are the next dispatches being sent to Rome?"

"Tomorrow."

"Then take this now." Making sure they were not being watched, the man reached into his tunic and pulled out a sealed scroll and handed it to Adolfo. "Remember, not a word about this or I will find you and kill you."

The man's last sentence hit home. Adolfo remembered how violent this man could be. He placed the sealed scroll into his leather bag. "I won't let you down," he said. Adolfo felt the hard pressure of the man's fingers through his tunic as he placed a hand on his shoulder.

"See that you don't. We'll meet here next month and I'll give you my next scroll. Now, you had better go back and attend to your duties before someone sees us. Remember, don't let me down."

Adolfo walked away, dreaming of his future life as a wealthy, powerful man.

The man grinned to himself as he tightened the hood of his cloak. He knew his master in Rome would be pleased that he'd resumed contact with a member of Pilate's own staff. Perhaps he might receive a rich reward for his success. He walked confidently out into the busy street and mingled with the crowds.

CHAPTER TWENTY

Flavius was on his way to visit Drubaal at the hospital, to see if he had recovered enough to give him any information about the attack and the abduction of Farrah. He saw Julius waiting by the cavalry block and stopped to speak to him.

"Good morning, Decurion," said Flavius.

Julius smiled. "Good morning, sir."

Flavius winced as he saw Julius's swollen eye. The deep bruising had now turned a vivid purple and green. He was angry. "I can't let Antonius get away with this," he said. "I must report this assault to the Commander."

A fleeting moment of panic crossed Julius' face. "No sir. Please don't do that. Thank you, sir, but I'm afraid you can't be with me every hour of every day and the Prefect is devious. He will find a way to hurt me, especially now he's been humiliated."

Flavius frowned. "Am I right in thinking you've had dealings with Prefect Antonius before?"

Julius hesitated, but under the tribune's steady gaze, he said, "Yes, sir – he was the Decurion who trained me when I first joined the Legion."

"Tell me what you know about him."

At first, Julius was reluctant to reveal what had happened between himself and the Prefect but Flavius persisted. As the story unfolded Flavius became more concerned about Antonius' behaviour.

"I promise you, Decurion, I will not report this to the Commander, but I will keep a close eye on Antonius. If he lays a hand on you again, I will make sure he suffers the full penalty for his crime."

Julius was about to reply when Antonius came swaggering out of his quarters. Seeing Flavius he stopped, surprised to see the Tribune standing there.

"Excuse me, Tribune," he said deferentially, "my men will be here soon. When the remainder of the Decurion's men arrive, we'll be riding out to continue the search for the Princess and ben-Ezra." He stepped forward, but Flavius barred his way. "If you don't mind, sir…" His instinct was to push past Flavius, but he thought better of it and waited until Flavius stepped aside. "Thank you, sir." He went to his horse and made a great show of checking it over.

Flavius looked Julius directly in the face and said in an imperious tone, "Don't forget what I said, Decurion."

"I won't, sir. Thank you, sir." He saluted Flavius.

Antonius snapped to attention and gave an exaggerated salute. Barely concealing his anger, Flavius stared at him for a long moment, then stiffly returned the salute, turned and walked away.

Making sure Flavius was out of earshot, Antonius immediately turned on Julius. "What have you been saying about me, you whoreson? Just because that strutting peacock has taken a shine to you, if I find out you've been spreading lies about me, I promise you...I'll make you wish you'd never been born!"

Julius ignored Antonius and continued to prepare his horse. Antonius brought his horse crop down viciously across Julius' back. Julius spun round, his fists tightly clenched, his face a mask of contempt.

"Come on then – if you think you're hard enough," Antonius sneered.

Julius quickly checked himself. He knew Antonius would love to see him severely punished, even executed, for striking a senior officer. He drew himself up to his full height, unclenched his fists and with a supreme effort forced himself to resume a relaxed expression. Then he turned away from the grinning man and adjusted the straps of his saddle.

Antonius was about to retaliate when his men arrived. They smartly saluted their Prefect, then gave a half-hearted salute to Julius before checking and mounting their horses. Antonius raised his voice. "Now, Decurion, get the rest of your men off their lazy arses and let's get out of here."

With a set expression, Julius moved away and rallied his men.

When the two Cavalry squadrons were mounted up and ready to ride, Julius cast a sideways look at Antonius and took a deep breath; he knew this day was going to be very unpleasant, especially if they didn't find any trace of the Princess or ben-Ezra. Time – and their options – were running out.

Flavius stood by the gate watching anxiously as Julius and Antonius led their men out of the garrison. He sighed deeply, feeling an uneasy sense of foreboding. He watched until the horsemen were out of sight, then made his way to the hospital.

Drubaal was propped up in bed, his head, arms and upper body encased in bandages. Flavius was shocked to see how badly hurt the Carthaginian was, but was relieved when the Garrison medical orderly assured him that his patient was making a slow recovery. Explaining the urgency of the matter, Flavius asked the orderly if he could question Drubaal. Reluctantly the orderly nodded. Flavius thanked him and as the orderly walked away to tend to an injured legionary, Flavius moved to Drubaal's bedside. He leaned over the hospital bed and softly called Drubaal's name. He let out a sigh of relief when the Carthaginian slowly opened his eyes.

Drubaal blinked as he saw the Roman looming over him. He gradually began to recognise Flavius. He tried to smile but it was too painful; he could manage only a lopsided grimace.

Flavius gently began to question Drubaal about the attack, hoping his savage head-wound had not wiped out the memory of that terrible night, a possibility he knew only too well after his own head injury.

Flavius' hopes were dashed when Drubaal was unable to tell him crucial details of what had happened, but he had recognised the leader of the attackers. He rasped out the hated name: "ben-Ezra".

It was obvious to Flavius that Drubaal knew nothing of his mistress's kidnap. He must have been unconscious when she was taken. He felt it was right that Drubaal should know, so he told the injured slave the terrible news.

At first Drubaal refused to believe Flavius, and cried out "No!" but on seeing the Roman's sad expression he realised with a heavy heart that it was true. Anguished sobs wracked the huge man's body. "My poor mistress!" he moaned. Tears coursing down his face, he whispered, "Master, I have failed you." Heartbroken and ashamed that he had been unable to protect the Princess, Drubaal tried to bury his ravaged face into his pillow. Flavius wondered if it was the pain of Drubaal's damaged body that had overwhelmed him or the pain in his heart. He laid a consoling hand on the big man's arm and noticed that the bandages wrapped around his torso had begun to show signs of seeping blood. He called out for the orderly, who quickly appeared.

The orderly took one look at the blood-soaked bandages and hurriedly went to fetch the duty doctor. The doctor examined Drubaal. Alarmed by the obvious pain and distress his patient was suffering, he politely, but firmly, ordered Flavius to leave.

As Flavius was leaving the ward, he turned back briefly to see the doctor carefully removing the stained bandages; he was shaking his head. He heard the doctor instruct the orderly to quickly fetch ointments and clean dressings.

Flavius cursed his impetuosity. Why hadn't he stayed quiet about the terrible news of Farrah's disappearance? He should have waited until Drubaal had recovered from his injuries before telling him. He remembered the remorse Drubaal had shown when Philo had been killed and knew, too late, that Drubaal would look upon his mistress's plight as his own failure to protect her. Feelings of guilt engulfed him as he walked out of the hospital, angry that through his thoughtlessness, the Carthaginian he had come to respect and admire had been caused further pain.

Julius and Antonius returned with their men at dusk. As soon as Flavius learned of their return, he rushed out to meet them, hope and expectation filling his heart. That hope was soon dashed when he saw they were alone. He had no time to speak to either man, for they quickly dismounted, left their horses with their men to take back to the cavalry blocks, and marched grim-faced to the Commander's office to give their report.

It was an agonising hour later that Julius told Flavius they had failed to find any sign of the Princess or of ben-

Ezra and that he and Antonius had been ordered to spread the search more widely. Flavius put on a brave face at the news, but deep down he knew it now seemed unlikely that they would find her alive. He tortured himself with the vision of her dead body lying somewhere out in the wilderness, her soft, flawless flesh being devoured by scavenging crows or wolves.

Julius was surprised by his senior officer's look of abject misery as he told him the news of their failure, and by his lack of comment on the situation. As he watched Flavius walk disconsolately back to his quarters, it was obvious to Julius there was something much deeper than duty as far as the Tribune's relationship with the beautiful Princess was concerned. Tomorrow the light cavalry squadrons would continue the search. He prayed silently to the goddess Fortuna, asking that next time they would strike lucky.

CHAPTER TWENTY-ONE

Farrah lay on the hard ground. She tried to move, groaning as pain shot through her body. She opened her eyes, then quickly shut them again. A wave of hopelessness swept over her. She wasn't waking from a nightmare; her surroundings were all too real.

She did not know how long she had been in the cavern, or if it was day or night. In this dark prison one miserable hour passed like another, her ordeal broken only by one of the women, Miriam, who brought her daily food and water and repeated the same warning: "Don't drink the water all at once as it has come from our precious supply jars. Our supplies are beginning to run low." She had explained that the cistern and rock pools would not be fully filled again until the winter rains and snow came.

Farrah slowly sat up as Miriam entered the cavern

again. Miriam looked at Farrah, and for a brief moment, she allowed an expression of sympathy to show on her thin face. Seeing Farrah staring back at her, her expression quickly became bland. She put a plate of greasy food and a cup of water on the floor.

Farrah looked at it and pulled a face. "I don't want it." She pushed the food bowl away.

"Suit yourself," Miriam replied, shaking her head. "We're hoping we have enough supplies to see us through the winter. I'd advise you to eat what you can now before they run out."

Miriam carried a garment over her arm. She threw it to Farrah.

"Here, put this on. The chief said I must bring it to you, to keep you warm. It gets cold in here and he doesn't want you to get ill." She saw Farrah hesitate and smiled grimly. "Believe me, you will be glad of it."

With that she walked away, her light footsteps echoing down the rocky corridor.

Farrah smelt the garment and threw it into a corner in disgust, pulling a face. Then she thought better of it and retrieved it. The chill in the cave was already beginning to eat into her bones, for her torn, flimsy clothes were not enough to keep her warm; if she was to survive the coming winter cold she would have to force herself to wear it.

She removed her tattered, soiled clothing, wincing as her arm caught her left breast. She looked at it and saw the source of the pain: bite marks and grazes, partly covered by congealed blood. Shuddering at the remembrance of her last encounter with ben-Ezra, she folded her spoilt clothing and hid it in a corner, then put on the coarse woollen garment. It scratched her skin and made her itch, but she was determined to get used to it.

The greasy meat looked unappetising, but she was ravenously hungry, so she forced herself to eat it, swallowing some of the water to help it go down and take away the taste. When she had finished, she wiped her mouth with the back of her hand.

As she placed the empty bowl on the ground she became aware of someone watching her. She looked up and saw ben-Ezra standing in the entrance to the cavern, leering at her. Farrah caught her breath, fighting the rising panic surging through her. She turned her head away from him, refusing to return his gaze. He had violated her several times, each more brutal than the last, his fists slamming into her when she had struggled against him.

He lurched into the cavern and dropped to the ground in front of her, forcing her head around to face him. Farrah gagged as the sour smell of stale wine enveloped her. She tried desperately to turn her face away again.

"Don't turn away from me," he snarled. He kissed her hungrily, forcing her lips open and ramming his tongue into her unwilling mouth.

After what seemed an eternity to Farrah, his repulsive kiss ended. She could do nothing as he forced up her arms and dragged the coarse dress over her head. A creeping dread ran down her naked spine as he quickly removed his tunic and loincloth, then pinned her down on the ground so she couldn't move. She shuddered at his loathsome touch.

His voice grew husky. "You're like a sickness I can't cure until I feel your body beneath mine – until I've tasted you."

Farrah bit her lip to stop herself from crying out as his teeth caught her injured breast, re-opening the wound. She knew it would be useless to fight him; she had learnt the hard way that it would only drive him to more sexual cruelty. Instead she lay there passively with gritted teeth and steeled herself for what was to come.

Hot with lust, his breath quickened as his excitement mounted. He forced her thighs apart and fell on her like a wild beast. The rank smell of him filled her nostrils and she stifled cries as ben-Ezra hurt her again and again. She knew he cared nothing for her pain, but sought only to enjoy his own selfish pleasure.

She had trained her mind to think of other things whilst the act took place, and she let her mind drift now. She conjured up the hot sandy dunes of her homeland, the desert hawks wheeling and swooping against a clear blue sky. She visualised herself sitting in the shade of a palm tree, eating succulent dates, in the oasis where her father's camp had once been set up.

Another tree came into her mind: one filled with almond blossom, its exotic perfume filling the air in her garden in Bethany; the remembrance of a magical afternoon spent with... no! The memory was too painful. She reluctantly forced herself back to the present and to a pain of a different kind.

Farrah thought her torment would never end, until with a grunt, ben-Ezra shuddered, then collapsed on top of her, panting heavily. Mercifully it was over. Until the next time, she thought despondently.

He stood up unsteadily and replaced his clothing. Without a word, he turned and weaved his way out of the room.

Farrah burst into floods of tears. Shivering with cold and shock, she pulled on her dress, then dragged her torn and bleeding body over to the small pot of water. She knew the water was only meant for drinking, but she always kept some of the precious liquid back to wash herself as best as she could. She tore off a strip of her old dress and carefully dabbed away the blood from her damaged breast, then dipped the fragment into the precious water, wincing with pain as she began to wash him out of her.

Ruth lay huddled in the corner of the cavern. Every day Miriam had been bringing her stale bread and water, for which she was grateful, but Miriam would not answer any of her questions: Where had her mistress been taken? Was she alive or dead? Since the day she had been parted from Farrah, she had been filled with abject misery for herself and for her mistress.

Incarcerated in this dank cave, she'd had plenty of time to recall her turbulent childhood, before Sheikh Ibrahim had rescued her. For eight of her fourteen years, she had been begging in the market place in Jerusalem. One day a wealthy foreign merchant had stopped in front of her. She had seen pity in his eyes as he had looked at her pathetically thin body covered in rags and filth.

"What is your name, child?" the man had asked her.

She had looked up at the stranger. "Why do you want to know? What's it to you?" Fear put an edge to her voice, but the stranger had smiled in understanding.

"I mean you no harm, I wish to offer you work in my household," he had said.

Taken aback, Ruth had looked deep into the man's eyes. What she saw there gave her an unexpected feeling of security. She'd lived on the streets long enough to know that he was no threat to her.

"I am Sheikh Ibrahim bin Yusuf Al-Khareem. What is your name, child?"

She had answered shyly, "Ruth."

"Well Ruth, my niece has need of a personal servant and I have chosen you – if you will come with me."

She had smiled, then meekly followed the stranger to his expensive-looking horse-drawn wagon.

At first, she had been frightened of the huge, fierce-looking man seated in the driving seat, but the Sheikh had put her at ease. "This is my personal bodyguard, Drubaal," he had said. "Drubaal, this is Ruth, my niece's new servant."

At first, Drubaal had looked at her strangely, but then he had suddenly lost his fierce look and broken into a wide smile. Nervously, she had climbed into the covered wagon and let herself be taken to... who knew where?

The Sheikh had taken her to a large house in Bethany and after a visit to the bathhouse, where she had scrubbed her hair and body free from encrusted dirt and lice, she had dressed herself in the clean clothes that had been left out for her. When she presented herself to the Sheikh he had nodded in satisfaction and taken her to his niece. On first seeing Princess Farrah, Ruth was struck by her great beauty and bearing and bowed low before her. Farrah, however, had been horrified.

"You expect me to have a street urchin as a personal body slave?" she had said, railing at her uncle. The Sheikh had stood patiently waiting for the tirade to cease. Then he had said gently, "I know how you feel about the people of this nation, and I can understand those feelings. You have much cause for hatred, but our quarrel is only with certain individuals. She is just an orphan who has no one to take care of her. Remember, your feet might easily have filled this poor child's shoes. Try to show compassion – if not for her, then for my sake."

That had been two years ago. Since then, she had served the Princess faithfully. Gradually her mistress had learned to accept her presence, even to show her some fondness. How could she have known that she and her proud mistress would share the same misfortune?

Ruth stood up as Rachel appeared, holding the usual stale bread and cup of water. Draped over her arm was some kind of garment.

"Where's Miriam?" Ruth asked. Rachel did not reply. "And where is my mistress? Is she still alive?"

Rachel laughed and put the bowl and cup on the floor, then threw the garment at her. "It's none of your business, slut." Without warning she sprang forward and gave Ruth a vicious slap around her face, hissing "That's for taking my man. It seems he prefers you over me, but I know him too well, he'll soon tire of your moon face and simpering voice, then he'll return to the woman who welcomes his lovemaking and knows how to satisfy his tastes." With that she spat on the floor, just missing Ruth's feet, turned and with her generous hips swaying, sauntered out of the cave.

Ruth took off her own filthy clothes, picked up the garment and put it over her head, smoothing the coarse material down over her body. It stank of stale sweat, but she had worn worse during her poor childhood. She soon began to feel the benefit of the thicker, warmer clothing. She had tried desperately not to cry out as Rachel's vicious slap had connected with her face. She tenderly felt around her cheekbone, flinching as she touched the point of impact. She grimaced at the thought that Rachel imagined she would actually welcome Abraham's sadistic attentions. He had subjected her to savage lust, punching and biting her into submission each time. As far as she was concerned, the quicker he returned to Rachel the better. She was welcome to him.

In the depths of her despair, she had prayed fervently after each encounter with him that she might die rather than bear the degradation and pain he inflicted on her. Her prayer had not been answered. Her new-found faith in the Lord Jesus' goodness and mercy was being severely tested. Perhaps the remarkable story of Jesus, the Son of God, as John Mark and the other followers called Him, being raised from the dead had been merely figments of their imagination conjured up as a way of dealing with the grief of losing someone they had dearly loved. And yet – John Mark had seemed so sincere in his belief, and Jesus' mother, Mary, was so sure that her Son had been sent by God; she and the rest of his Disciples had said they had seen Him after His death. Mother Mary's words came back to Ruth: "He will never leave you, whatever happens."

Ruth did not know what to think any more. Before her rescue by the Sheikh, there had been times when she had been afraid, but never had she experienced the abject terror she was feeling now. Would she die in this barren place, never seeing John Mark's lop-sided grin again? She knew now that she loved him, was sure he felt the same way about her, but even if rescue came, would he have anything to do with her now? She was a fallen woman, not worthy of his love. Deeply ashamed, she left the food and water where they had been put, hid herself in a corner of the cave and wept bitter tears.

The next morning Rebecca arrived, to be greeted by a jubilant ben-Ezra. He beamed at her. "Any problems on your journey?

She shook her head. "No. Josiah gave me two of his men to escort me here safely."

"Where are they?"

"They've returned to Jericho. They didn't want to linger here for too long."

Ben-Ezra nodded in satisfaction and took her in his arms. "I'm so glad to see you."

Farrah lay sleeping fitfully. She was woken abruptly by a kick to her shin. She yelped in pain and rubbed her sore leg, looking around to see who had hurt her.

A woman stepped out of the shadows. She stood for a long moment, her eyes registering every detail of Farrah's face and body. At first she frowned, then a cruel smile slowly spread across her face. When she spoke, her voice was low and husky.

"So, you are the fabled prisoner the others are talking about."

Farrah stared back at the stranger, taking in her oval face, framed by red hair wound into a loose plait hanging down to her slim waist. Farrah's eyes swept downwards and saw full breasts barely covered in a bright red top. The woman wore a black and red skirt which was pulled up on one side, revealing long, strong legs.

"What do you want with me?" asked Farrah, trying not to show her fear. "Who are you?"

The woman threw back her head haughtily "Who am I?" She moved towards Farrah, pulling a knife out of the skirt's waistband. "I'm Rebecca."

She snarled as Farrah shuffled backwards, trying to escape her. "Yes, you whore, you should be afraid of me." She brandished the knife before Farrah's face. "Go near ben-Ezra again and I will slice a piece off that beautiful face so all men will look at it with loathing."

Farrah knew it was useless to say that ben-Ezra wouldn't leave her alone. It would only increase the woman's hostility towards her.

Rebecca bent towards Farrah, the knife dangerously close to her face. "I will cut you anyway." Suddenly a deep voice filled the cavern, and she straightened up quickly.

"Rebecca! Leave her alone!" A shadow loomed across the two women – ben-Ezra. He grabbed the knife from Rebecca's hand and put it in the belt around his waist. They struggled for a brief moment as Rebecca tried to take it back off him. She screamed at him, "Rachel said you have been making love to her!"

Ben-Ezra grew angry. "Rachel would do well to mind her own business." His voice softened as he grabbed Rebecca's wrists and pulled her to him "Now, my little she-cat, calm yourself. How could any other woman take your place?" He lowered his face and kissed her passionately. She melted into his rough embrace, all anger forgotten. He frowned as Rebecca suddenly pulled away from him. "What's the matter?" he asked, disappointed.

"Not here, not now," she breathed. "I'm not going to put on a show for her." She pointed to where a red-faced Farrah sat, her arms hugging her knees. "What are you going to do with her?" She watched closely for his reaction.

He looked down at Farrah. "Sell her to the Nubian slave trader when he returns to the coast in the spring; it's why I don't want her harmed. The price will be much less if her face is damaged."

Rebecca frowned. "But surely the Romans are hunting for her. When you take her to the coast they will be watching."

Ben-Ezra grinned. "There are many inlets on the coastline. The slave-trader knows them all, and so do I. In any case, by next spring, surely the Romans will have given up the search for her, believing her to be dead."

Rebecca nodded in satisfaction. "Don't worry, I won't spoil her price, but put her with the others where I can keep an eye on her – and you, my love. But now, come with me and let me show you what you've been missing."

His eyes lit up and he grinned. He put his arm around her waist; she put her head on his shoulder and without a backward glance at Farrah, the two lovers walked out of the cave.

Farrah crumpled, shocked by what she'd just heard. Sold as a slave? She hoped she would be dead by next spring – or by some miracle, rescued, although there didn't seem to be much hope of that.

A little later Miriam appeared. She beckoned to Farrah. "Come with me, the master has ordered you to stay in the main cave with us now."

Reluctantly, Farrah got up and followed Miriam out. When they arrived in the much larger cave, Farrah was greeted by hostile stares from the other women.

Rachel laughed. "I told you Rebecca wouldn't like it, didn't I?" she gloated.

"Where's Rebecca?" another asked.

Rachel pointed towards another sheltered recess in the cave. "In there, with her man. They've got a lot of catching up to do." Her coarse laughter echoed around the cave walls.

Ben-Ezra lay next to a dozing Rebecca. He looked at the light sheen of perspiration covering her naked body and grinned. Their coupling had been lusty and loud, their separation over the past weeks having culminated in an explosion of pent-up lust. The cave was damp and he did not want her to catch a chill, so he pulled up the rough blanket to cover them both and wrapped her in his arms to keep her warm. His action was met with a contented sigh.

In his own way he loved Rebecca. They had been together for months now, but she still fascinated him. Not only did she have the power to satisfy his lust, her savagery and passion matching his own, he'd never known a more skilful practitioner in the way of lovemaking that he enjoyed. Nothing shocked her.

He had first come across her in the largest brothel in Jericho. Once he had tried her out, no other prostitute could satisfy him. He knew she wanted him too. When she had agreed to be his woman, he had gone straight to the brothel keeper and put in an offer for her. The brothel keeper had laughed and said he didn't have the power to sell her as she was the property of her brother, Josiah. She was the most popular woman in Josiah's brothel and earned him a lot of money. If he wanted the woman, he would have to make a deal with Josiah. Shocked to learn that Josiah treated his own sister so badly, he had thought of ways of rescuing her. What if he just ran away with her? But knowing Josiah's reputation, he had thought better of it.

Rebecca stirred and snuggled against him. "My love" she purred sleepily, sighing as he stroked her breast. When she finally awoke, she sat up. Leaning on one elbow she looked at him intently. "Rachel told me that you have spent a lot of time with the foreign woman. Is it true, Eleazar?"

Ben-Ezra silently cursed Rachel and her big mouth. He would make her pay for her gossiping. He thought quickly. "And you believe her gossip?" He turned to Rebecca. "Do you think I could ever love another as I do you? I wanted you so much that I was willing to pay your brother's asking price, even though I knew he had set it too high, but I was determined to have you for myself, so that no other man would ever touch you again."

Rebecca smiled "I'm so glad you did. You saved me from a life I hated."

"Your brother is a rich and powerful man with many men under his command." Ben-Ezra knew Josiah had many businesses under his control in Jericho too, as well as his protection rackets there and in Galilee, using gangs of thugs who had no qualms about violently extracting money from frightened business owners. "He is not a man to cross. Why would I risk his anger if I didn't love you?"

And yet, the beautiful Al-Maisan haunted his dreams. He had told her that she was like a sickness to him. Even now he could feel the touch of her silken body, taste her flesh and see her proud and haughty face. No matter how many times he had brutalised her, she had refused to succumb to him. He was convinced that given more time he would make her want him as much as he wanted her. Their first encounter had surprised him. It was obvious she had never been bedded before, that he was the first. He felt a wave of triumph wash over him. He had ploughed her before the Roman.

Desire coursed through his body. He turned to Rebecca. "Let me show you again how much I love you."

He pulled a laughing Rebecca back down onto the thin pallet. But as he made love to her, it was not her face and body he was conjuring into his mind.

Later, as he lay next to Rebecca, he thought about Josiah. He knew he must not do anything to alienate him. Knowing they shared a mutual hatred of Romans, he could become a powerful ally. If Josiah did join his men with his own, together they would make a formidable force.

After he had given Josiah the payment for Rebecca, he had put a proposition to him. At first, Josiah was sceptical. "Tell me what your plan is and I will decide if you are worth bothering with," he had said. Josiah had listened as ben-Ezra had outlined what was in his mind. After some thought, Josiah had come to a decision: he would have no hesitation in the two gangs joining together, adding that he had contact with a group of Zealots in Galilee who, he knew, would also be interested. The agreement reached, they had drunk a toast to their future victory.

As he lay there, ben-Ezra smiled to himself. He hadn't told Josiah the whole of his plan, for fear he would change his mind. He would tell him when the time was right.

Now living and sleeping in the main cave, Farrah had seen that for most nights couples would pair off and disappear into the recesses. The only exceptions were Miriam, who Farrah often saw sitting alone by the fire, and a woman Farrah had heard called Anna, who always stayed with her man, Isaac. They seemed devoted to each other and didn't join in with the nightly carousel of gang members.

Anna had taken to smiling at her whenever she had caught Farrah's glance. Rebecca had seen this and grown angry. "Don't make friends with the foreign woman if you know what's good for you, Anna!" she'd snarled.

Anna had been upset. She knew that Isaac had been angry at the way Rebecca had spoken to her and had tried hard to calm him down, reminding him that Rebecca was their chief's woman, and if he complained about her, ben-Ezra would surely retaliate. Reluctantly Isaac had nodded, knowing he would have to bite his tongue.

On this night, Farrah sat staring into the fire. Anna and Isaac had gone to another alcove, leaving her on her own. She looked up as Miriam entered the cave carrying two large jars of water. Some of the water slopped onto the floor. Farrah could see that Miriam was struggling with the heavy load and went to help her. She was shocked to see that Miriam's face was badly bruised, her left eye swollen. She wondered who had done this to her. She took one of the jars off her and carried it over to the other side of the cave. Miriam followed her. Having set down her jar, she smiled at Farrah. "Thank you, the jars were heavier than I thought."

Farrah frowned and led Miriam to the fire to rest and warm herself. She was angry, and said quietly, "This is no job for a woman, these jars are far too heavy. Why don't the men carry the water?"

Miriam sat down with a sigh. "They won't help me. It's my job to see to tasks like this."

Farrah was bemused. She had often wondered why Miriam was different from the other members of the gang. She decided to ask her.

"Miriam, you are kind, so different from these people, why are you with them?"

Miriam smiled wistfully. "I long to escape them. I am disgusted by what they do and everything they stand for, but I am as much a captive as you." She saw the shocked expression on Farrah's face. "You see, my husband was a wealthy silversmith, we lived in Tiberias. One day ben-Ezra and some of his gang came to our shop, intent on stealing the silver artefacts and jewellery. My husband was attending to a customer and Jonas, his young apprentice, was holding a tray of silver necklaces for the customer to look at. I was in the back room. Suddenly I heard shouting and angry threats. I ran out into the shop to see..." she took a deep breath, then continued – "to see ben-Ezra's men kill my husband, the customer and Jonas. They ransacked the shop, stealing everything we possessed, and would have killed me too had not one of the gang, Nathan, stopped ben-Ezra, saying he would take me as his woman. Ben-Ezra said Nathan could take me but I would be his responsibility. If he tired of me then he could do what he liked with me."

Farrah felt a wave of anger. "Ben-Ezra is a monster."

"I resented every moment of being with Nathan. I was racked with guilt and felt I was betraying my beloved husband, but at least Nathan kept me alive and saw that I wasn't too badly treated." She sighed. "Things changed when ben-Ezra and the others returned from Jerusalem without Nathan. I asked where he was and ben-Ezra told me he'd been killed when they kidnapped you. No other man has wanted me and without Nathan's protection I fear my days are numbered."

Farrah took Miriam's hand. "Can't ben-Ezra sell you as a slave? You might be bought by a kind master."

Miriam smiled wanly. "He has already said I am not pretty enough to earn him any money. I would only be fit to be a cheap household skivvy."

Farrah shook her head in disgust. "Do you have any other family?"

"No. My husband and I were not blessed with children.

Once I was sad about that, but now I am glad." Miriam looked at Farrah and said dejectedly, "Ben-Ezra will never set me free, I know too much about him, where his camps are and the people who work for him outside of the gang. He lets me live only to carry out menial tasks but when he's ready to leave here I think he will kill me."

"Have you ever tried to escape?"

Miriam patted Farrah's hand. "Where would I go? I would be on foot – he would soon hunt me down. No. I have accepted my fate. I used to sit alone by the fire dreaming of my freedom, but I know now my only hope of freedom will be when I am dead."

"How you must hate ben-Ezra and these people."

"I did hate them for a long time, but what's the good of blindly hating something you can't change?"

Farrah looked down as Miriam wiped a tear from her eye.

Unseen by them, Rebecca appeared and stood looking at them. "What are you two gossiping about?"

Miriam cowed in front of her. "I'm sorry, Rebecca. We've only been talking for a little while."

Rebecca was not convinced. "Stop this idle chatter. Go and get more wood for the fire, Miriam, I don't want it going out."

Miriam slowly stood up and walked round the fire towards the cave's exit. Rebecca stood in her way then gave her a vicious slap across her face. "Hurry up, or I will blacken your other eye!"

Head bowed, her face smarting from the slap, Miriam walked out of the cave.

Rebecca turned on Farrah. "Stop wasting Miriam's time."

Farrah wanted to lash out at Rebecca, but she knew it would only make her treatment worse, so, biting her lip, she turned her face away.

Rebecca stood staring at her for a moment, then, tossing her curls, walked off.

CHAPTER TWENTY-TWO

John Mark was worried. He had been coming to the Palm Tree Tavern every day for the past few weeks, hoping for news of Ruth. It had been several weeks now since she had visited them. She had told him once why she carefully timed her visits to his mother's house, explaining that she could only come when the stable-hand, Boraz, picked up fresh supplies from the Jerusalem market place. She would come with him, and make an excuse that she had to go and collect things for her mistress, then she would come to his mother's house. She'd explained that Boraz didn't care. He would pass the time drinking in the tavern, his favourite drinking place, while she ran her errands, making sure when she returned that the provisions were purchased quickly and hurriedly loaded onto the cart so it seemed they hadn't spent too long in Jerusalem.

John Mark had stayed in the courtyard, not venturing inside the tavern. Many times busy merchants had shouted at him to get out of their way as they manoeuvred their wagons into place to deliver various cheap wines, or by customers wanting to go inside. He'd asked them if they knew of the man called Boraz. Some had said they did know him. When he'd asked them if they had seen him recently, or the young girl that travelled with him, all said they had not seen him, or the young girl, for some time.

Downcast, he would return to the house, blaming himself for her absence. Had he been too forward with Ruth? Scared her off? He had dismissed those thoughts, for he knew she would not abandon her new-found faith and would still have visited the new friends she had made. Even if she was not interested in him personally, at least he could see her, talk to her.

It had been the same answer today. Nobody knew where the two of them were.

He turned to leave the tavern courtyard, desperately hoping that she might be waiting for him at the house, having arrived while he was asking questions at the tavern. He cheered up at the prospect.

He had only gone a few steps when he heard a man's voice calling for him to stop. He turned and saw a man coming out of the tavern. The stranger approached him.

"I hear you've been asking about Boraz and a young girl."

John Mark studied the man carefully. "Yes, I'm looking for them."

"Well, I used to drink with Boraz and I too wondered what had become of him. I knew he worked for an important merchant in Bethany, so I went there and made some enquiries." He paused for effect. "According to a local man, it seems there had been some trouble in the village. Boraz and some Roman soldiers had been found murdered in a house there."

"Murdered?" John Mark's mouth fell open in shock.

"The man pointed to a big house on top of a hill. He said that was where, a few weeks ago, he'd seen a lot of Roman soldiers hanging around. I was curious, so I went up to the house to have a look. The place had been ransacked and abandoned."

"What about the girl and her mistress?"

The man shook his head "I don't know anything about any women." He shrugged. "I'm sorry I can't help you."

John Mark was lost for words. His mind reeling, he nodded to the man and with shoulders bowed, walked away.

Deeply upset, John Mark entered the house. His mother had gone out; he was completely alone. He gave way to his grief, but then a new possibility struck him. Perhaps her mistress had escaped, taking Ruth with her. He couldn't bear the thought of not seeing her again. Ruth had been reticent in giving too much detail about her life and he did not know where her mistress's house in Bethany was. In any case, even if he did find out its location, he didn't think he could face seeing it.

Lost in his own worries, he hadn't noticed Peter come in. He jumped as Peter called his name. Turning to face Peter, he saw the expression on the big man's face and knew instinctively that something had happened.

Peter could hardly contain his excitement. "John Mark, I have wonderful news."

For a moment the younger man's face lit up. "Do you have news of Ruth?"

Disappointment overcame him as Peter shook his head. Peter saw the disconsolate look on the young man's face. "What is troubling you, my friend?" he asked.

"It's Ruth." The young man choked back tears. "She's gone and no one knows where. I don't know if she's alive or dead. I'm so afraid for her."

John Mark repeated to Peter all that he had been told by the stranger. Peter placed a conciliatory hand on his shoulder "I'm sorry, John Mark, but let's not jump to the wrong conclusions. She may well be safe somewhere with her mistress. I'm sure you will hear some news from her soon. In the meantime, I have some good news to tell you." He took a deep breath. "Philip reached Samaria; he's made many converts there. He's asked for John and me to go there to meet them and pray with them that they may receive the Holy Spirit."

John Mark managed a faint smile. "That is good news, Peter. When will you go?"

"When John returns from the city, we will make our plans, but I hope we will leave as soon as possible."

That night, after eating their evening meal, Peter and John sat talking together arranging their journey. Mary broke in, "It's wonderful news about Philip's work, but I must admit I'm worried for you. The journey is so dangerous, anything could happen to you – and what about us here? What about Saul of Tarsus? Oh Peter, you are our leader, our strength. Without you…"

There were murmurings of agreement from the other Disciples still sitting at table. Peter stood up and went to her, laying a soothing hand on her shoulder. He looked at the others. "My brothers, do you remember the answer Philip gave when I expressed the same worry to him?" He saw their blank look. "Let me remind you. Philip said: 'Not if the Lord travels with me.' I'm sure the Lord will protect us too. As for you here – my brother Andrew, Barnabas, and all of you my friends, even John Mark" – he smiled at the younger man – "must carry on the good work. John and I have made our plans – we leave as soon as the city gates open tomorrow morning." Mary tried to protest, but Peter held up his hand for silence. "The decision has been made," he said. John nodded in agreement.

Mary didn't sleep much that night. She was awake as the first glimmer of dawn broke and saw that Peter and John were already up. It was obvious they were eager to be on their way.

Wearily, she got up off her sleeping couch and began to prepare food for their journey to Samaria. When it was ready, she gave a bundle of bread, cheese and olives to Peter and a flask of goat's milk to John.

"I'll wake the others. They will want to say goodbye." Mary turned to where her son lay fast asleep, but Peter gently stopped her.

"No, let them sleep. They will need all their strength for the coming days."

Mary opened the heavy wooden front door as quietly as she could, then, poking her head out, she quickly looked up and down the street to make sure it was empty and safe. There was no sign of movement from the owners of the houses nearby. She was anxious, for after their Greek-speaking friends had been hounded out of those houses, families who supported the hierarchy of the Temple had been moved in. Mary was aware that there was an uneasy truce between the Disciples and the new occupants, who had said that as long as the followers of the new sect kept themselves to themselves and did not invite trouble to the neighbourhood, or try to convert them, peace would prevail.

Mary was momentarily startled as a stray dog came running down the street. The scrawny animal stopped as it saw her standing in the doorway and looked up at her expectantly. Seeing she had no food to offer, the dog shook itself and ran off. Making sure that no one was chasing after the stray, and the street was empty once more, Mary motioned to the men that it was safe to leave the house. The two men stepped forward and one by one kissed Mary's forehead in blessing and farewell. They intoned a prayer for the group and for themselves, then walked out into the street.

Mary watched until they were out of sight, then quickly returned inside, bolting the door behind her. Her nerves on edge, she jumped as she turned and saw her son standing there.

John Mark was visibly upset, his tone accusing. "They've gone! Why didn't you wake me up, mother? I wanted to say goodbye to them."

Mary went over to the table and began gathering food together ready for the morning meal. Speaking without looking up, she said "It was Peter and John's wish that I leave you all asleep. They said you would need your strength to face the coming days. I didn't argue."

"All the same, mother, I would have liked to have seen them off. I've already lost Ruth – if anything should happen to them…" He couldn't finish the sentence.

Mary smiled, put down the bread she was holding and went to her son. "I know, and I'm sorry. Have faith in the Lord, John Mark. You must believe that He will keep them safe." She ruffled his hair. "Now, let me get on with preparing the food." She returned to the table and busied herself laying out the groups' breakfast.

A little later, the rest of the Disciples began to rise from their beds. They too were disappointed not to have seen their friends off on their journey, but when Mary explained Peter and John's wishes to them they reluctantly nodded their approval and sat down to eat.

Aaron sat at his potter's wheel concentrating on turning a

new pot. He looked up quickly as he became aware of two men entering his shop. "Just let me finish this pot and I'll be with you," he said. He finished off the new creation, then gave his full attention to the strangers, who were looking through his merchandise.

"Can I help you?" he asked eagerly, hoping the strangers were new customers.

The taller of the men turned towards him. "Are you Aaron?"

Aaron hesitated to answer, not knowing if the strangers wished him harm.

The tall man smiled and said in a reassuring voice "Don't be afraid. We have come from Jerusalem. I am Peter and this is John." He pointed to John, who stepped forward, smiling. "We're looking for Philip. In his letter to us, he said he was staying with Aaron the Potter whose shop is in a street called Myrtle. There doesn't appear to be any other potter in this street."

Aaron was startled. The Lord's Apostles, Peter and John, here? He came out from behind the potter's wheel and bowed his head in reverence to the two Apostles who had known and travelled with the Lord Jesus and who were now forefront in spreading His Holy Word. "Yes, I am Aaron," he said. "Philip is lodging in my house. I will take you to him." He wiped his clay-clogged hands on a cloth. "Please follow me."

Aaron rushed excitedly into his house. "Where's Philip?"

Deborah heard the excitement in her husband's voice.

She put down the garment she was sewing and looked at him. "He's on the roof with Simon," she said. A shiver ran down her spine as she saw the two strangers standing in the doorway behind him. Her voice trembled. "Who are these men? What's happened?"

Aaron didn't wait to answer her but went outside again and ran up the stone stairs two at a time. When he reached the roof, he saw Philip and Simon sitting talking beneath a sheet of coarse material propped up on four sturdy poles, giving much needed respite from the hot sun.

Philip turned to him. "Hello Aaron, not at work in your shop?"

Aaron shook his head.

"Is everything all right, my friend?"

Aaron could hardly contain his excitement. "Philip. Your friends have arrived from Jerusalem."

"Where are they?" Philip stood up, a broad smile creasing his face.

"They are downstairs waiting for you."

Philip ran down to meet them, followed by Aaron and Simon. "Peter! John!" Philip grasped their arms in friendship. "It's so good to see you."

Peter's voice was warm. "It's so good to be here. You have worked wonders in bringing new converts to the Lord's cause, my friend."

Philip turned to Aaron and Simon. "Aaron you have already met." He gestured to Simon to come forward. "This is Simon, another willing convert." As Simon briefly bowed his head, Philip bade Deborah stand up. "And this is Aaron's wonderful wife, Deborah, who has looked after me so well."

Deborah's face flushed with pride. "It has been a pleasure."

Aaron cleared his throat, trying to mask his emotion. "My wife and I would be deeply honoured if you would consider sharing our home while you are staying in this area."

Peter looked at John, who nodded in agreement, then placed his hand on Aaron's shoulder. His face broke into a wide smile. "It is we who would be honoured to share your home."

After a hearty meal, Philip thanked Deborah, then excused himself from the table and took Peter and John aside. He spoke earnestly to them. "I have sown the seed of the Word of the Lord; it has taken and grown, I have baptised many new converts but only you Peter and you John can lay hands on them so they might receive the gift of the Holy Spirit. Will you do this?"

Both Apostles immediately agreed. Peter spoke: "Tomorrow, gather the converts together and we will lay hands on them. You have done well, Philip."

Philip smiled. "Thank you. I will ask Aaron and Simon to come with me. Together we will bring them to a quiet corner of the city where you may speak to them and lay hands on them."

Philip, Aaron and Simon left early the next morning.

A short time later, Philip returned to the house. "The converts are ready and are eagerly awaiting you."

Peter, John and Deborah followed Philip through the city. They found the converts waiting in a quiet area on the other side of the market place, away from the delivery carts making their way to the main part of the city. Aaron and Simon stood amongst them. Philip introduced Peter and John and a hushed reverence fell upon the gathering.

The Apostles began by speaking about their remembrances of being with Jesus during His time on earth. They then went on to tell the eager listeners some of His teachings.

Peter's expression was filled with zeal as he ended the discourse by saying: "My dear friends, the promise given to us by the prophets of old has been fulfilled. Jesus suffered a cruel death, but death could not hold Him and after three days God raised Him from the grave. We Disciples saw the risen Lord on several occasions. We witnessed Him being taken up into Heaven, and then, a few days later, as He had promised, the wonderful gift of the Holy Spirit was given to us."

He paused to let his words sink in. He looked around at the assembled gathering, then raised his eyes heavenward.

"Jesus is exalted now at God's right hand as the Son of God and Lord of the living and the dead. He has given his Holy Spirit to His followers as an assurance of His Lordship and as a foretaste of His return to be the Judge and Saviour of men at the Last Day."

John looked at the faces of the converts and saw their features filled with excitement. He said solemnly, "If you would receive the Holy Spirit, repent of all your sins and accept the Lord Jesus as your Lord and Saviour."

The air was filled with expectation. The people murmured amongst themselves. Then a man cried out, "I repent of all the bad things I have done. I believe that Jesus is the Son of God. Please, I want to accept the Holy Spirit."

Peter smiled at the man. "Ask and you shall receive," he said. He looked at John and together they intoned the prayer that Jesus had taught them: "Our Father…"

The group stood silently with bowed heads as they listened to the inspiring words. When the prayer had finished, Peter said "Come forward those who would receive this holy gift and we will lay our hands on you." They beckoned Aaron and Deborah forward to give courage to the others. Looking heavenwards, they laid their hands on them, praying for the Spirit to come to them and for the Lord to bestow His grace and mercy upon them.

Peter spoke quietly to John, who nodded in reply. They both looked at Aaron. Peter spoke. "You have done well, Aaron. We name you Deacon of this congregation."

Aaron was overcome with emotion at this gift. He took Peter's hand into his own and said, "Thank you, oh, thank you! I promise you both, I will work for the Lord until the day I die."

Deborah wiped away her tears as she too looked at the

Apostles, too moved to say how grateful she was for the honour bestowed on her husband. Aaron and Deborah stepped to the side as, at the Apostles' bidding, one by one the rest of the converts stepped forward to receive the longed-for gift.

Having received their priceless gift, some converts fell on their knees loudly praising God, while others lifted tear-stained faces to the heavens, mouthing silent prayers.

Simon had stood back, eagerly watching and waiting. He had expected the Holy Spirit, as the Apostles called it, to come with a flash of lightning and a clap of thunder, or at least be accompanied by heavenly rays of sunlight, but none of these phenomena had occurred. He was bitterly disappointed.

Then a thought came to him. If the Apostles laid their hands on him he would receive their power, and then he too could work miracles on others, but he would make it more interesting – dazzle them with some of his old tricks. His mind raced. He would travel to other cities, become famous – become rich. He wouldn't be so crass as to charge a fee for his performance; he would just make it known that donations would help him in his work. After all, it had already worked for him here, why not in other places? He made up his mind; he would offer Peter and John money for this power. Surely they would not refuse.

Simon approached Peter, a bag of coins in his hand. He held the bag out to Peter. "Take this money, give me the power too so that when I lay hands on someone, they will receive the Holy Spirit."

Peter could barely conceal his anger as he looked at the bag, then at Simon. He held up his hand to hold back a furious John. He rose to his full height, towering above Simon. His voice rose above the murmuring of the shocked converts.

"You and your money; may you come to a bad end for thinking God's gift is for sale! You are doomed! You have no part to play in this, for you are dishonest with God. Repent and pray to God for forgiveness for suggesting such a thing."

Simon stared back at the Apostle. Had Peter read his mind, or had his eager expression given him away? Trying desperately to conceal his humiliation and horror at Peter's words of warning, he countered "Pray to the Lord for me yourselves and ask that the things you have just said will not happen to me."

Peter and John shook their heads and turned away from Simon, signalling that to them, he no longer existed. A look of hatred crossed Simon's face. With a snarl, he turned and walked away, Peter's words ringing in his ears.

Philip was mortified. He approached Peter and John. "I'm sorry, I have failed the Lord. All of those hours I spent telling Simon about Jesus have been for nothing. My teaching has obviously fallen on deaf ears."

Peter laid a concilitary hand on Simon's shoulder. "No one has tried harder than you to further the Lord's work, Philip. There will always be those who refuse to listen. Pray that one day that unfortunate man will come to understand all that you have told him."

As Simon hurried away, he was angry but fearful. The Apostles were undoubtedly powerful men; what if Peter's warning came true?

He banished the terrifying thought. He must leave the area and go where he was not known. If he went far enough away, surely he could continue his magic tricks without the Apostles finding out.

Arriving at Aaron's house, he quickly gathered together his few possessions and made his way towards the edge of the city. He turned once to make sure he was not being followed by an irate member of the converts. Satisfied that he wasn't, he called down a curse on the city's inhabitants, spat on the dusty ground then quickly left the city.

A few days later, Peter and John drew Philip to one side.

Peter smiled at Philip. "You have done well, Philip. The Word will surely prosper here. We feel that it's time we returned to Jerusalem. Saul of Tarsus is spreading fear amongst our brothers and sisters; many have been arrested. We must re-join the other Disciples and continue to encourage the people there. On our journey home we will spread the good news to the villages we passed on our way here."

Philip nodded in understanding. "Yes, you are right to return to Jerusalem. For myself, I feel my work is done here. You have made Aaron a Deacon, and he is respected amongst the people. The faith will be left in good hands."

John looked into Philip's eyes. "Will you return with us?"

Philip shook his head. "No. I'm not yet ready. I feel a calling to go to other places. Gaza keeps coming into my mind. I feel drawn to it, for what purpose I don't yet know, but I'm sure the Lord will reveal it to me in time."

John smiled. "If the Lord calls you, then you must go."

"I pray the Lord will be with you Philip." Peter clasped Philip's arm in friendship. John followed suit.

Early the next morning, Peter and John said their farewells, then began their journey back to Jerusalem. After they had gone, Philip went up onto the roof of the house. He had asked Aaron and Deborah to leave him in solitude, to which they had readily agreed. He sat in the shade and spent the rest of the day praying for guidance. Over and over he heard a voice in his head saying: 'Go south. Take the desert road that leads from Jerusalem to Gaza'. He was sure now that this was the revelation from the Lord he had been waiting for. He bowed his head. "Yes, Lord, I will obey your command."

Excited at the prospect of his new adventure, he got up and hurried back downstairs. He knew it would be sad to leave Aaron and Deborah, but it seemed he had no choice in the matter. It was the Lord's will that he should go.

Deborah was preparing the evening meal. She turned to Philip as he came into the room. She was about to ask if everything was well with him, but seeing his expression, she hesitated. As Philip took her hands in his, she knew. "You're leaving us, aren't you?"

He nodded. "Yes."

"When?" Deborah felt her throat tighten as she fought to control her tears.

Before he could answer, Aaron came bustling into the house. "Good news, Philip. Some new converts have joined us today." His excitement evaporated when he saw Deborah's face. "What's wrong? Has something happened to Peter and John?"

"No. But I too must leave now." Philip said it as kindly as he could. He moved towards Aaron. "Thank you for your kindness to me. I will never forget you."

Aaron had known that this day would come, but now that it had it was still a shock. He tried desperately not to let his feelings show. Over the weeks he had come to love and respect this man who had suddenly appeared in their lives. Now he was going to leave them and he didn't know if they would ever see him again. He swallowed hard.

"How can we ever repay you, Philip? We thought we were lost to God, but not only have you restored our faith in Him, you have raised me up beyond all expectation to further the work you have begun here." He stopped, emotion overcoming him.

"I am happy you and Deborah have found God again," said Philip. "That is all the repayment I need, Aaron."

That night, as he lay on his mat, Philip decided he would not prolong the agony of parting from these good people. Early the next morning, after a hearty breakfast, he quickly gathered up his few belongings.

Deborah frowned. "You're leaving now?"

He smiled at her. "Yes. The Lord has called me to travel to new places. I have to answer that call." He took her hands in his. "Thank you for all your hospitality, Deborah."

Picking up his belongings, he moved towards the door. He turned to face Aaron and placed his hand on his shoulder. "I know I leave the Lord's work in capable hands. May the Lord bless and keep you both." With a final farewell, he left the house.

Aaron gathered a weeping Deborah in his arms as he too let his tears fall.

CHAPTER TWENTY-THREE

As soon as they reached Jerusalem, Peter and John went straight to Mary's house. They stood before the rest of the Disciples and told them about Philip's progress in Samaria.

"Philip is going to travel to other places to spread the Good News of the risen Lord," Peter told them. "May the Lord be praised, the Gospel seed is beginning to take root and grow. Let us pray for our dear friend."

All bowed their heads and prayed for Philip's safety and the Lord's blessing on his journey.

Philip had been travelling for days. Weary and footsore, he trudged along the dusty desert highway. He stopped and wiped the sweat off his face with the sleeve of his robe. The oppressive heat was beginning to sap his energy. He took a drink from the water bottle slung around his neck and decided that as soon as he reached some shade he would rest for a while.

An expensive-looking horse and carriage passed him by. He thought he could hear someone from inside the carriage reciting the words of the Prophet Isaiah, in a strange accent too, and wondered if his ears were deceiving him. He had to find out who the reader was.

He quickened his pace. As he approached the carriage he heard: "He was led like a sheep to be slaughtered; like a lamb that is dumb before the shearer, he does not open his mouth. He has been humiliated and has no redress. Who will be able to speak of his posterity? For his life is cut off and he is gone from the earth…"

Philip was dumbstruck. He looked into the vehicle and saw a richly-dressed foreigner reading aloud from a beautifully-decorated series of scrolls.

"Sir." Philip couldn't help himself. "Do you know what you are reading?"

The foreigner called his driver to stop the carriage, then looked at Philip. He said in a heavily-accented voice: "How can I understand what it means unless someone explains it to me? Can you do this for me, stranger?"

Philip felt excitement surge through him. "Yes, sir, I can."

The foreigner looked Philip up and down and nodded, satisfied that he seemed to be an honest man. He opened the carriage door. "Then come, sit beside me and explain."

Philip needed no second bidding. He climbed into the

carriage and sat down, waiting for the questions to begin.

The wealthy man instructed his driver to continue, then shared the scroll he'd been reading from with Philip "Now, tell me please, who is it that the Prophet is speaking about here, himself or someone else?"

Philip took a deep breath to calm his nerves. He knew he had to get the message through to this obviously important man. He began by saying "The Prophet Isaiah is foretelling the good news of the Lord Jesus."

The foreigner looked at Philip questioningly. "Who is this Lord Jesus you speak of? The Prophet does not mention that name here." He pointed to the scrolls.

Philip knew he would have to explain who Jesus was. "I think I'd better start at the beginning," he said. He went on to tell him the whole story of Jesus' life, death and resurrection.

The man sat enthralled by the tale. When Philip had finished, he was silent for a while, trying to absorb the information he had just been given. Then he said, "Thank you friend." He frowned. "But excuse me, I have not introduced myself. I am from Ethiopia and have the honour of being a high official at the court of Ethiopia's Candace, the mother of our young king. In fact, I am in charge of all of Her Majesty's treasure." His serious face suddenly lit up with a smile. "Although I am Ethiopian, I am also a Jewish convert. I have been to Jerusalem on a pilgrimage." He pointed to the scrolls. "As you see, I have been studying the words of some of the great Prophets.

They speak of many amazing things, and now you have explained to me the significance of their foretelling of this Lord Jesus, I begin to understand."

They had travelled a short distance when the Ethiopian suddenly called out: "Driver, stop the carriage!"

The carriage immediately pulled up. Philip wondered what was wrong. The Treasurer smiled at Philip, then pointed to a small oasis.

"Look, here is water. I would like to be baptised."

Philip's heart leapt with joy. This must be the reason he'd been called to travel to Gaza. "I will gladly baptise you, sir," he said.

Some camel traders had stopped to rest at the oasis and take water for themselves and their camels. They looked on intrigued as they saw the ornate carriage stop and two men climb out of it, one simply dressed, the other obviously wealthy. They watched as the men walked down to the water's edge and enter the water, stopping when it reached their thighs. They gaped at the simply-dressed man as he stood looking up at the sky. His lips were moving, but they were not close enough to hear his words. They wondered who he was talking to.

They shook their heads in disbelief when the man scooped up the precious water and poured it over the wealthy man's head. Shocked and surprised by this action, their eyes followed the two men as they came out of the water and returned to the carriage, where they stood talking for a while.

The Treasurer smiled at Philip. "Thank you, my friend. You have given me a great gift. I hope I am worthy of it. I will certainly tell the Candace about you and about Jesus."

Philip returned his smile. "God go with you as you journey back to Ethiopia," he said. Giving a final blessing, he turned and walked away.

The Treasurer watched him for a while, then climbed back into the carriage. At his command, the driver flicked the reins of the carriage horses and they moved off on the next stage of their long journey home. From inside the carriage came the sound of the deep, rich voice of the Treasurer joyously reciting psalms.

The camel traders scratched their heads and spoke animatedly to each other, both trying to make sense of what they had just witnessed.

Philip arrived in Azotus and toured the surrounding countryside. After a while, he left that region and continued his journey, eventually reaching Caesarea. He knew that it could be dangerous for him, as it was the seat of Roman government in Palestine and housed the Roman Governor's palace as well as a large garrison of soldiers. There were also many gentiles and pagans living in the city.

He found some clean lodgings owned by a local family. The next morning he began his first tour of the city. Never having seen such a large city before, he was astounded by the stunning buildings and the hustle and bustle of so many people. Even at festival time, Jerusalem was never this busy. He came upon the magnificent harbour, filled with galleys from Rome and ships from all different parts of the Empire. He thought the Romans were very clever to use such a beautifully-constructed port set in such a strategic position, for surely, from here, these ships could reach any part of the Roman world.

Close to the harbour, on a promontory jutting out to sea, he could see part of an impressive structure. He wondered if this was where the Roman Governor stayed when he wasn't in Jerusalem. If it was, it was not hard to see why it had been chosen as an official residence. The position and sheer beauty of the area would appeal to the Roman aesthetic mind.

Although the memory and name of Herod the Great were hated throughout many regions of Palestine, Philip had to admit that Herod's creation of this spectacular palace and port was superb.

That evening, when the air had cooled, Philip went up onto the roof of the lodging house and looked at those parts of the bustling city he could see from his viewpoint. He blinked as the rays of the setting sun projected a fiery glow onto the brilliant white marble façades of the pagan temples nearby. The effect was stunning, and frightening.

Philip frowned. If he did decide to stay in the city, he would have to tread carefully. Judging by the number of temples here, the citizens of Caesarea worshipped many foreign gods. He would have to find out if he could trust his landlords and whom else he could trust amongst the local citizens; only then would he tell them the story of Jesus.

As he looked at the sun, now beginning to disappear over the horizon, he said quietly: "Is this what you want, Lord? Is this why I'm here?" A feeling of peace came over him; he had his answer. "Then, Lord, this is where I will make my home."

Saul stood proudly before the assembled Sanhedrin.

"Speak, Saul of Tarsus." The High Priest, Annas, beckoned him forward.

Saul stepped forward and bowed before his superiors. "My Lord High Priests and esteemed members of the Sanhedrin. Even after the death of the blasphemer Stephen of Alexandria and the imprisonment of the converts here in Jerusalem, I must regrettably report their network of lies has now spread as far as Damascus." He paused dramatically to let his words sink in, and was inwardly elated as he saw the effect they were having on the gathering.

Annas turned in his seat and looked straight at Gamaliel. "Well, Rabbi, what do you think of this news? Should the Sanhedrin still ignore this new creed as you suggested? Tell me, what can be done?"

Gamaliel shook his head sadly and slumped into his seat, defeated.

"The dangerous ideas the Nazarene's followers still adhere to must be stamped out once and for all," spat Caiaphas. "If they cause an insurrection with their foolish assertions of a coming 'new age' their so-called Messiah has brought, then Rome will retaliate with violence so far unseen in this Country. Are we going to let that happen?"

"No!" wailed the members of the Council.

Annas held up his hands in exasperation "But how do you kill an idea, Caiaphas?"

"By destroying its source."

Annas stood up. "Members of the Sanhedrin, do you agree that the cult of the Nazarene should be wiped out in Damascus?"

All but Gamaliel, who sat with his head in his hands, shouted "Aye!"

Annas' voice rang out: "Saul of Tarsus, with my full authority and the authority of the Sanhedrin, I order you to go to Damascus and root out this evil. Arrest all those who follow this new religion and bring them back to Jerusalem. I will make an example of them that will put a stop to this abhorrent and dangerous blasphemy once and for all."

Saul bowed before Annas and Caiaphas. "My Lords, I promise to bring the blasphemers back in chains to stand trial before you."

Peter was hot and tired. He had been out preaching all day. As he wearily made his way through the winding streets leading back to Mary's house, he thought about the hearty meal he would eat that night.

He stopped as he saw a man hurrying towards him, a man who was constantly looking back over his shoulder. Peter recognised him as one of the servants of Caiaphas.

He had spoken with him several times and knew he was on the brink of asking to be baptised.

With one last look to make sure he was not being followed, the servant approached Peter.

"Thank the Lord I've found you, Peter." The servant steadied his breathing.

"What's wrong?" Peter could see the man was distressed.

"I was serving refreshments to the High Priests when I overheard a conversation between them – it was about Saul of Tarsus. As soon as I was free I went to the market place to see if you were there, but Barnabas was on his own. He told me you were preaching at the Pool of Siloam. I had to warn you..."

Peter looked questioningly at the servant. "Warn me? What has Saul of Tarsus done?"

"Early tomorrow morning he's going to Damascus to arrest the converts there."

Peter knew the servant had placed himself in great danger by coming to him. He was sure he could trust the man. His face was grim as he said, "Thank you. You must stay silent and return to the High Priest's house as quickly as you can before you are missed." Peter watched as the servant hurried away.

Peter sighed. He would have to break the terrible news to the other Disciples. With a heavy heart, he continued on his way, wondering if Saul's persecutions would ever end.

Later, as they were all gathered together for the evening meal, the conversations around Mary's table were filled with the Disciples' cheerful experiences of that day. Their animated chatter stopped abruptly as Peter stood up and faced them, his expression extremely grave.

Peter took in a deep breath, then began: "My dear friends, the days are darkening for us again. I have been reliably warned that Saul of Tarsus is leaving for Damascus tomorrow morning. He intends to arrest every convert in that city and bring them back here in chains to face the High Priests and the Sanhedrin."

Gasps and cries of "No!" filled the room.

Barnabas rose up out of his seat, his voice filled with anger. "How can Saul do this? What has happened to the man I once called friend?"

Other voices joined in the condemnation of the man from Tarsus. Peter's voice rose above the clamour. "We must offer up prayers for the safety of our brothers and sisters in Damascus," he said. The little group became quiet and bowed their heads as Peter prayed.

"Dear Lord Jesus, have mercy on your servants in Damascus, give them strength and courage to face their coming ordeal. We ask you to forgive their persecutor – even as you forgave those who persecuted you."

As one voice the group intoned "Amen."

CHAPTER TWENTY-FOUR

Saul of Tarsus strode along the Damascus road, a determined look on his face. Nothing was going to stop him from hounding out the blasphemers in that city and bringing them back in chains to face their punishment. The sun was hot and beat down on him and the small group accompanying him, but it did not deter him from his goal.

Elias, one of Saul's companions, wiped the sweat off his brow. He turned his head to look at Jacob, another member of the group "This is hard going, Jacob. I wish Saul would stop and rest, if only for a little while, in this merciless heat."

As he waited for Jacob's response, his attention turned to Saul, who had come to a sudden stop. He let out a cry as he saw Saul fall to his knees on the hard ground, and rushed over to him. He could see Saul shading his eyes against the bright sunlight and his mouth moving as if talking to someone. He heard a voice and thought it was Jacob.

He called out to his friend, "What did you say, Jacob?"

Jacob looked quizzically at Elias. "I didn't say anything."

Elias looked at the others "Did any of you speak just now?"

The rest of the small group shook their heads. Elias was puzzled. If Jacob, or any of the others, had not spoken, then who had? He looked around, but there was no one else there.

Jacob came and stood with Elias. "What's the matter with Saul? Is he ill?"

Elias put out a hand to steady Saul as he staggered to his feet. Perhaps Saul had heat-stroke, or had suffered some kind of seizure? Whatever it was, it had happened quickly and strangely.

Before he could ask what had happened, Saul's hands were scrabbling at his coat. With desperation in his voice, Saul cried out "Help me! I can't see!"

Elias was staggered. Saul, blind? How could that be? One minute he was striding along the road, the next… Grabbing Saul's arm, he called out, "Jacob, help me support Saul."

Shocked and bewildered by these events, Jacob took hold of Saul's other arm. Together they supported the distraught agent of the High Priest.

Jacob looked at Elias. "What do we do now?"

Elias thought for a moment, then came to a decision. "You, Jacob, must lead the others and take Saul to Damascus and leave him at the lodging house designated for us there and settle him in; I will return to the High Priests and tell them what's happened. I don't think Saul is in a fit state to carry on. They will have to send a replacement to finish the task. You" – Elias pointed to one of the Temple guards – "will return to Jerusalem with me. And you" – he ordered a second guard to come forward – "You will help support Saul in my place."

With Jacob and the Temple Guard supporting Saul, the group continued their journey, determined, despite this set-back, to bring the followers of the new cult to justice. Elias and the guard made their way back to Jerusalem.

Hot and tired after their long journey, Elias and the Guard reached Jerusalem and went straight to the Council Chamber to report to the High Priest. The Captain of the Temple Guard dismissed the Guard and told Elias to wait until the meeting of the Sanhedrin reached its conclusion. The meeting over, the High Priests sat watching as the members of the Council left the Council Chamber.

Troubled and irritated by the lack of news, Caiaphas turned to Annas. "Why hasn't Saul returned with any prisoners? He's been gone for some time now and we've heard nothing from him." He clenched his fist. "Where is the man?"

Annas' face was grim. "Where indeed? Something's happened, I'm sure of it."

He looked up as the Captain of the Temple Guard entered the Council Chamber and bowed respectfully before them. "My Lords, one of your agents is waiting outside. He wishes to see you. He says it's urgent."

Annas turned to Caiaphas "Ah, perhaps Saul has arrived."

"At last!"

Annas gestured to the Captain. "Bring him in."

The High Priests were shocked when it was not Saul the Captain escorted into the Chamber but Elias. Annas and Caiaphas stared haughtily at him as he bowed before them.

Caiaphas leaned forward. "What are you doing here, Elias? Why aren't you in Damascus with Saul?"

Elias was nervous. Beads of sweat began to appear on his furrowed brow as he tried desperately to formulate the right words. He had to give his report some credence. He knew that what he had to say would not go down well with his masters.

"Answer Lord Caiaphas's questions!" snapped Annas.

"Yes, Lord Annas. I'm sorry, Lord Caiaphas." He swallowed hard. He must tell them exactly what happened, however unbelievable it sounded. His words came out in a rush.

"My Lords, we were travelling along the road to Damascus when Saul of Tarsus suddenly fell to his knees. I went to him. He was shielding his eyes with his hands and babbling about a bright light. He appeared to be talking to somebody – but there was no one else there." He thought it best not to reveal that he too had heard a voice. "Saul suddenly cried out, saying that he'd gone blind. I came straight back here to let you know."

Annas let out a sigh of frustration. "What are you gabbling about, man?"

"I'm sorry, my Lord. It's just difficult for me to try and explain what happened."

"You'd better tell us your story again. And this time, speak more coherently."

"Yes, Lord Annas."

Elias repeated the story, more slowly this time. When he'd finished, Annas laughed.

"This is utter madness. Saul was perfectly well when he left here. How could he have suddenly lost his eyesight?"

Elias shook his head. "I don't know, my Lord."

Annas stopped laughing and stared icily at Elias. "I've never heard anything so ridiculous. There's more to this story, isn't there?"

"No, my Lord. I can only report what I saw with my own eyes."

Caiaphas too was not convinced "You said you have come straight back here?"

Elias nodded. "Yes, Lord Caiaphas."

"What has happened to Saul and the others who accompanied him?"

"As far as I know, my Lord, apart from the guard who returned here with me, Jacob and the others have taken

Saul to the lodging house of Judas in Straight Street, as you had arranged."

Caiaphas leaned towards Annas and said quietly "Lord Annas, I don't believe for one minute that Saul has suddenly gone blind. Perhaps it's a ruse to get out of doing his duty."

"If it is, he will face grave consequences."

Caiaphas shook his head. "We can't let this situation go on."

Annas' voice grew stern. "No we can't. We won't! Saul must be brought back here to face us." Annas turned back to Elias. "Elias. It is our opinion that whatever game Saul of Tarsus is playing, he is no longer fit for the task we set him."

Elias was convinced that Saul had lost his sight, but it was obvious that the High Priests did not believe it. He made no further comment, knowing he must tread carefully to avoid the High Priests' anger.

Annas conferred briefly with Caiaphas, then looked back at Elias. "We place you, Elias, in charge of the group. Make sure the blasphemers in Damascus are dealt with." He turned to the Captain. "Choose men to go to Damascus with Elias and find out what Saul of Tarsus is up to. They must bring him and any prisoners back here. If there are no prisoners, then Saul must be brought back here alone."

"Yes, my lord." The Captain bowed.

Caiaphas spoke up. "Impress upon your men that only Saul and the converts are to be arrested. The last thing we need are the Damascus authorities becoming involved. If a diplomatic incident occurs, it will not go down well with our Roman masters."

"I will make sure your orders are carried out, my Lords." The Captain bowed again and hurriedly left the chamber.

Relief flooded over Elias. As the bringer of bad news, he'd expected the High Priests to have vented their fury on him. Instead, they had done the opposite and turned their anger on Saul, then promoted him to be the new leader of their agents in Damascus.

He had never really liked Saul of Tarsus; he had just pretended to for his own safety, as he knew Annas and Caiaphas favoured him. Knowing that, Saul had brooked no argument from anybody else. Elias had witnessed on many occasions just how ruthless Saul could be. Remembering the jabbering man kneeling on the dusty road, his sudden blindness and the weakness of his body, Elias knew that now the tables had turned, and those favoured days were over for the man from Tarsus. He smiled inwardly. What satisfaction it would give him to have Saul at his mercy!

Hiding his elation, Elias bowed to the High Priests.

"I thank you for this great honour, my Lords. I promise that I will do everything to bring the blasphemers back here to you to face their just retribution."

"Make sure that you do." With an impatient wave of dismissal Annas sneered, "Now get out!"

Elias bowed again, then followed after the Captain.

CHAPTER TWENTY-FIVE

Farrah sat cross-legged on the stony floor, fascinated as she watched two of the women grinding barley flour with clay pestles and mortars preparing the mixture for baking bread. When the grain was ready, it was passed to two more women who mixed it with water; the dough was then fashioned into small shapes. Rachel was in charge of placing the shapes onto an iron pan, which she then placed on the hot cooking coals of the fire.

The first woman sighed as she worked the pestle in her mortar. "How I wish I could have bought my stone quern and clay oven. It would be so much easier to make bread." The second woman laughed. "You've got your own quern and oven? Come up in the world, have we?" She was greeted with a hateful look from the first woman. "Oh, I forgot. Your man might have made your oven, but he stole the quern on a raid didn't he? You could never have afforded to buy your own."

Without taking her eyes off the cooking pan, Rachel warned the women, "Now, now, you two."

The second woman raised her hand in mock protest. "I'm only having a joke."

"Well stop talking and get on with your work. There's a lot of baking to do if we all want to eat tonight." She didn't hear the whispered curse in reply.

When the first batch of bread was baked, Rachel laughed as she saw the concentration on Farrah's face. "The first time you've seen bread being baked, is it? Of course it is. Your ladyship couldn't have cared less how the rich foods you ate in the past were prepared by your servants. Not that they would have placed coarse barley bread on the table."

Farrah was in no mood to tangle with Rachel. She got up and moved to a corner and sat alone.

Later, after the evening meal had been eaten by the gang, Rachel handed Farrah a bowl containing chunks of boiled, salted fowl. "This is all you're getting tonight," she said.

Farrah grimaced as she forced down every unappetising mouthful. The food was always bad, but she needed to keep up her strength. She still refused to give up on the idea that one day Flavius would come for her.

Rachel got up and moved closer to Farrah, then watched her closely as she finished the food, placed the empty bowl on the ground and wiped her mouth with the back of her hand.

"Not so grand now, are we your ladyship? What would your fancy Roman say if he saw you now?" Rachel's lips curled into a sneer.

Farrah refused to rise to the bait. Instead she stared over Rachel's shoulder, her attention caught by a movement at the entrance of the cavern. She gasped in shock and surprise to see Miriam leading Ruth into the room. It was the first time she had seen her young servant in weeks, since the day they had been brought to the cave. Ruth had been pretty and lively then, but now she was a shadow of her former self: gaunt, thin-faced, her long hair a dirty, straggly nest of tangles. Farrah realised that she too must look the same to others' eyes.

Ruth stumbled, and had it not been for Miriam holding her up, she would have fallen headlong onto the stony ground. Farrah rose up quickly and went to help Ruth.

"What have you done to her?" Farrah glared at Rachel.

"Why should I do anything to her? Abraham tired of her days ago, he's back with me now, where he belongs."

Farrah and Miriam helped Ruth to sit down with her back to the wall for support. Farrah was deeply concerned.

"She's sick, she needs medicine."

Rachel laughed. "Who cares if she lives or dies?"

Farrah thought quickly, then rounded on her "She too is meant for the slave market. If she dies, then ben-Ezra will lose valuable money. What do you think he will do to you if he finds out you didn't help her?"

That statement hit home. Rachel knew all too well what ben-Ezra's reaction would be to a lost sale. Her life would be forfeit too. She stood up, threw Farrah a withering look then retreated into another part of the cave complex. Miriam drew closer to Farrah.

"Quickly, before Rachel returns, you must listen to me," she said. "I have been watching Ruth for the last couple of weeks. I don't think she is sick – I think she is carrying a child."

The news hit Farrah like a thunderbolt. "Are you sure?"

Miriam nodded. "She has shown all the symptoms of early pregnancy. Please don't mention this in front of Rachel – the child must be Abraham's. If she discovers the truth, Rachel will find a way to get rid of Ruth. Oh, she will make it look like an accident so ben-Ezra won't blame her, but she *will* kill her."

She turned away from Farrah as Rachel entered the cavern, a small vial of liquid in her hands. She held it out to Farrah.

"Here. Give her this."

Farrah took the vial, carefully removed the leather stopper and placed it to Ruth's scabbed lips. Ruth tried hard to swallow the potion without coughing, but her mouth was too dry. Eventually she managed to swallow a few drops of the bitter-tasting liquid. It did not stay in her system for long; soon after, she leaned over and vomited the liquid onto the floor. She dry-retched for a while, her stomach having nothing left inside to lose. Exhausted by the effort, she lay back against the cold wall and closed her eyes.

Suspicion began to gnaw at Rachel, but she kept that suspicion to herself. She would keep a close eye on the girl, to see if she was right.

Farrah felt anger well up inside her. Ruth would not be able to hide her condition for too long. Rachel would realise who the father was. The weeks ahead would be worrying. She wasn't concerned by what ben-Ezra might do; she was sure he would just try to fix it with the slave trader for a two-for-one deal.

Then a thought struck her. If Rebecca hadn't arrived when she had and taken ben-Ezra's unwelcome attention away from her, she could have been in the same situation as Ruth. She silently thanked all the gods whose names she knew, as well as those she didn't. Now she must concentrate on looking after her poor servant and helping her as much as she could through the coming dangerous weeks.

That night, ben-Ezra took Abraham to one side. "It's time to remind Josiah of my plan, give him the opportunity to prepare, if, as I hope, he still agrees to join with us. You will ride with me, Abraham. We leave for Jericho tomorrow at first light. We must travel before the rains begin."

Early the next morning, without waking the rest of the gang, ben-Ezra and Abraham rode out to Jericho. Several days passed before they returned. Ben-Ezra was relieved: Josiah had liked his plan and agreed to join forces. He would go with his men to the allotted place at the chosen time. Ben-Ezra chose not to tell this to Rebecca. She would be told when he was ready.

Rebecca tried to wheedle out of ben-Ezra where he and Abraham had been, but he refused to tell her, leaving her frustrated and annoyed that he should keep things from her. When Miriam came to her and said "Rebecca, our water supplies have almost gone. If the rains don't come soon we will all die," Rebecca took out her frustration on Miriam and slapped her hard across her face. "You useless whore, it's you who has wasted it!" shouted Rebecca. "Every time you carry the jars in you slop the water all over the floor."

Farrah was incensed by this wanton act of cruelty and rose to Miriam's defence. Rebecca turned on her, her hand raised, ready to strike. "Mind your own business!" she hissed.

Abraham came into the cavern, rubbing his hands together and smiling. "Dark clouds are beginning to build, and I think the rains will come very soon. If I'm right, it won't be long before rainwater starts to flow into the cistern. Then there will be plenty of water for us all." He looked at the still angry Rebecca. "Where is Eleazar?"

"The last time I saw him, he said he was going to check on the food supplies," Rebecca replied tersely.

Abraham turned and walked out of the cavern to find ben-Ezra and give him the good news. Uttering a curse at Farrah, Rebecca followed him.

CHAPTER TWENTY-SIX

Three days had passed since Saul's companions had brought him to the lodging house in Straight Street, Damascus. Every day they had left him lying on a thin mattress placed on the floor of his room while they went into the city seeking converts to arrest. Hour after hour, blind and desperately ill as he was, Saul's tortured mind had conjured up terrible visions of the frightened men, women and children crying out to him as he'd thrown them into prison. Faces, some with a pleading look, others with a look of pity for him, continuously passed before his sightless eyes. One man was predominant in these visions: Stephen of Alexandria.

As he lay there now, the vision of Stephen appeared to him. He groaned at the memory of that stoning pit, of the young man suffering under a barrage of stones, and most of all, his words. Despite the terrible thing happening to him, Stephen had called on Jesus of Nazareth to have mercy on his tormentors and at the moment of death, he had asked Jesus to receive his soul. Saul was bemused. Why had this same Jesus, whose followers he'd so relentlessly persecuted, appeared to him as he had made his way along the Damascus road?

Again and again he had relived that moment when the strange, unearthly light had appeared. At first, he'd thought it was the heat of the sun playing tricks on his eyes, some kind of mirage. But the light had grown so intense that he had been forced to shield his eyes from it and had fallen to the ground. Then he'd heard that voice: 'Saul, Saul, why do you persecute me?' Frightened, he had asked 'Who are you?' The voice had replied 'I am Jesus of Nazareth. Stand up and go into the city and you will be told what you have to do.' He had stood up and opened his eyes, crying out in terror, "I am blind". His shocked escort had led him by the hand into Damascus to this house and left him alone here in this room.

His remembrances stopped abruptly as he heard a sudden noise. Someone had opened the door and come into the room, closing the door behind them. Then he heard footsteps coming towards him. He called out "Who's there? Is that you Jacob?" There was no reply. Suddenly, very afraid, he shuffled back against the wall.

The newcomer stood looking down at the pitiful sight before him. He saw Saul flinch as his soft voice broke the menacing silence. "Don't be afraid, Saul," he said. "My name is Ananias. I have been sent to you by the Lord Jesus."

Saul was amazed. "Ananias? I had a dream about a man called Ananias. Are you really that man?"

Ananias knelt down beside Saul. "Yes. Saul, my brother, the Lord who appeared to you on the road to Damascus has sent me to you so that you may recover your sight and be filled with the Holy Spirit."

Ananias placed his hands across Saul's sightless eyes and softly intoned a prayer. Then, taking his hands away, he waited.

Saul immediately felt a deep joy course through his being. A few moments later, he slowly opened his eyes. Although his vision at first was hazy, he gradually began to make out the outline of a man kneeling next to him. He stared at the outline until his eyes focused and he saw Ananias. He grabbed hold of Ananias' hands and said joyously "I can see. I can see!"

Ananias gave a prayer of thanks, then helped Saul to stand up. At first, Saul was unsteady on his feet. Ananias waited until he could stand without help, then let go of his arm. "Where are your companions?" he asked.

"Out in the city searching for converts."

Ananias frowned. "I pray the Lord will protect His followers." He pointed to the door "Now, you must come with me, Saul."

Saul hesitated. "Where are we going?"

"The Lord has instructed me to baptise you."

"Baptise me? Me?"

Ananias smiled. "The Lord thinks you are ready now."

Bemused, Saul followed Ananias out of the room and down the stairs to a passageway leading to the inner courtyard of the house. Before they reached the end of the passageway, Ananias stopped. "Wait here, Saul, I must make sure the courtyard is safe to enter."

Saul waited as Ananias checked. Ananias was soon back, a smile of relief on his face. "The courtyard is empty." he said.

In the middle of the courtyard stood a well. Ananias walked over to it, then beckoned Saul to follow him. As he walked out of the passageway, Saul had to shield his eyes against the sunlight streaming into the courtyard. They soon adjusted to the brightness, and he went to the well and stood waiting expectantly by Ananias' side. Ananias took hold of the chain fixed to the well's pole and hauled up a wooden bucket filled with water. He stood the bucket on the side of the well and scooped some water out of it with his hands. As he baptised Saul, he intoned a heartfelt prayer of thankfulness and joy to the Lord.

Tears stung Saul's eyes as Ananias baptised him. How loving and forgiving was the Lord Jesus after all the terrible things he had done to His followers! He knew that he would follow Jesus for the rest of his life.

Seeing Saul begin to regain his strength, Ananias said to him: "Saul, I must tell you that at first, I was reluctant to come here. I'd heard the stories concerning you and your treatment of the converts in Jerusalem. Then the news came that you had been given authority by the High Priests to come to Damascus to arrest all of the Lord's followers here." He took a deep breath. "When the Lord asked me to come to you, I am ashamed to admit that I told Him I did not want to, but the Lord said, 'You must go, for this man is my chosen instrument to bring my name to the nations and their kings and before the people of Israel.' The Lord also said He would show you all the things you must go through for His name's sake."

Ananias smiled. "How could I argue with that?"

Saul mused on the words Ananias had repeated; He, Saul, a chosen instrument? He would bring Jesus' name before the nations? Which nations? Their kings? Which kings? And the people of Israel? He was hated throughout Judaea. Who was going to believe he was a changed man? And what things must he go through for Jesus' sake? It seemed a daunting task that had been asked of him. He shook his head. "Ananias, I don't know if I can do these things the Lord has asked of me."

"The tasks set before you do seem frightening, but you will be doing the Lord's work, Saul. He will be with you every step of the way." His face suddenly showed concern "You cannot stay here, Saul, it's too dangerous for you now. How will you explain your regained sight to your companions? They must certainly not know of your baptism. I think it best you leave here. I have trusted friends you can stay with." He searched Saul's face for a reaction to his statement, and saw a brief hesitancy there. "Will you come with me, Saul?"

Saul pondered his predicament. The men who had travelled with him would most certainly arrest him for blasphemy if he told them the truth. He shuddered at the thought of the High Priests' revenge. His new life would end before it had begun. And yet, it seemed the Lord Jesus had chosen him for a purpose, a purpose he knew he had to fulfil.

He came to a decision. "Yes, Ananias, I will go with you."

Ananias was relieved. "Good. Now, put up your hood and let us be on our way before your companions return."

Ananias walked out of the lodging house first, checking that there was no one waiting outside the house or walking down Straight Street. Satisfied that the street was empty, he said "Quickly Saul, follow me."

As they travelled to the other side of the city, Saul's body felt weak through lack of food and the after-effects of his fever, but his spirit was soaring. He was embarking on a new, different kind of journey, this time to further the work of the Lord, not destroy it.

Ananias took Saul down a side street, then stopped before a small house. The house was owned by Jonathan, a cloth merchant, and his wife Calisto. They too were converts to the new religion.

"I know you will be happy here with my dear friends," said Ananias, knocking on the door.

Jonathan opened the door. "Ananias. It's good to see..." He stopped, fear engulfing him as Saul stepped forward. What was this man doing here with Ananias? Had Saul arrested Ananias and forced him to betray the converts? Not possible. He knew Ananias would never betray them. He looked at Ananias, who stood calmly by Saul's side with no trace of fear on his face. Why then was Saul here? He stared at Saul. The man looked gaunt, half-starved.

Seeing Jonathan's pale, troubled face, Ananias smiled. "There is nothing to fear, Jonathan, all is well. Please let us in and I will explain everything to you."

Jonathan stepped aside and let the two men enter his house. Calisto came into the room. She smiled when she saw Ananias, but stifled a scream of fear on seeing Saul. Ananias reassured her that Saul was now a friend, a friend in need. As she listened to the story of Saul's conversion, tears stung her eyes. Convinced that Saul had changed, she graciously bade Saul to sit at their table and eat with them.

As Calisto prepared nourishing food, the smell of her cooking made Saul realise just how hungry he was. He smiled at Calisto and thanked her as she placed the appetising meal before him, then eagerly ate his first meal in Damascus.

CHAPTER TWENTY-SEVEN

Quintus frowned as he looked at the gaunt figure of Flavius standing before him. His face was pale and drawn, and it was evident that this once supremely fit young man, who prided himself on his athletic physique, had lost weight. Since the abduction of Princess Farrah, he had watched the gradual decline in the Tribune. He should have listened to the trusted body slave, Gebhard, when he had come to him raising concerns for the Tribune's health. Instead, he had dismissed the German with the instruction to take better care of his new master.

He blamed himself. He should have stopped Flavius from visiting Bethany so many times. He had guessed that the friendship between Farrah and Flavius had moved on to something more, but he had kept quiet, telling himself that after all, Flavius was an intelligent man; he would surely know that any further relationship between them would not be tolerated. Dear Gods, the woman was a foreign princess! A distant relative of the King of Nabatea! Now he had to tell him the bad news. He knew it would hit Flavius hard, but it had to be said.

He cleared his throat. "I've ordered that the search for the Princess be called off. It appears that after all these weeks, with no sighting or news of her whereabouts, she must be dead. I can no longer afford to waste valuable manpower on a hopeless cause."

He felt a pang of guilt as he saw the downward turn of the mouth, the fleeting glimpse of pain cross Flavius' face. His mind raced. He had been partly to blame for this awkward situation, so he must help to remedy it. He hoped Pilate didn't know about the relationship. If he did, he had not said or done anything to stop it – yet.

If the Governor wished to punish Flavius, he would surely bear in mind that he was a member of his own family, however distant, and probably not dismiss him outright from the Army, but might demote him and have him transferred immediately to a different legion in another part of the Empire. Flavius' father would want to know why, and Pilate would reluctantly have to tell him the truth. It would cause a huge scandal. He would understand if Pilate blamed him, as Flavius' commander, for letting things get out of hand. They all had to deal carefully with a powerful Senator, an esteemed member of the Curia, especially one in favour with the Emperor;

a Senator who could exert influence and have all of their futures hanging by an easily-cut thread. He must make sure Flavius himself didn't confess to Pilate his love for the Princess. For all their sakes, it would be better if Pilate knew nothing about this whole rotten mess.

Quintus looked directly at Flavius. "Tribune, it has come to my attention that you have a personal interest in Princess Farrah." He saw Flavius move as if to speak but obviously think better of it. Instead the obviously-shocked Tribune stared at him.

Quintus continued, "I suggest that from now on, you forget everything concerning your association with the Princess. Governor Pilate must never know of it, or the consequences will be dire for you. Is that understood?"

He tried hard to hide his frustration as he saw Flavius' embarrassed look. Even so, he could not stand by and watch the Tribune's career and future prospects be ruined because of his failure to deal with this problem in its early stages. He must keep Flavius busy, give him something else to think about.

He rifled through some maps laid out on his desktop, giving himself time to think. Then he remembered a series of recent complaints he had received about trouble in the prominent merchants' area of the city. Investigating that might help Flavius concentrate on his duties. He looked up at Flavius and said in a gruff tone, "Tribune, I want you to lead a detachment of legionaries to the Valley of the Cheesemakers; I've had reports of looting from premises belonging to certain influential merchants. I want you to find out what the situation is and deal with it appropriately. Take Centurion Sextus with you." He saw Flavius' puzzled look. "Yes, I know Sextus is more than capable of dealing with this, but I want you in charge."

He sighed impatiently as he saw Flavius' hesitation, and in a clipped voice added, "This is a direct command, Tribune. Go and find Sextus and his men and get to the Valley of the Cheesemakers." His irritation rose sharply as Flavius continued to stand there. "Now, Tribune!" he barked. "The bloody merchants won't wait forever!"

The severity of the Commander's tone made Flavius snap to attention. "Yes, sir." He saluted stiffly and left the room.

As the door closed behind Flavius, Quintus shook his head wearily. He felt some sympathy for the Tribune. He knew how easy it was for legionaries to fall in love with women they could never hope to marry. He had personal experience of that, and knew how it felt to love and lose someone.

Throughout his army career, he had purposely avoided marriage, but he had been involved in many easily-broken relationships. He had made love to countless women in many countries wherever his legion had served. Only one of those women had stirred his heart. She had been his first sexual conquest. He conjured up the face of the girl with the corn-gold hair belonging to a tribe living in a village close to the fort where he had served as a young officer with the Legion Tenth Gemina in Germania. Not speaking her language, he had named her Azurea in honour of her large, brilliant blue eyes. Their illicit love affair had eventually produced a son, one he could never acknowledge as a legitimate heir.

After his cohort had successfully put down a rebellion in another area, he had returned to the village and looked for her to tell her that his legion was moving on, a prospect he knew would deeply upset her. He'd searched everywhere but couldn't find her. He had asked one of her friends if she knew where she was. He still remembered the hateful look on the girl's face as she spat at him: 'I don't know where she is. The girl who was once my friend, who you called Azurea, has been cast out of the village with your bastard son for co-habiting with you, Roman! No one is allowed to help her for fear of punishment by the village elders.' With that she had turned her back on him and walked away. Shocked, he had stood silent with gritted teeth, but he had been powerless and afraid to defend Azurea and their child for fear of retaliation by the villagers and his Commander.

When he had first joined the Legion, he had resolved that nothing was going to stand in the way of his military career. And it hadn't. He had left Germania when the Legion transferred to Petavonium in Hispania. The years passed by, and he'd been promoted and transferred to this legion, the Tenth Fretensis, working his way up through the ranks until he had eventually become the Commander of the Antonia. But throughout the years, Azurea had always been a guilty secret in the back of his mind. He had often wondered what had become of her. Was she still alive? And what of his son, who had apparently inherited his dark hair and his mother's blue eyes? If he had survived he would be about eighteen summers old now, a man.

The guilt of not coming to Azurea's aid when she most needed him surfaced and tortured his mind. He guessed these feelings were what Flavius was experiencing now. He would be the worst kind of hypocrite to discipline him for loving someone who, according to Roman law, was deemed 'inappropriate'.

He grimaced. His prediction that the young aristocrat would be trouble had been right. He swept the maps off his desk onto the floor with a clenched fist, angry with Flavius for the painful memories his actions had evoked.

Light rain began to fall as Flavius found Sextus on the parade ground, putting his troops through their paces. He approached the Centurion, who smartly saluted him. At Sextus' command the troops stood to attention.

"Tell the men to stand easy, I need to talk to you," said Flavius.

"Sir." Sextus turned to the troops "Stand easy, men."

Flavius was impressed by the troops' immediate response to their Centurion's command. As Flavius told Sextus the Commander's orders, he saw the brief look of bewilderment on the Centurion's face. He was grateful that Sextus kept his opinion of those orders to himself.

"Choose the right legionaries for this, we don't want to inflame these merchants any further," added Flavius.

Sextus quickly chose the legionaries he wanted for the job. Flavius nodded, satisfied with the choice.

Mounted on Saturn, Flavius, followed closely by an ever-watchful Sextus, led the patrol as it made its way through the wet, congested city. "Get out of the way!" Flavius shouted as some men got too close to the horse. Wary of the big black stallion's hooves, and Flavius' boot kicking out at them, the men quickly jumped aside.

As the patrol approached an alleyway, Flavius heard a woman scream. He halted the troops and looked down the alleyway to see an angry mob. "Centurion Sextus. See what all the commotion's about," he ordered.

Sextus saluted and taking two legionaries with him, forced his way to the front of the baying mob. A woman was laying badly injured on the rain-soaked ground, a pile of stones on and around her. He swiftly left the scene and reported back to Flavius.

Flavius ordered two other legionaries to follow him and went to look for himself. "What's going on here?" His voice was gruff. The image of a young man dying in a pit, his head and body smashed by stones and rocks, came back to him. Why had that scene affected him so much at the time? Was this woman another of the Nazarene sect? He looked at a burly man, who Flavius took to be the leader of the mob. In his hand was a small, jagged rock, "What are you doing?" he shouted.

The man replied defensively. "She was caught in the act of adultery. Our Law says we have the right to kill her for this sin."

Flavius bristled. "I am sick of your so-called laws. You Jews forget you are governed by the laws of Rome."

Sextus stepped forward, speaking quietly "Sir. He's right. Stoning for a woman caught in the act of adultery is one of their ridiculous religious laws. Rome can't interfere. Take my advice, sir. Come away."

Flavius remembered Quintus and Philo's words about Jewish religious laws having to be tolerated by Rome, but it still rankled that a conquered race was allowed to exercise them. He tried hard to control his mounting anger, but could see that Sextus was wary of getting involved and decided to bow to the more experienced man's advice. He looked down at the pitiful woman lying half dead at his feet, nodded, and ordered the soldiers to continue to the Valley of The Cheesemakers to question the disgruntled merchants.

The culprits appeared to be known to the merchants, and they gave Flavius the names of the suspected thieves. Some of the names were familiar to Sextus.

"Where can we find these criminals?" Flavius asked Sextus.

"Usually in the back alley hovels, the poorer side of the city, sir."

"Let's go."

Flavius let Sextus lead, as he had a better knowledge of

those areas. It didn't take long to find the criminals lurking in their filthy hovels. Flavius moved Saturn aside and ordered Sextus to arrest them. The Centurion threatened them with torture if they did not acknowledge their guilt and name their leaders. They were only too ready to confess. Two men were named as the ringleaders of the gang.

The Romans moved on to the leaders' lair, where they found the men skulking in a corner. Bitter and angry with ben-Ezra and the helpless situation concerning Farrah, and, to him, the senseless scene of mob rule he had just witnessed, Flavius, at that moment, hated all Jews, their idiotic religion and their thieves and cut-throats. He would make sure these thieves would be tortured. Seeing their pain might ease his own. He barked out an order: "Bind the ringleaders and take them back to the Antonia for punishment."

The two felons protested loudly, cursing all Romans and lashing out with their feet as the legionaries struggled to bind their hands. With a few punches and well-placed kicks the legionaries soon had them under control.

The rest of the gang thought they would be allowed their freedom as a reward for giving up their leaders. But Flavius' voice rang out "Kill them all!"

Panic set in as the felons tried to escape. They were brutally cut down.

Simon the beggar was sitting in his hut, counting the coins he had been given by gullible pilgrims that morning.

He stopped counting as he heard the sound of marching feet. He moved to the doorway, pulled back the top half of the ragged covering and cautiously looked outside to see what was going on.

He shuddered. Roman legionaries!

As some of the legionaries stood guard outside two of the hovels close by, the rest forced their way inside. He recognised the Tribune in charge: it was the lover of Al-Maisan. Shaking with fear, he quickly let the door covering fall back into place and hid himself in the darkest recess of his hut, praying that the soldiers were not going to arrest him too. He heard clipped commands followed by shouts, curses and the screams of dying men. His relief was enormous when the echoing sound of iron-shod boots on the dirty cobblestones gradually faded into the distance.

He waited awhile, then went to the doorway. Pushing the ragged curtain aside, he looked out into the alleyway. He recognised the dead men lying on the blood-soaked ground and felt sick. He'd been lucky this time. How much longer would his luck last? He made up his mind. He would find his granddaughter and leave Jerusalem. They would travel northwards and find a small town of no interest to the authorities and stay there until springtime.

Flavius and Sextus reported to Quintus. The Commander was pleased with the outcome of the successful mission. He ordered Sextus to take the felons to the dungeon, then sat back smiling at Flavius. "Well done, Tribune. That's more scum off the streets. If we're lucky they might know ben-Ezra's whereabouts." He caught a glimmer of hope in Flavius' face. "Look, boy, don't get your hopes up. They might not know anything about him." He softened his tone. "But there's always a chance. Go to the dungeon and see if my persuaders have got any information out of the thieving bastards."

Flavius saluted and left the Commander's office. On his way to the dungeon, he briefly watched some of the junior officers exercising on the exercise ground, something he had not felt like doing since he had heard about Farrah. He had lost heart. He chided himself. If he wanted to keep his toned physique he would have to make the effort.

He entered the dungeon, quickly covering his nose and mouth with his hand as a sickly, rank smell hit him. He heard Sextus' voice issuing orders to the torturers. He moved deeper into the dungeon and saw the Centurion standing apart from the prisoners, who were both chained to the wall. Two torturers stood close to brightly-burning braziers which cast flickering shadows on the dim, dank walls. Flavius wondered if this was what Hades looked like.

He swallowed hard as he saw, resting in the fires, white hot blades and pincers, their covered handles poking out of the braziers so the torturers could go about their business without harming themselves. He had told himself that the prisoners deserved everything that was coming to them, but if these horrific instruments were to be used on the prisoners, he pitied them. Deep down, he felt a pang of guilt that he had not ordered them put to the sword in a clean kill.

Flavius moved to the Centurion's side. One of the torturers, heavily muscled and dressed in a blood-soaked tunic, partly covered by a thick leather apron, approached one of the prisoners. Flavius flinched as the torturer began to systematically beat the man's naked body with iron-tipped rods. Flavius wanted to cover his ears as the man screamed, and shut his eyes against the horrific sight of the felon's barbaric treatment, but steeled himself to watch as the man's skin became more and more lacerated, his blood splattering the floor.

Next to him the second prisoner shook with fear as another of the torturers moved towards him holding a searing hot knife.

"Tell me what I want to know or…" Sextus ordered the torturer to brandish the weapon closer to the criminal's face. "Where is ben-Ezra?"

The terrified prisoner's voice rasped out "I keep on telling you, Roman, I don't know. We've never been part of his gang and we don't know where his hideout is."

There was an unearthly howl as the torturer held the knife across the prisoner's eyes. The man's bowels gave way with shock and pain. He let out a low moan and with head lolling, sank into merciful unconsciousness.

As the torturer withdrew the knife, Flavius could see the prisoner's blackened eye sockets and the charred flesh around them. Part of the man's cheek had been burnt to the bone. The smell of burning flesh turned Flavius' stomach, but he fought back his nausea. It would not do to show weakness in front of the Centurion.

"Enough!" Sextus' voice rang out. "We shan't get any more out of them now. "Revive them, then work on them again later. Keep them chained up until tomorrow. The bastards might be more amenable by then." He pointed to the blood and foul waste matter on the floor. "And clean up that mess."

The torturers saluted the Senior Officers, then fetched water and began to sluice the blood and waste away.

Flavius and Sextus returned the salute. Seeing Flavius' pale face, Sextus smiled and said, "Don't worry, sir, they won't hold out much longer, not if I know those torturers."

Flavius did not return the smile and made no comment. He just wanted to get out of this monstrous place. Outside the dungeon he took in a great gulp of fresh air, trying to drive out the stench from his nostrils and the taste of bile from the back of his throat.

Tired and dispirited, Flavius made his way back to his quarters. He threw his helmet onto his bed then stood motionless as Gebhard unbuckled his elaborate belt carrying his sword and dagger and removed his armour, metal-studded skirt and padded vest.

"My breastplate and greaves have blood and gore on them." Flavius pointed to the discarded armour thrown into a heap on the floor. "Clean and polish them until they shine."

Gebhard bowed. "Yes Tribune. It shall be done."

"Make sure it is!" Flavius barked "Fetch me clean undergarments and a tunic." Flavius watched the slave with narrowed eyes as he fetched the clean clothes. "Give them to me. I'm going to the baths, I stink of the dungeon."

"Shall I come with you, Tribune? Help you to dress and bring back the clothes you are wearing now to be washed?"

"Look, I'm quite capable of dressing myself!" Flavius snapped back. "Just get on with cleaning my armour." Carrying his clean clothes, Flavius strode out of the room.

Gebhard was astonished by his young master's behaviour. He shook his head. What had happened to the Tribune who had once seemed so happy and proud? He had guessed some time ago that the amulet the Tribune constantly wore around his neck was some kind of protective good-luck talisman. If it was, it was failing. In its place something dark had entered his master's soul. He made the sign for warding off the evil eye.

Sad and bewildered, he looked down at the heap of dirty armour on the floor, then fetched his oils and polishing cloths. He picked up the breastplate, poured some of the oil onto it, took a cloth and began the arduous process of ridding it of the foul mess. He would do his best to ensure the armour gleamed ready for the next day.

At the baths, Flavius undressed and threw his sweat-stained garments onto the floor. A slave bent to pick them up, asking if he should take them to be washed. The answer came swiftly and firmly. "No! Take them away and burn them!"

Flavius lay still on the marble slab as the bath-house slave's strigil scraped the sweat and dirt off his body. His muscles were tense and he was filled with frustration. He cursed his situation, wishing he had never come to this godforsaken country. He had been met with nothing but trouble and horror since the day he arrived. Only Farrah had made his time here bearable, and now she was gone. Anguish swept over him as he whispered softly, 'Farrah, my love, where are you?'

He would have to learn to live without her. He still had many months left to endure life in this infernal land of fanatics and cut-throats before he would be free of the army and could return to Rome. He reluctantly had to admit that his father had been right about one thing: life in Judaea had made him grow up. Too quickly.

With these torturous thoughts running through his mind, he gave himself up to the bathing process, hoping it would calm his frazzled nerves, help remove the stench and the terrible scenes he'd witnessed in that nightmare dungeon – and soothe the ache in his heart.

Later that day, the two prisoners in the Antonia dungeon died under torture. If they had known the whereabouts of ben-Ezra, their secret had died with them.

CHAPTER TWENTY-EIGHT

Taking advantage of a brief dry spell during changeable weather, Drubaal stood on the empty Antonia training ground. He flexed his aching muscles, careful not to tear open the angry-looking scars running down both arms, his side and across his thigh, but determined to carry on with his exercises and training. Most of all, he wanted to try out his new sword.

As he swung the weapon around, the long, curved, highly-polished iron blade glinted in the sunlight. The balance was perfect. He held it in his right hand, concentrating on strengthening his right arm as the tendons in his left arm were taking longer to heal.

He grimaced as he lifted his new curved sword above his head and brought it down in a swift stroke, slicing in two a melon 'head' on an upright pole fixed in the ground. He breathed hard at the effort, but despite the pain, he knew that each day he was becoming stronger. He examined the cut he had inflicted on the fruit, then checked the weapon. He nodded, satisfied.

As one of his previous swords had been so badly damaged in the attack, he had been left with only the one that had been brought back to the fortress along with his injured body. He had been surprised to learn that Decurion Julius had received permission from the Commander to instruct the fortress armourer to make a new curved sword exactly to his specifications, ready for use when his left arm was strong enough. He had visited the armoury with Julius and carefully explained to the armourer how he wanted the sword to be fashioned. Earlier that morning he had gone with Julius to see the finished article. The armourer had handed it to him to check that the specifications were right. He had inspected it carefully, pleased that the armourer had fully followed his instructions: the curve of the sword was precise, the hilt was made from metal covered in leather for grip, the guard was fashioned in iron and decorated with intricate patterns. The armourer had also made two beautiful wooden scabbards covered in red leather in which to hold both swords.

Drubaal had hefted the sword in his right hand, hoping it would not be too much longer before he could wield both swords again. After thanking the armourer, he had turned to Julius and smiled, finding it difficult to say words of gratitude for the Decurion's kindness.

He had suddenly become aware of someone standing on the edge of the training ground watching him. It was Julius.

"I see you're trying out your new sword," said Julius. "It looks very dangerous. I would not want to be faced with that in battle." Smiling, he walked over to Drubaal. "It looks like you're regaining your strength now."

Drubaal nodded. "In my right arm, yes."

"I'm sure it won't be too long before you can use your left arm as well and terrify everyone with both your deadly swords."

Drubaal looked at Julius. "I am grateful for this gift, Decurion. I will never be able to repay you for the cost of this sword and scabbards."

"I didn't pay for them. After the Commander gave his permission, I happened to mention it to Tribune Flavius. It was he who paid the armourer."

Drubaal was astonished. He was fast changing his mind about the Tribune. At first he had been wary of his increasing attachment to his mistress. He would not stand by and see the Roman hurt her in any way. Since he had come to know Flavius better, it seemed he had misjudged him. He was a decent man, not like most Romans. Now this business of the new sword and scabbards had cemented that opinion. Having no money of his own, he wondered what deed he could do in the future to repay the Tribune for his act of kindness.

"Why should the Tribune be so generous to me?" he asked.

331

Why indeed? It was a question Julius had asked himself several times. He looked across the training ground and nodded in the direction of the Commander's office. "Why don't you ask him yourself? He's coming this way."

Knowing Drubaal to be a proud man, one who would prefer to speak with the Tribune privately, Julius made his excuses and walked off in the direction of the cavalry block.

Drubaal decided he would use this chance to thank the Tribune and show the young Roman his progress. He was sure he would be pleased. He frowned as Flavius drew closer. Seeing the anger and distress written on his face, Drubaal knew that something had happened. He slid the weapon into its ornate scabbard and anxiously waited to hear the Roman's news.

When Flavius repeated the Commander's order, Drubaal breathed hard in an effort to hold back his anger, then drew himself up and looked defiantly at Flavius. "No! She can't be dead! I will never give up hope until her body is laid out before me."

Flavius said sadly, "I'm sorry, Drubaal, but it seems all hope is gone."

Drubaal was filled with anguish. He bowed his head, fighting back tears of despair. During the Tribune's many visits to him in hospital to check on his recovery, both he and the Tribune had always believed she would be rescued. With his eyes filled with unshed tears, Drubaal raised his head and stared hard at Flavius "Has my master, Sheikh Ibrahim, been told about his beloved niece?"

Flavius shook his head. "The Commander has no idea where the Sheikh is at present and I don't think Governor Pilate would have informed him, even if he knew where he was. He would not want to draw the Sheikh away from his mission for King Aretas."

Drubaal's voice was as cold as ice as he said, "I tell you this, you Romans may have given up the search – but I never will. As soon as I am able to leave this fortress, I will look for the Princess myself."

Flavius shook his head. "I would strongly advise against that action. If the Roman Army, with all its resources, can't find her, then how will you on your own, my friend?"

Drubaal's mouth was no more than a slit. "I will find a way."

Over the past few weeks, Quintus had become more and more concerned by Flavius' actions.

He had seen the young Tribune's dark shadowed eyes, seen his handsome features grow hard and the mouth become permanently set in a cruel line. Flavius had become ruthless in his dealings with any felon. Several of the legionaries who served under him had complained about his unfairly harsh treatment. He had himself noticed that Flavius no longer exchanged friendly banter with the other officers in the bathhouse; in fact, he had barely said a word to them for weeks, seemingly preferring to be on his own. It was obvious to Quintus that the young Tribune was struggling with lack of sleep and his increasing bitterness at the loss of Princess Farrah and, most of all, his growing hatred of the Jews.

This situation could not continue. Governor Pilate was due to arrive in Jerusalem for the Jewish Festival of Lights. If only he could persuade Pilate to take Flavius away from Jerusalem for a while. But what excuse could he give the Governor without giving away the young Tribune's secret? He had wrestled with the problem for days, but could not find an answer.

The day after he arrived in Jerusalem, Pilate requested Flavius' presence at the Palace.

Pilate finished signing the last of the dispatches for Rome. "See that these go with the others tomorrow," he said. He handed the dispatches to Scribonius, who bowed and left the room. He turned his attention to Flavius and appraised the gaunt figure standing at attention before him. He frowned as he saw the young Tribune standing ram-rod straight, seemingly on edge.

"Stand at ease, Tribune," he said.

Flavius made a supreme effort to relax.

"You look unwell, my boy. Are you suffering from some malady?"

"I'm tired, Governor Pilate, that's all. I've been constantly seeking out and rounding up various felons for punishment. Some have proved more troublesome than I first thought. As a result, some of my men have regrettably been injured."

"I see. Have you gained any information from the

captured criminals about the Princess's whereabouts?" Pilate looked straight at his young relative and thought he saw a momentary sad and bitter look flash across his face; then it was gone.

"No sir. Unfortunately there has been no further news of her."

"A pity." Pilate drummed his fingers on his desk. Trying to keep his frustration out of his voice, he said "How is the Sheikh's bodyguard, Drubaal? Recovering, I hope."

"He is well, sir. In fact, we have difficulty keeping him in the fortress. He wants to search for the Princess by himself. It has been explained to him many times that if the might of the Army can't find her, then the prospect of one man searching on his own is futile and the search could take years to accomplish with no end result. It would also put his life in danger again, a prospect his master would not like."

Pilate nodded. "No, indeed he would not. I have recently received a communication from the Sheikh. He has been delayed and won't be returning to Jerusalem for several weeks. When he does, it will be my unpleasant task to tell him about the Princess – something I am not looking forward to. I know the disappearance of his niece will devastate him."

Pilate sighed. "Well. First things first. Let's get this damnable festival over with." He stared at Flavius again and scowled. The young man had been in Judaea for a relatively short time, but it seemed the place had already changed him. He knew how that felt. His mind was made up.

"I'm waiting for a new Senior Tribune to replace one who is about to finish his tour in Caesarea and will shortly be transferring to Gaul," Pilate went on. "Apparently, this new man is known for his adherence to discipline and is considered to be an officer who will not tolerate sloppiness in any shape or form. However, I gather it is considered that he is not quite ready for this appointment. Therefore, I want you..."

Flavius wondered exactly what that meant. Perhaps the new man had not yet become brutal enough. Flavius felt sorry for the legionaries who would undoubtedly suffer under his command. He suddenly felt ashamed, remembering his own recent behaviour. Seeking to appease his own heartache, he had sometimes cruelly brutalised the local people, and treated his own men too harshly.

He was brought out of his reverie by the sound of Pilate's raised voice.

"Tribune! Did you hear what I just said?"

Flavius snapped back to attention, his face flushed with embarrassment. He would have to admit to having a momentary lapse of concentration. "No, Governor Pilate. I'm sorry Governor Pilate. It won't happen again, sir."

"Hmm. No it won't! Pilate's voice held a note of sarcasm. "Now that I have your undivided attention, Tribune, I will repeat what I just said. When I return to Caesarea, you will be coming with me. Until the new man arrives, I want you, Flavius, to be my temporary Senior Tribune. What do you say?"

Flavius was astonished by the Governor's offer, which had come as a complete surprise. He swallowed hard, thinking fast. What if Farrah was found safe and well and returned to Jerusalem and he wasn't there to see her? On the other hand, he wouldn't be staying in Caesarea forever. If she *was* found, then he could see her when he returned to the Antonia. It might do him good to get away from this city and its unhappy memories for a while. In any case, it was not wise to refuse the Governor of Judaea's offer.

He drew himself up "It would be an honour, Governor Pilate."

"That's settled then. Lady Claudia, I know, will be very pleased to see you. I will make arrangements with Quintus Maximus and send for you when I'm ready to leave. Until then..."

Pilate turned his attention back to the various documents spread out on his desk. Flavius saluted and quickly left the room.

When Pilate told Quintus of his plans to take Flavius to Caesarea with him, the Commander felt a weight lift off his shoulders. He readily agreed with the Governor that his idea of temporarily replacing the departing Tribune with Flavius was an excellent idea.

Later that day, Adolfo, as he had dutifully done these past weeks, went to the appointed alleyway and met with the man who promised him everything. He took a rolled, sealed scroll from the man and placed it in his bag.

"When are the latest dispatches being sent to Rome, Adolfo?"

"Tomorrow," replied Adolfo.

The man smiled and walked away.

Adolfo made sure the way was clear, then hurried back to the palace before he was missed.

CHAPTER TWENTY-NINE

The Disciples told the converts that while the persecution of the followers of Jesus continued, it would not be safe to celebrate the Festival of Dedication, also known as the Feast of Lights, in the Temple or in any of the synagogues, for fear of arrest by the Sanhedrin. They remembered only too well the day Jesus had come into Jerusalem and visited the Temple to honour this feast. As He was walking through the Temple precincts, angry men had surrounded Him. If He had not escaped they would have stoned Him to death there and then. So it was decided that the feast days should be held in their own, or their friends' houses instead.

At sunset on the first evening of the Festival, the Disciples gathered together in Mary's house. Peter stood before the assembled gathering. He took a taper and lit

THE POWER AND THE GLORY

it from an oil-lamp standing on the table. He moved across the room to where a chanukiah, a nine-branch candelabrum, stood near the window. He held the taper over the Shamash, the ninth and tallest container on the chanukiah, filled with olive oil, then began the retelling of the story known to all Jews, the story that was now over one hundred years old.

"I light this Shamash in remembrance of the rededication of the Temple after the defeat of the Seleucids and their evil leader, Antiochus Epiphanes, who murdered our people, defiled the Temple and banned our religious beliefs and observances. He tried to force our people to either worship the pagan god Zeus or die. But the children of Israel would not give up the worship of the one true God," he added proudly.

He went on to recount the inspiring deeds of Mattathias the Hasmonean and of two of his sons, Simon and Judah Maccabee, who gathered an army and fought the Seleucids; of Judah's routing of four Seleucid armies and of his re-purifying of the Temple. Although the Disciples had heard the story many times before, they sat enthralled as Peter came to the end of the stirring tale.

"The Eternal Light which had constantly hung in the Temple had been extinguished by the Seleucids. A jar of oil was found in the Temple, and Judah used it to relight the Eternal Light. But there was oil for only one day. By God's miracle, the oil replenished itself and the Eternal Light burned for the full eight days of Purification, giving enough time to prepare fresh supplies of oil."

Peter lit the Shamash, then took it to light the wick in a small container of oil on the left of the chanukiah, reciting the accompanying prayer: "Blessed are you, Oh Lord our God, Ruler of the Universe, who has sanctified us with Your Commandments and commanded us to kindle the lights in remembrance of this Holy Festival."

The gathering replied as one: "Amen."

The observance completed, Peter pointed to the table. "Come, sit and eat."

They were all looking forward to the special meal Mary had spent most of the day preparing. They chatted amongst themselves as Mary and John Mark served up the food. After mother and son were seated, Peter blessed the delicious fare, then joined his hungry friends as they helped themselves and began to eat.

Barnabas sat next to his sister. He smiled at her. "This food is delicious, Mary. These pancakes are very tasty."

"I should hope so." She playfully nudged his arm with her elbow. "By the time the eight days are finished I will have used up a whole month's supply of oil."

"Hey, Thomas!" John Mark leaned forward and removed the large earthenware plate of goat's cheese from the obviously hungry man's possession and placed it on the table in front of him. "I'd like some of that before you eat it all." John Mark laughed at the Apostle's answering scowl. After cutting off a piece for himself, he passed the plate to his Uncle Barnabas, then poured out a cupful of creamy milk from a large jug set in the middle of the table. After taking a long drink of the milk, he looked at his piece of cheese, then turned to his mother. "I've forgotten why we also eat cheese and cheesy pancakes at this celebration," he said.

Mary raised her eyes heavenward. "You young people have memories like sieves. We eat these things because of Judith."

A spark of remembrance of his biblical lessons as a child came back to him. "Oh, yes. Wasn't she the beautiful widow who helped to free us from the Assyrians?"

Mary nodded. "Yes. Judith was one of the most beautiful and bravest women in our history. As well as celebrating the heroic Maccabee family's exploits, this is her time for remembrance too. I will never forget to praise her. If she hadn't had the courage to kill the Assyrian general Holofernes, then I don't know what would have happened to this nation."

"But why is it we commemorate her with foods like cheese?"

Mary sighed in mock annoyance. "General Holofernes desired Judith, but not only was Judith very beautiful, she was clever too. When the general threw a banquet for his servants in his tent, he invited Judith too. As a present, she gave him some salty fried cheese. He didn't realise it was to make him thirsty so he would drink more wine. When the servants were dismissed, Judith was left alone with him. Overcome with passion for her, he thought to defile her, but drank himself into a stupor instead. It was then she cut off his head." Mary reached for another piece of cheese. "Using his own sword too."

John Mark looked down at his cheese and pulled a face. "That's horrible," he said. He put his uneaten slice of cheese back onto the table. "Judith was lucky not to be killed."

Peter had overheard the conversation between Mary and her son, and he leaned towards John Mark. "Yes, but we must remember Judith had constantly prayed to God and put her trust in Him. He kept her safe and answered her prayers. It is a good lesson for us all. During these troubled times we must also continue to place our trust in God."

John Mark became serious "Stephen trusted God, so why did God let him die?"

Peter put his hand on the young man's shoulder and spoke kindly. "It is not for us to know how God's mind works, but it must be part of His greater plan. Perhaps one day He will permit us to know what it is."

John Mark bent his head so that Peter would not see the tears that threatened to fall. In a brief space of time he had lost his best friend and the girl that he loved. He pushed his plate away, suddenly losing his appetite.

The next seven nights continued with the appropriate prayers and the lighting of the oil wicks. Then on the last evening of the Festival, when all eight wicks had been lit, the final festival prayers had been said and everyone was happily full and complimenting Mary on her food, the atmosphere changed. Thomas had asked "Is there any news from Damascus?"

A sudden gloom descended on the company, and Peter's smile changed to a frown "I have heard nothing, Thomas."

Those around the table began to question each other. Each one shook their heads. It was John who spoke. "Don't you think it strange we haven't heard anything at all, Peter?"

The other Disciples murmured amongst themselves, agreeing with John's question.

John Mark tried to lighten the dour mood that had settled on the room. "Perhaps no news is good news, John."

"I hope you are right, John Mark." Peter tried desperately to hide the constant worry that had plagued him since Saul had left Jerusalem "We must pray that the Lord will protect our brothers and sisters in Damascus."

CHAPTER THIRTY

Quintus looked at the ramrod straight figure of Flavius standing before him. "Stand easy, Tribune," he said. He scowled as Flavius continued to stand rigidly before him. "I said, stand easy!" He felt the tension emanating from the young Tribune. He cleared his throat and continued, "Orders have come from Governor Pilate. He is leaving for Caesarea tomorrow morning. You will ready yourself to depart with him and report to the Governor's residence at dawn. Is that clear?"

Flavius had been waiting apprehensively for this order to arrive. Now that it had, he would have to put that apprehension aside. He saluted stiffly. "Yes, Commander."

Quintus looked at the obviously torn Flavius. "It will do you good to get away from here for a while, Flavius, and this promotion, albeit temporary, will look impressive on your Legion record and will, no doubt, help towards your future career."

Flavius's downcast expression did not change. Quintus got up from behind his desk and walked round to face the Tribune. He could not let this young officer ruin his career before it had begun. It was time for straight talking.

"Whatever your problems are, Flavius, face them like a man and put them behind you. It's not wise to dwell on personal regrets and maudlin thoughts, they could cost you your life." He grew angry at Flavius' continued lack of response. "Look! I have tolerated your behaviour long enough. No more! You have been given a wonderful chance by the Governor to further your political career. Don't waste it."

He saw Flavius's face change. It seemed his stark message was beginning to get through to the young officer. He softened his harsh tone. "Now I suggest you sort out your equipment and tie up any loose ends before you leave."

Flavius saluted "Yes, Commander."

"Good luck."

"Thank you, sir."

Flavius saluted again, then turned and left the room with the Commander's harsh words ringing in his ears. What Quintus Maximus had said was true. He had been so wrapped up in his selfish misery that he had forgotten where his duty lay. If he was to help his career by serving Pilate, then that was what he must now focus on. He would try to make his father proud of him. He straightened his back, squared his shoulders and marched towards Zeno's workshop to tell him that Saturn had to be groomed and made ready for the following morning. He then made his way to his quarters.

On Flavius' orders, Gebhard began to pack his master's clothes and equipment for the coming long journey and his stay in Caesarea.

Later, Flavius went looking for Julius. He found him at the pens checking on his horse.

"I leave for Caesarea with the Governor tomorrow," he said.

Flavius saw the downcast look on the younger man's face. He knew it must be a great disappointment to him that he would not be accompanying him to Caesarea. "It's a pity you can't go with us, Julius. There may have been an opportunity for you to see your family."

"I would have liked that, sir, but I've not been ordered to travel with the Governor."

"I'm bound to see your father some time at the Caesarea garrison. Would you like me to pass on a message to him?"

Julius' face lit up. "If you could just let him know, sir, that I'm well, that I miss him and my sister very much and that I shall write to him soon."

"Consider it done, Julius." Flavius could see that something else was troubling Julius and guessed what it was: Antonius. He would not be there to protect the Decurion from the Prefect's bullying.

"If you have any further problems with the Prefect, go to Chief Centurion Sextus and tell him," he said.

Julius smiled wanly. "Will he believe a mere Decurion over a Prefect, sir? I don't want to make matters any worse than they are."

"I know Sextus is a hard man, but I have come to believe that he is fair and very proud to serve this Legion. He would not want an outsider coming in and tarnishing the Legion's reputation."

Flavius could see that Julius still looked doubtful and tried to reassure him. "If, whilst I'm in Caesarea, you have cause to make an official complaint against Antonius, and it's ignored, when I return for the Passover Festival next year, I will back you up. I'm sure Governor Pilate will believe me."

He studied Julius for a moment "There is something I'd like you to do for me." He saw Julius' puzzled expression. "Will you keep an eye on Drubaal while I'm away? I'd like to know he's being well looked after. Despite recovering from his physical injuries, the Princess' disappearance has affected him badly. He doesn't have any other friends here, so perhaps you could speak to him from time to time when your duties allow and help ease his loneliness."

Julius was surprised at Flavius' request. First the new sword, now this. Why was a Roman Tribune so worried about a Carthaginian servant's wellbeing? He wondered if it was something to do with the missing princess, but it was not his place to question a senior officer. Instead, he nodded and said "It will be a pleasure, Tribune."

"Thank you, Julius." Flavius's expression grew serious

"I meant what I said about Antonius. I will stand by you."

Julius saluted Flavius, then watched him walk away. He trusted Flavius and knew he would keep his word. He frowned. If only he too had been chosen to travel with Pilate's entourage, been able, for a while at least, to get some respite from the Prefect's threats. He missed his family desperately and would have given anything for the chance to see them, however briefly. Downhearted, he turned back to his horse. Sensing its master's unhappiness, the horse nuzzled his hand as if trying to offer some comfort. Julius stroked the horse's strong withers. "I know you will never let me down, old friend," he murmured.

Up in the hills, the weather had turned considerably colder. Torrential rain ran in rivulets down the craggy hillsides, creating pools of water in the rocky hollows. It gushed down the channel, replenishing the cistern deep below in ben-Ezra's cavern hideout. Inside the cavern, fingers of chill wind clawed their way through every fissure, the cold and damp causing its inhabitants to shiver and suffer with snuffling noses, coughs and aching bones.

Farrah and Ruth sat huddled together around the fire. Because of the weeks of sickness she had suffered, thankfully now diminished, and the lack of nourishing food, Ruth's pregnancy hardly showed, something she was grateful for. She had no wish to tangle with Rachel, who, she knew, still eyed her with suspicion. She was terrified at the prospect of giving birth whilst a prisoner of ben-Ezra.

She wondered where the birth would take place. Would it be in some foreign land? Would she and her child be slaves to a cruel master or mistress? She doubted any of her future owners could ever be as kind as the master she had lost, Sheikh Ibrahim. The terrible fate awaiting her overwhelmed her. She could no longer hold back her bitter tears.

CHAPTER THIRTY-ONE

"Wake up, Tribune. You must wake up."

Flavius groaned at the sound of the insistent voice. He opened his bleary eyes, turned over and froze as he saw a shadowy figure standing by the side of his bed.

"Sir, it is Gebhard."

Suddenly alert, Flavius sat up. It was still dark, the room barely lit by oil lamps.

"What time is it?"

"It will soon be dawn, Tribune."

As if to verify that fact, a cock-crow sounded in the distance, heralding the coming day.

Gebhard's voice held a note of urgency. "Sir, you have to get ready. You must not be late."

With a deep sigh, Flavius reluctantly forced himself out of bed. He could imagine Pilate's anger if he was kept waiting. Looking around, he saw that all of his armour had been cleaned and his spare clothes and equipment packed ready for him.

Gebhard helped Flavius to dress and put on his armour, then the slave handed him his sword, dagger and helmet.

"Thank you, Gebhard."

The slave bowed.

"And thank you for looking after me these past few months, I know it hasn't always been easy for you."

Gebhard smiled, hiding his true feelings "It has been a pleasure, Tribune."

"I shall see you when I return to Jerusalem with the Governor next year." Flavius didn't add that the thought of returning to Jerusalem, with its bitter-sweet memories, was something he would not enjoy, but as part of Pilate's entourage, he knew he would have no choice.

Gebhard bowed again and watched as Flavius left the room.

As Flavius entered the front of the house, he saw Zeno waiting for him. Saturn had been made ready for the journey to Caesarea. Flavius smiled. "Thank you, Zeno, for making sure my horse has been well looked after. I will see you again next spring."

Zeno bowed. "I am glad you are satisfied, Tribune." Flavius led Saturn outside. He checked the saddlebags, packed by Gebhard, one last time, satisfying himself that he would have all that he needed to begin his duties in Caesarea. He placed them across the horse's back, then turned as he heard a noise behind him and saw Julius walking towards him. Zeno bowed again and left the two officers on their own.

"You're up early, Julius."

Julius saluted. "Tribune, sir, I just wanted to wish you good luck. You will be missed here."

Flavius put his hand on Julius' shoulder. "Thank you. Don't forget what I said, Julius. I meant every word." He took hold of Saturn's reins. "Now, if you will excuse me I have to report to the Governor."

Julius stood aside as Flavius mounted up.

Flavius gently reined in the powerful horse, which he knew was eager to be free of the confines of Jerusalem. Saturn would relish the exercise he would have on the long journey to the Coast. He patted the silky neck of the magnificent black horse, bending forward to speak quietly and calmly to him. Saturn tossed his thick mane as if in reply to his master's voice, then stood calmly waiting. Flavius flicked the reins and Saturn trotted forward. With a wave to Julius, Flavius rode out of the Jerusalem Garrison.

He reached the palace just as the sun began to rise.

Joel stood amongst the crowd watching the departing Romans, Pilate in their midst. He hawked and spat on the ground as the Governor and his escort passed by. As the eyes and ears of ben-Ezra in Jerusalem, he had done all that his friend and chief had asked of him: to recruit those men who shared his hatred of their oppressors. He knew ben-Ezra would be pleased by the number of men he had rallied to his call. Now he must wait until the spring, hoping the order would be given to strike. The skilled blacksmiths and armourers were already busy making many weapons. They would work in their secret hideouts all through the winter until every man owned at least one weapon, making them a force to be reckoned with. When spring came, they would be ready.

Flavius rode through the city as one of the many soldiers escorting the Governor. He stared at Antonius, who was leading the cavalry surrounding Pilate. He hoped the Prefect would leave Julius alone. If not, he vowed that he personally would see that the arrogant man would pay for his bullying.

As they rode along, Flavius could feel the hostile stares of the Jews on his back. He turned in the saddle to see a man with a hate-filled expression spit on the ground as Pilate rode by. Flavius narrowed his eyes, looking for any signs of trouble. None was evident, but he saw men grimly staring at the procession and stony-faced women with loathing in their eyes, murmuring to each other behind their hands. The hatred of the watching Jews was tangible. Flavius half expected that at any moment a dagger would come flying through the air and strike him in the back.

He heaved a sigh of relief as they rode through the city gates and out onto the highway.

A mixture of excitement and regret coursed through him as the horses picked up speed and headed down the road to Caesarea.

36675884R00214

Printed in Poland
by Amazon Fulfillment
Poland Sp. z o.o., Wrocław